PIECES of US
BOOK 7 IN THE BACK TO BILLY SAGA

A novel by:
Michael Anthony Giudicissi

Copyright © 2023 by Michael Anthony Giudicissi All Rights Reserved

No part of this book may be reproduced without written permission from the publisher or author, except for a reviewer who may quote brief passages in a review; nor may any part of this book be reproduced, stored in a retrieval system, or transmitted in any form or by any means electronic, mechanical, photocopying, recording or other, without written permission from the publisher or copyright holders.

This manuscript is a work of fiction. Any names, characters, businesses, places, events, locales, and incidents are either the products of the author's imagination or used in a fictitious manner. Any resemblance to actual persons, living or dead, or actual events is purely coincidental.

Mankind Media, LLC Albuquerque, NM
Email: billythekidridesagain@gmail.com

Editor: Melanie Hubner
Book Design & Layout: Mary Dolan
Cover Art: Fivrous

9 781088 086933

Retail: $18.00

In the end, we must all go...and all that we leave behind are pieces of us.

Michael Anthony Giudicissi

1.

A flat, pale light nagged insistently at the bedside window near Trisha Davis's head. That the blind had been left slightly open made it even worse as the young woman blinked her eyes heavily, trying to ascertain where she was, and where she had been? The stillness of the morning only served to confuse her more, being that the last few days in Lincoln had been anything but. Truth be told, Trisha felt as though she'd been having some sort of half out of body experience, if there even was such a thing. Ever since that tourist, Martin Teebs, had confessed his love for a beautiful woman from the past that could serve as Trisha's twin, she was inexorably being drawn closer and closer to the edge that she feared she might see if she opened her eyes fully. She'd spent all of Sunday walking around Lincoln, nearly catatonic, and increasingly unaware of who she really was. Attending the pageant to support her friends was supposed to provide some relief for the young woman while she struggled to understand what was happening to her, but the violence that rocked the event sent her nearly into shock. In what seemed like just a couple of minutes, Carl Farber had wreaked devastation on the whole of Lincoln, killing one man, and severely wounding two others. Even her new friend Martin hadn't escaped unscathed as he was taken down by a bullet that came flying into the fray at precisely the wrong moment, and hitting the wrong man.

That moment, the second that Martin was shot, was when something happened to Trisha that she could not explain. The young woman had never given birth, so she couldn't be sure, but the feeling surely had to be similar. As the stray round tore into the arm of Martin Teebs, Trisha Davis went cold as if her soul, nay her very identity, were wrenched from her body in most painful fashion. For a minute, or maybe less, afterwards, Trisha could still see what was going on. Jane Gordon stood off to her left, a wisp of smoke rising from the barrel of her .9mm pistol. If she'd shot Martin, it would have to be an accident. Trisha couldn't think of a single thing Martin could have done to incur that kind of wrath. More likely, Jane shot Farber, as that man had fallen after taking a shot to the chest that seemed to come from her direction. Exactly why Jane would shoot the older guy she'd been playing around with and stringing along escaped Trisha, but she made a mental note to ask Jane as soon as she saw her. Now Trisha remembered the emptiness of her being after Martin fell. Brief flurries of visions crossed her eyes, but nothing that she could hold onto long enough. Her breathing became labored and she feared she might pass out. At one point, thought Trisha, she must have….as she came to at the pageant grounds, only to find that she was completely alone. Scared at first, then amused, she finally became angry that she'd been left like so much post pageant trash fluttering around in the wind. Why didn't someone help her? Check on her? Take her home? When she finally came around, she rose from the bleachers and walked through the eerily quiet town to the house she'd been watching for the summer. As out of sorts as she was, Trisha could only acknowledge that she seemed to be the only one moving through the tiny town at that moment. If that struck her as weird, she couldn't be bothered to even check on it, tired and uneasy as she was. She'd arrived at her house just as the sun got lost on the far side of the Capitan Mountains, closed the door, and dragged her aching body to bed without even changing clothes.

Now, as the annoying light forced her from her cocoon, Trisha had to face the remains of the day, and see how life would go on in Lincoln after the bloody episode.

She wearily sat up in her bed, as tired physically as she'd ever been. Breathing heavily she swung her legs over the side of the bed and made her best attempt to stand up. It was as if she was sitting in cement, such was the force needed to break the bed's inertia but after a couple of tries she was able to gain her feet.

"What the actual fuck is going on with me?" she wondered aloud. Softly padding over to the window she looked out upon the small slice of Lincoln that she could see. If she had expected a line of police and FBI vehicles to line the streets, still trying to find that murderous loser Farber, she was disappointed. The town was as still this morning as it had been last night. Thinking that she'd eventually get out and see where everyone had gotten off to, Trisha trudged to the shower, stripping her clothes off along the way. As the steamy water began to cloud the mirror, she caught one last look at herself and wagged her head disapprovingly at what she saw. "Girl, you haven't looked this bad in….well….ever," she declared at the matted hair, bagged eyes, and pallid skin. Wanting to erase the vision from her mind she slipped into the shower for a long luxurious scalding, designed to wash away what was left of yesterday's misery from her body, mind, and soul.

20 minutes later, Trisha stepped from the shower, feeling lighter and more alive than she had in the past 2 days. She admired her naked body in the mirror. Even though Lincoln had no gym for her to work out in, she'd stayed fit over the summer by running, hiking, and generally treating her homestay house as a jungle gym. "Not bad for not

having an LA Fitness within 500 miles," she mused as she flexed her shoulders and biceps. This was the body men pledged to kill or die for. This was the physical realm that men wanted to enter and swore they'd never leave. To Trisha, this was her temple, and not just anyone was invited to worship there. She'd been with men who'd have paid their last cent to enjoy her charms, only to cheat on her as soon as the newness wore off. Nowadays she was less concerned with the physical expression of a relationship and more focused on the emotional one. Hot guys in LA were a dime a dozen. Now Lincoln, that was another matter, but still every male tourist that came to town couldn't help but wonder what it would be like to be invited into her pants, and she could have had her pick of the litter.

But she never did.

Not once during this long summer did she connect physically or emotionally with anyone that had anything to offer her that she wanted.

Until she met Martin Teebs.

Physically Martin was nothing of the sort of hardbody that Trisha was used to dating. His face brought the word 'ordinary' to mind. In short, if he'd been walking down Hollywood Blvd and Trisha had passed him going the other direction…..she'd never have even known he existed. In fact, except for Martin's drooling stare the first time she met him at the courthouse, she'd still never have known he existed in Lincoln, even as they both temporarily occupied the tiny town. It was that night, that one night at the brewery when Trisha was a couple of beers into her feel good, that Martin came clean and spilled his story to her. While she didn't know it at the time, that moment she first heard about Rosita was a beginning. It was the start, almost as if someone was pulling on a long zipper on a bag, trying to release the truth. While it took days for the rest of the zipper to open up, it was inexorable and each day that Trisha woke up, she felt it more and more. It was a slow tug on her soul as the real Rosita seemed to occupy more and more of Trisha's real estate. On that final day….yesterday, Trisha was moving as if under the weight of 2 people. At the time she couldn't tell if it was the burden of knowing Rosita's end, or if it might just be a new beginning, a metamorphosis for the 19th century beauty?

Martin…..

Now that Trisha seemingly had shed the influence of Rosita, it left her with a clean and clear picture of Martin Teebs. No longer did the memories of a long dead woman cloud her judgement. Now she could see Martin for who he really was, and what she really felt about him. Surprisingly Trisha still felt some connection to the sad, strange man. With no attraction to him, she still had one burning emotion that only he could quench.

She wanted Martin Teebs to want her….as badly as he wanted Rosita, and she didn't understand exactly why?

That Martin was able to brush Trisha off as just some sort of vehicle to reach Rosita bothered her. She'd listened to the man lay his soul bare about this mystery woman that she looked so much like, that she became jealous of Rosita Luna. Surely, Trisha would never respond to Martin's advances should they ever happen, but just to know someone hungered for her mind and soul as much as for her body would reinforce the fact that not all men were worthless pricks attached to the rest of their anatomy. Glancing back into the mirror at her full breasts, her damp hair cascading around her shoulders, Trisha determined that yes, she could play up the Rosita angle enough to make Martin crave her. She'd read enough in Farber's book to know what happened to Rosita during Martin's frequent absences. She could fill in the gaps for him almost as if the real Rosita had come back to life, and Martin would not be able to withstand it.

Step 1 was to get his attention, step 2 was to seek him out and let him know his woman had returned. Deciding that a topless photo texted to him would definitely get his attention, Trisha walked back to the bedroom to retrieve her phone. It was nowhere to be seen on her bedside table, nor was it tangled in the bedsheets she'd turned inside out during the course of her sleep. The living room, kitchen, and bathroom further failed to yield her prized iPhone. It was unlike Trisha (and every other 24 year old) to be more than arm's length from their phone but try as she might, she couldn't find it. Failing every other option, she got dressed to walk down to the pageant grounds, on the off chance she left her phone there, and no one had walked off with it. She knew Martin was staying at the Patron House. If she happened to see him, she'd just have to move right to step 2, knowing their time together in Lincoln would be short.

Dressed, and walking out the front door, Trisha gulped in lungfuls of the clean mountain air as she began walking into town. Even from her moving vantage point she could tell that something was amiss.

Just where the hell was everyone?

2.

"Well shit, Martin," was all Steve could manage in the flat morning light. Just in front of him, the dusty silhouettes of Billy Bonney and Rosita Luna faded from sight, on their way back to a time which Steve would give his left arm to visit. Martin quick-stepped back to the rental car driven by his wife Lilly, grabbed his suitcase, and tossed it into the back seat. Steve squinted his eyes to see if the woman was smiling, but if she was, it was hidden behind a dark scowl.

Steve's friend, Martin Teebs had just made the most fateful choice of his life, running back to the now frigid arms of his wife rather than the electric embrace of his lover from another time, Rosita Luna. Right up until Martin pivoted in the middle of Route 380, cutting through the heart of Lincoln, Steve would have laid money that he couldn't afford to lose, that Teebs would choose the great beauty from the past. Why hadn't he?

The skinny tires on Lilly's rental car screeched away in protest as the back of Martin's head grew smaller and smaller in Steve's vision. He thought, although he couldn't prove it, that the big man might have looked back for just a moment, a single tear streaming down his face. As the hum of the tiny engine faded in the background, Steve kicked his boot tip into the tire of his truck. While he didn't appreciate being left holding the bag in any situation, he couldn't help but feel that this time he was left holding….well, nothing. No Billy the Kid to talk to. No Martin Teebs to explain time travel to him. No chance to get back to Lincoln circa 1878 and see the real Lincoln County War go on. No…..with Martin, Billy, and Rosita's sudden departure, Steve was left with nothing but a nasty gash on his head that would leave a handsome scar, and the brief memories of talking face to face with the west's most infamous outlaw.

Talking to himself as he sauntered around to the driver's door, Steve asked, "What in the actual hell am I supposed to do now? Huh? Go back to looking at fake Billy the Kid pictures in Facebook groups? Try to explain to the damn media where that asshole Farber up and disappeared to? Give tours of the hospital room where I had coffee with Billy the Kid?" Steve snorted in laughter and disgust at the thought of any of it. He'd gotten so close….so close to his dream of really living the Lincoln County War, and in a flash, it had been stripped away from him like a guy's last dollar at a strip club.

Climbing into the cab of the massive pickup, he slipped it into gear and slowly started driving west towards Capitan. While the buildings in Lincoln all looked the same as they did the day before, they now had new meaning. Steve had impossibly met the guy responsible for all of this to still be standing. Through his buddy Martin Teebs, he'd gotten the chance, however briefly, to cross the great divide in time and sat at the hospital bedside of one Billy the Kid. The brass ring was that close….and then, it was gone. When Billy faded from sight, so too did Steve's chances to get answers to so many questions that he had. Steve rolled through the quiet street back to his life, the one he had before Billy the Kid and Carl Farber came to interrupt.

"That's that," Steve said to his dashboard with a sigh, "The Kid's gone and disappeared from Lincoln yet again."

Suddenly an icy chill shot through the big cowboy. Sure Billy, Martin, and Rosita were gone……but so too were two other people. Kevin Barrow and Trisha Davis. The doppelgangers of Kid and Rosita melted away during the furious shootout the day prior and hadn't been seen since. To be honest, Steve wasn't sure they ever actually existed. If they did, someone was going to come looking for them. When that someone came, they were going to ask when they were last seen. When that answer was given, it would have been someone putting out the trash or letting out the dog on a Tuesday morning in Lincoln. That person would have seen a big pickup truck roll into town, stop on the eastern edge of the village and have a big cowboy get out with two young people who looked naggingly familiar. When that person told detectives what they saw they would mention only one person who was last seen on that early morning with Kevin and Trisha, standing on the side of the only road through Lincoln, New Mexico.

Steve….from Capitan. If Trisha and Kevin were alive, Steve would be the last person they'd been seen with. If they weren't well…."Aw, shit," said Steve as he pushed harder down on the gas pedal and melted into the distance.

3.

Two days after arriving back in New Jersey from their trip to New Mexico, Martin and Lilly sat at their kitchen table, drinking coffee and each lost in their own thoughts. Both now fully aware that the last five years of their life had been rewound, they had several conversations that bogged down in fits and starts, trying to make sense of it. Somewhere between Martin choking on a glob of green chile enchiladas in the Patron House Bed & Breakfast, and Lilly pounding firmly on his chest to dislodge the killer *comida*, Martin had gone on a fantastical voyage that spanned some 40 years of his life, right up until his death. While Death came to claim Martin in those final moments, it somehow allowed him to slip through its boney grasp and reunite in the otherworld with his great love, Rosita Luna, and the son he'd never before met, Martin Jr.. While Martin's life was slipping away from choking both in the here and now and the afterlife, Lilly's insistent hammer blows plucked Martin's happiness from the grasp of Rosita and brought him back to a day 5 years prior in their lives. Now, sitting here, both remembering all that had gone on in that 5-year period, words escaped either of them.

"So, umm….what's on the schedule for today?" Martin asked Lilly formally. Knowing that just 3 days ago, another man named Dallas Jones had been inside of his wife, Martin had adopted a strict hands-off policy towards Lilly until he could make more sense of their relationship. The fact that he had been inside of the beautiful Rosita Luna the same day (7 times, to be exact) made his conundrum even more difficult to navigate. On the same day, both he and his loving wife had slept with other people who they seemed to have far more interest in than each other.

"Not sure hon. Maybe, I don't know…..see a movie later?" responded Lilly somewhat cautiously. She'd purposely dropped Martin off to see his girlfriend from the past that day, giving him an ultimatum to choose, by day's end, either Rosita or herself. Of course, after a solid knock on the skull during a minor car accident, Lilly was suddenly awash in 5 years worth of memories, few of which involved Martin. She'd purposely slept with the handsome B&B proprietor in this version of her life just as she did in the first one. That Martin found out about it, and seemingly didn't mind at first shocked Lilly, and then annoyed her. She wanted some sort of passion from the man she married. Even if disguised in anger, something, some kind of dramatic, escalating emotion would be better than the droll everyman sitting in front of her.

"Ok, let's play it by ear Lil," said Martin as he rose to fill his coffee cup and walk into the living room. Martin padded his way towards the couch in the utter silence of an early weekday morning. While Martin should have been at work that day, he'd taken the balance of the week off for he and Lilly to figure out how their lives would move forward, but talk of coffee and movies was all they were able to manage.

Billy, Martin thought…..what was he doing now? When was he, as in, what year did he and Rosita go back to? Was he fighting the Lincoln County War, or did they return to a time later? Was Rosita able to find their son Junior in the time warp? If not, where was the boy, and who was caring for him? The possibilities seemed all bad and made Martin's head hurt. He'd stood on the road two days prior and made the most fateful choice of his life. His great love and the mother of his child Rosita Luna stood there, waiting for her man to run into her arms and disappear back to a time that Lilly could never even imagine. Equidistant in the other direction, Lilly, car horn blaring, challenged Martin to make his decision or be left behind. In one of those moments in life that seems to play in ultra slow motion, Martin scanned the playing field like a baseball manager, waiting to see what his next move would be. The smart thing to do would be to go for the sure thing…Rosita. She was madly in love with him, would do anything for him, and would remain by his side until he drew his dying breath. Lilly was a wildcard. Sure, she loved Martin, but not enough to keep Dallas Jones outside of the place where only Martin should be invited in. Lilly had shown in her time that she tolerated most of Martin's foibles, but the deep burning, love and lust that she might have felt for him when they met was gone. 6 feet under, never to be exhumed.

Martin knew all this as he stood there, Rosita waving her arms to beckon him home, Lilly blaring the car horn to bully him back to their predictable lives. If his memory served him right, he stepped in the direction of Rosita, Billy, and Steve and had made his mind up to go, just go back to the warm embrace of the past. As he neared and Lilly tossed his suitcase in the road, a ghastly vision appeared in Martin's mind. In it, a broken, frail Rosita Luna held a gun to her head, demanding Martin come no closer. In the moment before he dove to stop her, she pulled the trigger, her skull coming apart on the wall of Paulita Maxwell's bedroom in Fort Sumner. By the time Martin arrived a split second later, Rosita was already dead. Numb with shock, he stood there knowing that this was his fault, and no one else's. He was the one that came and went from Rosita's life, leaving her when she needed him most. As her blood seeped into the floorboards, drop by drop, the recognition that he had caused all of this and it couldn't be undone seeped into Martin's soul. He simply had no control over his travels through time. If he had, he'd have taken the first exit to 1878 with Rosita, thrown away his return pass, and never looked back. He'd have been there to protect her from the horrific bastard, Carl Farber. He'd have been there for the birth of his son. He'd have taken care of, and provided for Rosita for the rest of their happy lives together. He'd have fought bravely with his pal Billy in the Lincoln County War and beyond. He'd have done all these things and more, except…he never did. He couldn't. Just when he'd settle into old Lincoln on one of his trips back in time, some stupid thing would happen and he'd be catapulted back to the future. He'd leave at the most inopportune times, never returning in time to fix whatever he'd just screwed up. It was heartbreaking and comical at the same time. Just when things were going according to Martin's dreams, he wound up exiting stage left and there wasn't a thing he could do about it.

Standing there on that night, trembling, Rosita's broken lifeless body floating in his hands, he knew he'd never recover from this. There was no coming back. Even knowing that he'd gotten a rewind and Rosita was alive again, Martin knew, in that final moment, just days ago, on Lincoln's main street, that he was going to take her down that horrific road again, sooner or later. He was going to take the one he loved most dear, and force her into an unthinkable choice….and there'd be no way he could stop her.

Again.

While Martin may not have been running at Lilly in that moment, he was most definitely running away from Rosita, as fast as he could. To love someone so much you must let them go is the ultimate sacrifice, and Martin had made it. He sat heavily on the couch, tears teasing the corners of his eyes. He'd never see Rosita again. He'd never meet his son. He'd never see his pal Billy. In the blink of an eye he'd thrown away everything he felt dear and replaced it with…..

This.

This house, this relationship, this life. This prison…..

"What did I do?" Martin whispered to himself hoarsely, "Oh my God, what did I do?" If Lilly heard him, she didn't want to interrupt his confessional. Martin had determined that he would put Billy and everything else in his rearview mirror, and this was his chance. His pity party could last a few more minutes, then he could march upstairs, empty his desk and bookshelves of Billy books, and force the young outlaw from his mind. He could erase the bookmarks on his computer, delete the photos, burn the notes he'd been taking for another book he thought he might write someday, and just move on. Essentially, Martin could be a man of his word. His word that he'd given to himself, and to Lilly. He could put on his big boy pants and make the best life possible out of this life, and the past be damned. "Yeah," he again said to himself with more confidence than he truly felt, "that's just what I'm gonna do."

"What? What are you doing Martin?" asked Lilly casually from the other room.

Martin walked firmly back into the kitchen and stated, "I'm going upstairs to clean out my office. All that Billy the Kid stuff. The books, everything. It's over Lil. I made my choice and that part of my life is over." Lilly looked both pleased and a little sad at the missive, but simply nodded and replied, "Ok Martin, if that's what you want to do." Martin nodded his head solidly and walked up the stairs, carefully balancing his cup of coffee. Each step seemed to get progressively steeper and higher, almost as if something were trying to prevent him from the deed. Nevertheless, Martin reached the landing and turned towards his office, just in time to hear his phone ring. Surmising maybe Colin was calling to see if he was ok, Martin reached for it and went cold when he saw the name of the caller.

Steve, from Capitan.

4.

"Why!? Why *Billito!*?" demanded Rosita Luna, "He lays his soul bare for me! And then!....." A long pause ensued while Rosita either waited for Billy to finish her thought or she waited for her frantic mind to catch up and do it herself.

"And then he left again Rosie, right?" asked Billy meekly.

"*Si,*" Rosita said sadly, tears beginning to well up in her eyes, "Why?" she asked simply for what Billy hoped was the last time.

Billy huffed and sighed, wishing he had the answers that the beautiful woman wanted, but none were forthcoming. If Billy had any money, he'd have bet every last dime that Martin, or "Teebsie" as Billy liked to call him, would have jumped at the chance to finally establish himself in old Lincoln and as the soon to be husband of Rosita. Even in those final moments when Teebsie began making his way towards Steve's truck, the time travel express loaded and waiting for him, Billy could see the sense of peace in the man's eyes that soon, and finally, he'd be home once and for all. Billy remembered an awkward step by his friend, almost as if he'd sprained an ankle, and Teebsie's victory run slowed. There was a blaring of the car horn at the control of Lilly Teebs, and the world seemed to turn to slow motion. Billy sensed something change in his friend, his eyes clouding with doubt, or was it maybe fear? If Billy could somehow will them back to that moment, he'd run into the street, catch his friend by the shoulder, and guide him quickly to Rosita so the two lovers could escape this time that neither of them seemed to belong in, together. Instead, on unsteady feet, Teebsie turned in mid stride and with just the barest of a parting glance, ran back to his wife and his old, modern day life. Rosita screamed, horrified at what she was seeing, but she and Billy were already on their way to 1877 by then. Billy sincerely hoped that Martin had not heard the scream, knowing his friend would yet again be haunted by an image of his love that he'd carry with him for rest of his days.

"I dunno Rosie, I wish I did." replied Billy finally. Rosita cast sad glances back and forth across Billy and up and down the street. It was almost as if the young woman wasn't in the same reality as everyone else. As if she couldn't believe she'd been sentenced to this place yet again without Martin and with no possibility of parole.

"This man, he makes the love to me," began Rosie in a dialect that made Billy smile, "He makes it in the bed, then on the dresser, the down the stairs…."

"Oh, ok now," interrupted Billy, "Don't need to know every detail."

"On the kitchen table, outside over the wall…."

"Easy now Rosie. That's just for you and Teebsie to know…"

"He even makes the sex up against the woodpile!" snapped Rosita.

"Look here Rosie, I get it. You two are in love. That's what lovers do." said Billy carefully, now wondering if he was ever going to get to see his great love, Maria Hidalgo again, or if time had conspired to rob him of his happiness too?

"And now you say we are in love *Chivato*? Where is this love? Where is this man who loves me?" Rosita asked weakly, "He is in another time, with his Lilly and I shall never see him again. This, you call love?"

Billy let his tired eyelids sag and block out the late summer sun. He'd faced down the Murphy/Dolan gang, shot Joe Grant at point blank range, and even fired the bullets that took down Sheriff Brady, but now Billy wanted to escape his current predicament. Not only did the young woman demand answers from him, if Billy was truthful, he wanted answers about his friend for himself. Billy had nearly been killed by Farber. The same Farber that escaped his own time and wound up somewhere in the past. Perhaps Farber was right here in Lincoln right now? Billy had always looked at Martin as a father figure….and if not, at least as a much older brother. Now he'd been robbed of something that he wanted, needed, and probably would never have again. Why Teebsie, why… Billy wondered to himself.

Reaching for his saddlebags, Rosita spotted the well-worn copy of Sergio Bachaca's book, The True Life of Billy the Kid, that had returned her and Billy to their own time. Looking at it with a mix of revulsion and awe, she couldn't help but speak up. "This book," she said, wagging her finger in its direction, "this book is the key to the travel the time?" Billy just gave a sad half smile and nodded his head. "Then you shall give it to me *Bilito, si?*" asked Rosita in what was more of a demand than a question, "And you will teach me how to use it to travel the time, *si*? I will go and make Martin answer me to why he left. I deserve at least that." Billy had heard a number of bad ideas in his life. Hell, sometimes the worst ones came from his own mouth, but this seemed to be the worst of the worst. Right before their very eyes, they saw Martin make his own choice, of his own free will. Billy tried to picture Rosita showing up on Martin's doorstep, eyes burning bright for her man, only to have Lilly answer the door. In Billy's mind, Lilly wouldn't fight fair and the two would roll on the Teebs' very green lawn, scratching, clawing, and pulling hair until one cried uncle. He could see Teebsie rush to the door to see what the commotion was, only to be startled to see Rosita lying there in the throes of a knock down drag out fight. Martin wouldn't be able to comfort the woman with Lilly there and he'd simply have to tell her to leave, just as he'd done to Billy all those years ago. Rosita's heart, already frail and damaged, would break even harder this time and she'd probably wind up......

No, thought Billy, I can't even think about that again. Rosita's first end was too horrific and Billy didn't want to invite it back into his mind. No, he absolutely couldn't allow this. It was up to him to protect Rosita from herself.

"No Rosie, and I ain't kiddin," he announced firmly, "I can't allow it. This thing is....I don't know…dangerous. It ain't to play with." Rosita eyes boiled while staring at the young man. Billy was her good friend but she didn't expect to be treated this way when he knew how much she was hurting.

"Fine!" she snapped back, "then you go and bring him to me. He will have to look me in the eye and tell me he loves his Lilly, and not me. If he can do that, I will let him go."

"Rosie," Billy began gently, "I done tried that the last time, remember? Tried gettin him back here for Junior. It didn't work then and it ain't gonna work now. Whatever Teebsie's got going on in his head, it took him away from us and I don't expect he's coming back no how." A heavy tear escaped Rosita's eye as it ran down her face and chin, and fell heavily on the dusty main street.

"No." she whispered weakly to herself. Billy was unsure if she was responding to him or accepting her own fate. Noiselessly, more tears began to rain from her chocolate colored eyes but she refused to make a sound. Standing proud and brave, she wore the tears like her own badge of honor...or maybe it was courage? So long did they both stand there in silence that Billy began shifting on his feet uncomfortably. He finally decided to speak.

"Look, Rosie," he began, "Let's give Teebsie a couple of weeks. Maybe a month? He might just realize what he's lost and show up on his own....you know how he likes to do that." Rosita glared from behind her tears but said nothing. "If he's not here by say, October, I'll see about using this book to try and find em, ok?" Rosita's eyes softened almost imperceptibly at the thought but still she remained silent. "So lemme hang onto this," said Billy, gesturing towards the book, "and I'll put it to good use when the time comes, ok?"

Rosita stood there sad and shaking. While she wanted to tell Billy everything, she didn't want to burden the young man further. They both knew the history of what was about to happen in Lincoln in just a few short months. While everyone else would be surprised at the advent of the Lincoln County War, Billy and Rosita surely would not. After all, they'd lived through it already. It was September. Over the coming winter each faction would position themselves for control of the county. Billy and his Regulator pals would be summoned to protect Tunstall's interests. The war would flare with the murder of John Tunstall the next February, and the rest...well, the rest would go down just as the history books demanded. History, thought Rosita, couldn't be changed, could it? If that was so, a bumbling man from the future, dressed in jeans and a shirt with cats and fireworks on it would once again show up in Lincoln the night before Billy and his pals would murder Sheriff Brady. That was history. That's what had already happened in Rosita's life. Wouldn't it happen again? For a moment, Rosita relaxed, a feeling of warmth spreading throughout her body. Martin would be back. He had to. His presence in Lincoln and in her life was preordained, wasn't it? Nothing would change and Martin would be back in her arms. Nothing would change and.....

The memory of that horrid night in Fort Sumner stabbed at her mind. In the nanosecond that it took for her to decide to pull the trigger, she imagined a better life for Martin if she were not in it. She was broken, frail, and unrepairable. The weight of her sad existence would be a life sentence for Martin, burdened with taking care of her and Junior for the rest of his days. Never would she regain the light and the beauty she once had, because Carl Farber had stolen it. All she would have been able to offer Martin was pain, anguish, and an anchor to a woman that barely resembled the one he fell in love with. Billy looked at the quiet woman, deep in thought, as tears again rolled down her cheeks.

"What Rosie?" implored Billy, "What did I say?"

Rosita sighed and wiped her eyes, "*Billito*, this time again we have. Will it be the same as the first time?"

"You mean, is it gonna turn out the same way?"

"*Si*, can the history be changed?" asked Rosita.

Billy turned his eyes towards the sky, contemplating the question. In his life, at least the historical one, he'd just arrived in Lincoln after riding with the Jesse Evans gang. Just 2 months ago, he'd killed that loudmouth blacksmith back in Arizona. He hadn't even been hired on by Tunstall yet, although he knew Dick Brewer would come calling within a few weeks. While Lincoln and everyone in it seemed to be on the same trajectory that history said they would, Billy and Rosita might not? After all, Billy had used Bachaca's book to foil Garrett and live a long, somewhat happy life the first time. If nothing else, that taught him that history could be changed, even if it shouldn't be.

"Well, I'm guessing it can," he admitted, "Cause Garrett didn't kill me the way all them books said he would."

"But now that is a new history, no?" asked Rosita, "can that change, or will we all wind up in July in that same….." Rosita stopped herself before she had to face the gruesome mental image again. Billy tread carefully into the conversation, not wanting to open old wounds.

"It can Rosie. I'm sure of it." he concluded simply. Rosita, unsure of whether Billy was telling the truth, or lying to spare her, simply nodded her head. One other question had nagged at her since their return, and she figured now was as good a time as any to discuss it.

"What happened to this Trisha and the Kevin?"

Billy looked out towards the Tunstall Store, where a carpenter was banging nails into a sign that read simply, "Bank". People milled up and down the main street, oblivious to what was coming, and unaware of what had just happened, albeit 140 years in the future. The only ones who knew or felt anything were standing right here. "I've been wonderin about that myself Rosie," said Billy with a nod, "cause it don't feel right, what happened and all."

"*Si Billito*, I feel this the same, as if something of me I left behind. *Intiende*?"

Billy knew exactly what she was talking about because he felt the exact same thing. Something was missing. Something was amiss. Some small piece of Billy Bonney was missing and try as he might, he couldn't figure out what it was. Unable to solve the mystery at the moment, he put as good a spin on it as he could, "Yep, but I bet it's just all the stuff we gone thru in the last few weeks. It's a lot."

Rosita eyed Billy, knowing he wasn't telling her the truth, but too tired to push the conversation further. Suddenly feeling sick to her stomach, she grimaced and simply said, "*Gracias Billito*, I shall go home now," and walked away. Billy watched her go, finally disappearing around a curve in the road. He shook his head at the task in front of him. If he was ever to reunite Martin and Rosita, he was going to have to have an even bigger reunion first, and he wasn't at all sure how he'd even find his way there to attend?

5.

"So now that we've got some time to talk, just what in the hell did you do to me Martin?" asked Steve directly into his mobile phone.

Martin thought for a moment before he answered. Did he do this? Was all of this time travel and circular living a product of him, or was something else at work here? Martin was an unspectacular man, given to leading an unspectacular life, right up until he didn't. Steve's question cut to the very core of the past 5 years of Martin's life. Who did this? Why? And how? Martin yearned to blame this on Sergio Bachaca, the now dead author who somehow weaved the vile Carl Farber into the story. Even still, Bachaca, if his final words could be proven true, could only be guilty of adding Farber to an already incomprehensible situation, but not creating it. No, someone else had done that. Some entity that remained unknown was fucking with Martin royally, and seemingly continued to do so. If there was some cosmic puppet master, Martin would love to get face to face with the wizard and duke it out, once and for all. He'd wrestle back control of his future and die a boring, but once again sane man.

When running for Lilly's car just a few days ago, intent on returning to his mundane life, Martin assumed that once free of Lincoln, all of his problems would be over. Sure, he'd miss Rosita terribly, and probably never recover from the experience, but at least he could settle back into his regular routine and this chapter in his life would be over. Thinking carefully about the situation he'd left behind however, Martin quickly realized that words like "normal" and "regular" were to be exorcised from his vocabulary. Sure, Rosita and Billy were gone. Sure, he was back in New Jersey with Lilly. Sure, the investigation into the disappearance of Carl Farber would never bear any fruit. Old Steve might spin a yarn or two over the next few years, but he was 2000 miles away and Martin assumed that would be enough of a buffer zone. The only thing (or things) that would cause a ripple in his peaceful harmony went by the names Kevin Barrow and Trisha Davis. Martin still struggled to understand if they were even real people? He'd seen Rosita emerge from Trisha just as he was shot mistakenly by Brandon at the pageant. It was as if there were some metamorphosis right before his very eyes. In one moment it was Trisha Davis of Los Angeles, and in the next it was Rosita Luna of Lincoln. The nagging question then was….where did Trisha go? The same question existed for Kevin Barrow as the bullet from Farber's gun extinguished all that was left of the young man and left only the real Billy Bonney in his place.

What the hell had happened?

"Hey Martin! You still there?!" bellowed Steve into the phone as Martin realized his thoughts had overtaken his actions and he'd never answered the man.

"What do you mean Steve?" asked Martin with caution, "I mean, I didn't really do anything."

"Bullshit Martin," cackled Steve with a laugh, "I'm here having to paste 5 years worth of pages back onto my calendar and you're trying to tell me it ain't your fault? You outta take me for someone smarter than that." Martin sighed heavily on the phone, unable to answer Steve's question…or his own for that matter.

"Look, Steve. This is as messed up for me as it is for you. I just got back here to New Jersey and I'm hoping that this all just goes away. As for the do over on the last 5 years, I can't explain it. I wish I could," answered Martin thoughtfully before he continued, "or, actually maybe I don't wish I could. I'm not sure I want to know any more."

"Well Hoss, I sure as shit want to know more, *comprende*? Aside from everything else, guess who in the hell is the last man to be seen with that Barrow kid and the Davis girl…or at least everyone thinks it was them."

"Ummm, you?" Martin said, sounding like a little boy about to be scolded by his father.

"You're damned right it was me Martin! And all of that, every last bit, is thanks to you!" Steve's accusation hung in the air for a time before Martin could answer.

"Look Steve, I'm sorry. Really. I know that doesn't help much right now, but I swear to you that I'm not doing this. If I had any control over this I'd turn the ride off. Shit, 5 years ago, or…." Martin stopped as he struggled to get the timeline right, "or a month ago, I don't know, I put this all to rest. I'm having a barbeque in my backyard and Billy the Kid shows up at my doorstep. I didn't ask for that! I didn't want that! I was willing to just let it be. You can be pissed at me if you want Steve, but you're pissing up the wrong tree!" Martin, surprised at how much emotion he was able to muster, noticed his rapid breathing and his eye twitching. This entire experience had taken a toll on him, and now he was being forced to pay the bill.

"Sorry huh? Ok then Martin. You can be sorry. I can accept that. Shit, if you get this figured out maybe we never have to get old?" Steve laughed into the receiver.

"You're already old Steve," joked Martin in return.

"Ok then, old…er, how's that? The problem is those kids. They were there and now they're not. Billy and Rosita are gone and I'm hoping they stay that way. They took that blasted book with them so that's covered. The only thing that might cross me up is that phone. The Davis girl, shit…I mean Rosita had it while we were in the house that morning. I didn't go back to look, but I'm sure the cops did, and I know they haven't found it. Where the hell is it Martin?"

The phone, thought Martin. Where did it go? Rosita had sent him a photo from it, presumably with Jane's help, on the morning he was released from the hospital. While the rest of that day was a pleasant blur of talking, kissing, and lovemaking….Martin was sure he remembered at least a couple of selfies of himself and Rosita.

"Shit!" he said aloud before he even thought to stop himself.

"Well now, what did you just remember?" asked Steve with a lilt in his voice.

"I took some pictures of Rosita and me with it…that day. The Monday. We were in bed, on the stairs, in the kitchen, up against the woodpile…."

"Whoa son, I don't need to know all that."

"If someone finds that phone and sees those pictures, it's not Steve from Capitan they're going to be looking for, it's me!!" screamed Martin loudly enough that Lilly rushed to the bottom of the stairs and yelled up to make sure Martin was ok.

"Haha," laughed Steve at his friend's predicament, "technology will trip you up every time. I'm glad I grew up before all this shit was invented. Some of the stuff I did? Let's just say I can't run for President….cept you can't prove any of it!"

"Wonderful, I'm so happy for you Mr. President," said Martin drolly, "In the meantime, what the hell do we do about this?"

"Could Rosita have taken the damn thing with her? What would be the point? It wouldn't work back then." asked Steve.

"It could be. Geez, I hope she did. In a day the battery will be dead and that will be that." surmised Martin.

"Well, no one's found it...so that's a good sign. I say we just shut the hell up about this thing and let it die down. You understand Martin?" asked Steve in a question that was clearly a command. Lacking any better plan, Martin simply agreed, "Um hmmm." While Martin's current life was without much in the way of excitement, it probably wouldn't have the Feds knocking on his door any time soon. That Steve believed the phone was now gone also gave Martin some measure of relief. If he could just give this a little more time, the past might just be in the past....and stay there.

"Besides, when I drove out of Lincoln the other day, the Sheriff and his boys stopped me to say hey," mused Steve, "they'd have been some shit detectives if I was hiding two adults in my old truck and no one noticed."

"Alright, I got it Steve. We keep quiet about this and let it fade away. Copy or roger, or whatever the hell it is that you guys say," said Martin sarcastically.

"Don't you worry about what we say, tenderfoot. Just do me a favor and don't go winding me back in time anymore. I don't wanna wake up tomorrow and be going to my birthday party when I was 9 years old. Lost my virginity that day to old lady Smithers at the skating rink. It was like wrestling with a bagful of wet mothballs. It's haunted me ever since." Steve laughed hard enough that Martin had to question whether he was kidding or not.

Fade away, Martin thought. Would this experience ever really fade away? While he felt sorry for the Davis and Barrow families, he wanted nothing more to do with his one week in Lincoln. Rosita and Billy were back where they belonged. Bachaca's book was in the past and no longer a threat, and now Martin was reasonably sure that Trisha's iPhone was also gone, never to be seen again. As long as that phone stayed gone, the pictures of Martin and Rosita would never be seen. Rosita taking it with her to the past was just about the best thing that could have happened to it.

6.

Trisha stayed inside the rest of the day, still freaked out by the lack of any movement about town, and the fact that the internet was down in her house. Even if she'd had her phone, the high mountain walls that ensconced Lincoln prevented any reliable cell signal from reaching the small town. In a home, with a working internet connection, she'd have been able to message her family and friends to let them know she was ok. As it was, no one had heard from her in two days and they were likely worried sick.

The next day, she rose and dressed for work, despite the fact that she wasn't sure that anyone else would actually show up. Braiding her hair and slipping her boots on, she walked gingerly from the front door of the house, stepping her way east towards the courthouse. Squirrels jumped playfully from tree to tree, as the birds serenaded her journey. A few deer lazily laid in the tall grass and swung their heads to look at her as she walked by. All in all it was an ideal morning save for one key thing.

There were still no people around. None. As in, zero…and it was freaking Trisha out. It seemed as if the town had been abandoned after the violence of Sunday afternoon, but no one had bothered to tell her. Cars remained parked where they were, the pageant grounds and sets were untouched. Even the blood of Martin, Farber, and Steve was still coagulated in the dirt next to the courthouse. Trisha had known something was wrong on Sunday as she worked her way back to her house, but now she was downright scared. If everyone else had left, why didn't someone take her with them? Why did not a single truck come blasting through town, rattling the old buildings like old metal fillings in your teeth? Had the Sheriff blockaded the town to the east and west, trying to find the mystical portal that the creep Carl Farber had crawled through? No answers made sense to her as she approached the deathly quiet building. It was clear that putting her uniform on today was a waste of time. No tourists stirred, waiting to get a look at The Kid's final stand against Olinger and Bell. Trisha looked around in circles, fists balled in anger and fear, for any sign of human life, getting more panicked by the second. Eyes darting from building to building, head on a swivel, she finally released every bit of emotion in a long, high pitched, blood curdling scream.

"WHERE…ARE…YOU!?"

The words tore at her throat, making her gag when she was done. Tears began to fall as the pretty woman feared she'd never escape the prison that had been born of Lincoln, NM. She fell to her knees in the middle of the street, weeping loudly, hoping that someone might hear her cries and save her from this madness. Just then, she heard someone clear their throat, and her eyes snapped to attention towards a bench near the courthouse entrance.

"Hey, Trish," called the young man, "It's ok. I'm here."

Looking at the distraught woman from behind his own scared eyes was none other than Kevin Barrow.

7.

Upon hanging up the phone, Martin began rummaging around the spare bedroom that served as his office. Without a plan, he started to scour the shelves of every one of his Billy the Kid books, creating a neat stack near the door. Down from the walls came his Billy poster, along with the framed photos of Lincoln that he'd put up. As the office grew more sterile, the pile of historical rubble grew in concert. Three times Martin had to stop himself from doing the accounting on the amount of money he was getting ready to throw away. Logic dictated that he perhaps sell the books, but bartering for fifty cents at a garage sale over the written lives of his friends was something Martin didn't think he could bear. At first, the idea of a huge bonfire appealed to him, but his selfish thoughts were quickly banished. Martin could quickly and easily donate his books to the Waldwick Public Library where someone else could learn from them, but hopefully not learn enough to screw up the tally of lives that Martin had.

Making a mental note that he needed to find some strong boxes, Martin next sat at his computer and clicked the history tab on his web browser. Unsurprisingly, his screen was filled with links that referenced Billy, the War, the Regulators, and just about every other keyword attached to New Mexico Territory, circa 1878. Highlighting as many as he could at a time, Martin made liberal use of the delete button as his friends, and his memories of them, were reduced to so much digital trash. Pausing a few times to catch his breath, Martin talked to himself, "It has to be this way. You have no future if you're stuck in the past. You made your decision, don't second guess it." His eyes closed heavily as if he was unable to look at the screen, a wave of nausea sweeping over him.

"Who are you talking to Martin?" asked Lilly, who'd padded quietly up the stairs.

Martin's head snapped around, surprised that his wife had heard his self pep talk, "Wha? What did you say?"

"You were talking to someone. I heard you." said Lilly with a knowing smirk. Martin drew a deep breath and held it for a few seconds before releasing it. He raised his head to smile at his wife.

"I was talking to me Lil," he replied, "Telling myself that I had done the right thing, and that all of this stuff needs to go. That's what you heard." Martin stared directly at

Lilly, almost daring her to try to pick apart his story. Although her eyes clouded over a bit, she gave no inclination that she would. After a few seconds, she spoke, "Um, Martin? I've been meaning to ask." Lilly stopped and took a deep breath to brace herself for either the question or the answer. "Am I in any of these books?" she asked, pointing to the impressive stacks Martin had created. Martin looked confused, trying to figure out how to answer without hurting his wife's feelings.

"No," he said with a shake of his head, "I mean, how would you be?"

"You said I had a life, 5 years of a life that we're doing over. I owned that B&B Martin. I sold it to you. I lived in Lincoln. You're telling me there's no mention of Lilly Teebs anywhere? In any of these?" Martin shrugged his shoulders and lifted his hands. "Well, no Lil. That's recent history. These are all the history of Billy. There'd be no reason for you to be in these." Lilly looked at the floor and slowly nodded her head. "What about Austin, Martin? Where can I find out more about him?" A deep stab of sadness and regret lanced through Martin, knowing that at some point, Lilly was going to need to know more about what happened to her son, and that he would be powerless to help her. The knock on her head had given Lilly recall of the last 5 years of her life, but like Martin, she had no ability to understand where those 5 years had gone, along with the people in them.

"I'm not sure Lil," Martin said slowly, "It happened. I'm sure of it, all of those things. I know Austin exists…or existed, or…I don't know. Junior did too. You saw the photo." Lilly looked up from the floor to stare at Martin solemnly but said nothing. "I'm just not sure there's any record or, you know, anything that could prove it?" While Martin had unreliably found a way to travel back through time, he hadn't found a way to travel to this 60 month wrinkle in time that he'd created. How could he travel back (forward) in time to meeting Warner Smith III, his Denver real estate agent? How could he, if he was foolish enough to try, travel back to that night in Fort Sumner when he was gut shot alongside Tom Folliard? For that matter, how could he place himself in Mr. Talbot's office and ace his sales interview again, sending him on journeys across the country, and getting him access to his dear New Mexico on a regular basis? This was the rub. While Martin seemed to be able to jog through time, sometimes at will, there were two versions of history now, and he was only permitted to explore the current one.

Lilly raised her head, intent on not sulking her way into a depression over something she couldn't change. "How about that Steve? He's a detective, right? Isn't this what he does? Maybe he can find something?" Lilly asked hopefully. Fresh off his call with Steve, who was as confused as the rest of them over what had happened, Martin knew the old cowboy wasn't going to be able to help out this time. "I don't think so Lil, at least not right now. Steve's trying to get his bearings over this thing too." Lilly just shook her head at the news and turned to walk away without a word. She and Martin's brief spray of happiness and recommitment after returning home had fizzled and they were both left as something less for the knowledge they had. Who would have thought that infidelity, having children out of wedlock, publishing said story for the world to read and mock, and shacking up with other bit players could possibly affect their marriage? That 5 years of Lilly's life had been magically erased seemed cruel and unfair, being as she'd brought an entirely new life into the world. In some desperate way she hoped those 5 years had been totally erased from history. She couldn't bear the thought of Austin, lost and alone. At best, his dolt of a father might have swooped in to take care of him. Lilly winced at the thought that if the *best* thing she could hope for was Dallas taking care of the boy, the lesser options must be positively horrid. Just a few steps down the hall a question formed in her mind and she turned back to Martin's office. Unable to help herself, even if she didn't want the honest answer, she propped herself in the doorway once again.

"Martin, are you in any of these books?" she asked curiously. Martin raised his eyes at the towers of paper. These books represented many thousands of dollars and many hours of his unsatisfying work at the ad agency. He'd chased every bit of knowledge about The Kid through them, but ultimately they all failed to deliver. The one book that didn't was the one that Martin no longer had. Sergio Bachaca's book about Billy tossed Martin to and fro in time, allowing him to experience what others only dreamed about. Martin didn't need to inventory the stacks of texts in front of him, for he knew that book wasn't in it. It was with Billy….and Rosita.

"No Lil, despite everything that happened, Martin Teebs never showed up in any history book. I guess that means that maybe all that stuff really didn't happen? I just don't know?" Lilly pasted a faint smile on her face and nodded, walking down the hall and into the master bedroom. Martin thought more about it and was glad his name didn't grace any book about Billy the Kid. The FBI was searching for the missing Davis and Barrow kids and made it clear they'd want to talk to Martin again at some point. He could only imagine sitting beneath a bright light in some industrial looking, shitty interrogation room, being blasted with questions about why his name, Martin Teebs, was laced into every historical text about Billy the Kid? They'd dig deeper because, well that's what the FBI does, and they'd find no ancestors of Martin's with that name anywhere in the 1870's or near Lincoln, New Mexico. Then there'd be more investigations, Steve would be pulled into it all, Lilly would have to come clean and at some point, the world would know that Martin Teebs had either time traveled back to 1878, or he'd simply gone insane, taking his wife and friends with him on the journey.

"No thanks," said Martin to no one.

Rising from his chair, he began to put some of the books into a few boxes he'd collected and smiled, knowing his secret was safe. Someone would read all of these books, judging themselves an expert in the Lincoln County War. Someone would smugly walk around at parties and drop nonsensical, arcane knowledge to bored partygoers. Someone would gird their digital loins up at every mistruth and mistake published in social media groups, judging themselves to be the person to set these history newbies straight. Someone would do all this, but these books would never betray the name Martin Teebs. No researcher was ever going to find out about Martin's part in the war or his days in Lincoln. Ever.

Days. Lincoln.

Lincoln. Days.

Lincoln County Days.

"Oh shit!" exclaimed Martin as he remembered the tiny book that Farber had ghost-written. It told everything about his life in Lincoln and even about his time travels! Farber had even written himself into the final few pages, presenting himself as a conquering hero. Anyone with that book could follow the trail of Carl Farber and Martin Teebs all the way from Lincoln, NM to Waldwick, NJ. While Steve had burned one copy, the second one remained. Martin knew it to be so because he'd just seen it, in Trisha's house, just 2 weeks ago.

"Oh no, no, no…" Martin said to himself. Burying his eyes in his hands, he tried to remember what Trisha might have done with it. If the FBI hadn't found it yet, they certainly soon would. Martin had to get that book out of that house. Darting for the phone, he found Brandon's number, the same one he'd called to set up the tour of Lincoln. Martin slumped in his chair as the phone rang and Brandon's cheery "Leave a message!" rang in Martin's ear. Explaining that he needed to be called back right away, and to not say a word about it to Steve, Martin hung up, the phone slipping from his grasp and falling onto the floor.

Behind him, the cursor of his mouse blinked patiently where he'd left it, waiting to erase more of the older history that had been searched on Martin's computer. Had Martin looked over his shoulder he'd have seen the next two Google search entries, dated July 15, 2021, entries that he himself had never made:

Search results for: Kevin Barrow
Search results for: Trisha Davis

8.

A few days later Rosita woke early, just at sunup. It wasn't for any other reason than her roiling stomach every morning. While it hadn't yet been long past when her period was due, she had gone through this with Junior, and she already knew she was with child. Retching into a small pail she kept at her bedside, she lay there sweating and waiting for the morning sickness to pass. Some days it did quickly, and others she'd continue to struggle for an hour before it would let go of her.

The reality that she was once again pregnant, once again alone, and once again going to be a single parent saddened the beautiful woman and tore at her soul. Her first son, Martin Jr. was nowhere to be found, lost in some time fold that she, Billy, and Martin had somehow escaped. While she had only known the boy until he was 2 years old before she had died, she remembered every line and curve of him, his smile and his twinkling eyes, the way he laughed so hard his entire body shook, and the way he desperately needed a father, to the point that he began calling Billy Bonney "dada". Billy had used that wretched book back then to travel to Martin's house in New Jersey, in Martin's own time, in order to bring him back for his son. The meeting had quickly gone off the rails and Billy returned, but Martin did not. While Rosita had not confided in Billy that she was once again pregnant, it wouldn't be long before she was showing and she wouldn't have to tell anyone. After considering how to handle the situation for a few days, she finally sent for Billy to visit her home one late afternoon. It was nearly October and Rosita was already 2 months into the new pregnancy with this new baby Teebs. A careful knock at the door prompted her to rise and peek out the window to make sure it was the Kid.

"Hey Rosie! How are ya?" Billy asked, his voice full of glee. Rosita smiled in return and welcomed the boy in.

"*Hola Billito*, please come in and sit down," Rosita beckoned Billy in and motioned towards a chair at her table, "Would you like some *cafe*?"

"Naw, thanks though. Just took a big swig outta the horse trough!" Billy joked, to which Rosita at first looked on in horror, and then in laughter when she realized he was kidding, "What's up Rosie?"

Rosita's smile tightened a bit, nervous as she was about this conversation. After breathing deeply and smoothing her skirt, she spoke. "I'm pregnant *Billito*, with *Martin's* child," said Rosita flatly, and then added, "again." Billy's eyes opened wide with surprise at the news. He wasn't surprised that Rosita was able to get pregnant so easily, it was more of the "holy cow, are we going through this again" thought that caught Billy's attention. Wanting to measure his response, he simply smiled and said, "Ok."

"The way *Martin* ran back to his Lilly, I think he would not care," confessed Rosita, "but a man should know when he is going to be a father, do you not think so?" Billy threw his head back for a brief moment before deciding that yes, Martin should know. Billy had been there the night that Rosita died, watching Martin cradle her lifeless body in his arms. That night, Martin had to make a fateful choice. Stay with Rosita until morning when she would be buried, or meet his son Junior for a few fleeting moments before Billy and Maria would have to ride off with the boy under the cover of night? Martin's tortuous decision was to stay with the woman he loved, in hopes that somehow he'd get to meet Junior later in his life, or perhaps in some other one?

"Yeah Rosie, of course Teebise should know about his baby. The only question is, how in the hell are we gonna tell him?" Rosita pursed her lips and furrowed her brow as if trying to think of an answer, although she already knew what it was.

"The book, no? I know that you don't want to use this *Billito*, but I think that we must." she said softly. Billy thought back to his last conversation with Martin in the hospital. Martin was clear that he had to move on with his life and that Billy should move on with his. He warned Billy to not use the book to find him, and that Billy the Kid belonged to history, and Martin Teebs belonged to….well, nothing.

"Rosie, that last morning when we was all still in the hospital, Teebsie said something to me. Something like 'don't come looking for me with that book because you don't belong to ne no more'. He was real clear about it too. What do you suppose that meant?"

Rosita's head bobbed around for a moment, trying to find something that made sense in her response. "*No se'Chivato, ustedes son amigos.*" Billy removed his hat and rubbed his eyes.

"I don't know neither Rosie, but he was clear that I shouldn't try to go back," Billy took a deep breath and let it out before continuing, "But I guess this is some special kinda circumstance." Rosita brightened at the thought that Billy might be in agreement. In just days, maybe even hours, she would be able to let Martin know about his new child and maybe this time he would decide to come home to stay? While she was unsure how he'd take the news, she was optimistic and happier than she'd been in weeks.

"So *Billito*, when will you go? Now?" she asked excitedly. Billy held up his hands to bring her excitement back down to earth.

"Whoa now, easy. I ain't even got that book here. I gotta go and fetch it at the Coe's place. Need ta let them boys know I gotta git for awhile too. It's a long trip to New Jersey, Rosie, a week by train from the railhead in Las Vegas. Then I gotta see if I can find Teebsie and if'n he'll come back?"

"And then?" Rosita asked, "You must do the same travel in the reverse? The same time to come back to Lincoln?"

Billy nodded, "Yep." Rosita closed her eyes tightly and hung her head. Instead of hours or days, she'd wait weeks to get an answer to her prayer. Waiting, hoping, and praying that her Martin would come back. What would she do if he didn't? How could she possibly hold things together if she was once again abandoned? She began shaking her head firmly.

"No, no!" she yelled, surprising Billy, "I will not think like that! *No mas!*"

"Rosie?" asked Billy gently.

"*Billito*, I won't be the poor sad woman, hoping that you can bring my man back. *Martin* will see that we belong when you find him, and he will come to me. I will not think anything else. No more." Billy smiled at his friend's strength and nodded his head.

"Ok, I'll git to Frank's place in the morning and get on my way."

"No! Wait *por favor?*" asked Rosita urgently, "so that you would go from here *Billito?*

So I can see that you have gone to my *Martin?*" Rosita implored. For Billy, it was only another 20 miles or so in the saddle to return to Lincoln. If it meant that Rosita would be ok for the time he intended to spend away, then it was a small price to pay for his friend's happiness.

"Sure Rosie, I'll come back here by tomorrow afternoon. Maybe you can even pack me a lunch for my trip!" Billy joked. Rosita smiled and began to cry, not tears of sadness, but of happiness and relief that she and Martin might get their one more chance. Billy had already decided to try for Lincoln in what he thought was the time they just left, around the year 2021. Trains were faster in the future and it could save him days if he could just find some way to pay for a ticket. In any event, those details could wait until tomorrow when with book in hand, Billy the Kid would once more attempt to cross the great divide of time and push himself to Lincoln, New Mexico at a time over 140 years distant in the future.

"No problem," he said to himself with a smirk, "I'm coming for ya Teebsie. See you soon my friend."

9.

Amazed that there was actually some life in the otherwise abandoned and forgotten town, Trisha sprinted for the porch yelling, "Kevin! Oh my God Kevin!" With the idea that maybe she'd just been having a very bad dream, or maybe just a bad day or two, the hope that she was about to be paroled from Lincoln gave her reason to smile. Leaping up the 2 steps to the porch she skidded to a stop in front of a calm looking Kevin Barrow. "What is this? What happened?" she demanded of him, waving her hands wildly, until her manners caught up to her and she backtracked, "Are you ok? You were shot? You don't even have any…."

"Easy Trisha," Kevin said, using his hands to emphasize the point, "I'm fine. I didn't get shot though? That's crazy. What are you talking about?" Not ready to believe that her eyes and ears had betrayed her, she stepped forward to inspect the man. Wearing a short-sleeved shirt, it was easy to tell he'd not been shot in the arm, and there was no padding of bandages anywhere around his chest. In fact, Kevin looked the picture of health, save for a worried look on his face. Trisha breathed heavily as she quietly looked over the young man. Finally, swallowing hard, she spoke again, "What's going on here?"

"That's what I'd like to know actually," replied Kevin calmly. Trisha's eyes darted around town again, hoping that maybe her friend's presence would have restored Lincoln to something other than an isolation cell.

"Kevin, are we dead? Is it all over? Is this it?" Trisha couldn't believe that it could be so. Heaven was promised as some airy place, high in the clouds where you would live in love and light with all those that had gone before you. This wasn't heaven. This was Lincoln, NM, a place she'd never have even heard about if not for her freewheeling friend Jane Gordon. No, heaven was exactly as it had been described to her, decided Trisha. This place, this place must be Hell.

Kevin looked thoughtfully at the beautiful woman. In any other circumstance he'd have told her she was crazy, but something in her question caused him to pause and evaluate his answer, "I don't know Trisha. I mean, I don't feel dead, do you?"

"No," she snapped, "I don't feel dead, but this place doesn't do much to make you feel alive either. Where the fuck is everyone Kevin?!" Thinking back to what Trisha had said just a moment ago, Kevin had to revisit one key point.

"You think I was shot? What's that about? I barely remember getting ready for the second show on Sunday?" he protested. The strange conversation had taken a turn to be even more strange. Anyone in Lincoln would know that Carl Farber had gravely shot a young man portraying Billy the Kid during the final show of the pageant. Now Kevin was telling Trisha that he didn't remember being out there for the 2nd show, much less the final one.

"Carl Farber shot you Kevin, with Steve's gun. You cried out for Mr. Teebs to help you and then the whole world went to shit. How do you not remember this? Please tell me that if I've gone insane, I didn't make the trip on my own?" demanded Trisha. Kevin looked seriously at the woman, wondering if now was the right time to tell her what he'd been holding back? Deciding that nothing would change unless she knew the truth, he told her everything.

"Look, Trisha," Kevin began, "This is weird, but I never did anything other than that first show. I remember vaguely Mr. Childs talking to us before the second one, up in the courthouse, but I never did it. As a matter of fact, it seems like nothing else happened, or I must have blacked out because when I finally realized where I was, everyone was gone. It was completely quiet and I haven't seen another person in town for the past 2 days."

"So where have you been this whole time?" she asked.

"I've been right here. I....." Kevin wanted to go on, but the thought of a long stay in a mental health facility made him think the better of it.

"You what?" asked Trisha suspiciously.

Resigned to the fact that he wasn't going to get away without having this conversation, Kevin took a deep breath to relax, and hit Trisha with both barrels. "I got in my car that night and drove to my place in Capitan, or, I tried to. All I wanted to do was have a shower and go to bed. You know where Capitan is, right?" Trisha nodded earnestly, urging Kevin to get to the good part. "Well I drove on out right there," he said, pointing westward on Route 380, "and everything looked the same, as best I could see in my headlights, except for one thing." Trisha was almost waiting for the dramatic music to start, knowing the punchline was coming. "I never got there." said Kevin as he tried to avoid Trisha's probing eyes.

"Why Kevin? Did you get lost?" Even as she said it, she knew it was a ridiculous question. Capitan was 10 miles to the west on the only road in the area. If you drove for 10 minutes, and didn't careen off the road into the high desert, you'd have no choice but to get there.

"No, I didn't get lost," Kevin said with what seemed like a chuckle, "I drove for almost an hour Trisha, and all I ever saw were hills, mountains, and grass....but it's like I made no progress. I was just out there driving, but not going anywhere. After awhile I got spooked and turned back to Lincoln…"

"And then?" she asked, pretty sure she didn't want to know the answer.

"And then," he began, "as soon as I turned around, I was back here in less than a minute."

Trisha suddenly felt very sick to her stomach, a cold sweat spreading across her face. She spoke, but not to Kevin. She'd had enough time in church and reading the Bible to know what had gone on. She urgently wanted her words to exist, to be in the universe, so there'd be a record that she said them.

"So we're trapped. I get it. This isn't Heaven or Hell Kevin." she offered.

"So, what is it?" asked the young man.

"It's purgatory. We're here. Alone. Being judged. Until we either figure some way out, or someone comes to save us."

10.

"'Brandon, please?" implored Martin into his phone, "I need that book out of that house. I know this doesn't make sense to you. I'm not sure how it could. But you saw Farber. You know something strange is going on, right? The more I tell you, the deeper you get into this thing, and believe me…this is not something you want to get more involved in!"

Finally done with his diatribe, Martin waited to make sure Brandon was still on the other end of the phone.

"Martin, it's not that I don't want to help. Really. That Farber dude was a real piece of crap," he began, "And whatever the hell happened to him there at the end? Look, I've seen some shit in combat you'd never want to see but that? That was the weirdest damned thing I've seen in my life."

"So you'll do it?" Martin asked hopefully.

"Martin, Trisha hasn't been seen around here for weeks. The owner of the house is out of the country or something. What do you expect me to do, break in?" Brandon waited for Martin to tell him that, absolutely no, that's not what he wanted.

"Well?" offered Martin cautiously.

"Seriously!?" Brandon exclaimed, "You really want me to break into someone's million dollar home just so you can have a crappy little book?" On the other end of the phone, Martin rubbed his eyes and shook his head, knowing his options were running low.

"Of course not Brandon," Martin finally said, "Unless that's something you were agreeable to maybe?"

"Martin, forget it! This is where I run my business. I make my living. I'm not busting out a window and looking for some homemade book that you think the FBI is desperately after. C'mon man, if the FBI wanted to talk to you, don't you think they'd be at your place right now? It's the freaking Federal Bureau of Investigation Martin."

"I suppose," Martin mumbled in return, peering out his office window just in case a cavalcade of blacked out Suburbans were parking on his front lawn.

"So, that's it. You ain't going anywhere and they're not looking for you, right?" reasoned Brandon, "Besides, you didn't have anything to do with Trisha disappearing, did you Martin?" The way Brandon asked made Martin think that maybe people did believe that he'd done something to Trisha, and it make him angry, and scared.

"Of course not!" Martin shot back, "C'mon man, all I did is talk to her. Don't say that."

"Hey, I'm sorry Martin. You're just freaking me out a little about some book that says I don't know what, but you're afraid implicates you in something. It's a natural reaction to be suspicious."

"Yeah, I understand," said Martin quietly, "don't worry about it." Martin's mind started wandering to what other people he might call on for help as Brandon bade him goodbye.

"Hey, I gotta go Martin. Big tour coming through today. Take care man. If I hear anything about Kevin or Trisha, I'll let you know." Brandon was about to hang up when a thought occurred to him, "They mighta just run off together for awhile. Seemed like they got on pretty well. Probably show up after their first little lover's quarrel, huh Martin?" Martin knew that was absolutely not the truth, but saw no reason to argue the point.

"Yeah, maybe that's it. Well, I hope they're happy." he said grimly.

"Gotta go Martin, bye." said Brandon quickly and hung up. Martin reasoned that Brandon might be right. The FBI had agents on the case for two weeks now. They certainly would have checked the home Trisha was in, and if so, someone there would either have read the book, or moved on by now. Why was he worrying so much? Deciding to just let it go until and unless anything else happened, he turned his attention back to his computer, where he'd been deleting history and bookmarks of anything related to Billy. Sitting down on his chair, he looked up at the next two items in his search history, dated July 15, 2021, and his jaw fell on the desk.

Search results for: Kevin Barrow
Search results for: Trisha Davis

What?! Martin hadn't even known those kids in July! He'd only met them on his first day in Lincoln in August. Who the hell was searching on his computer for two people that he didn't even know existed? Lilly? She barely even wanted to go to New Mexico, and had almost no interest in all things Billy the Kid. Martin felt a little dizzy, his brain swirling like in one of those detective shows on TV when a person realizes that someone smarter than themselves is expertly setting them up. Was it Farber? Martin certainly knew Farber, but before Carl's awakening, did he remember anything about his last life? Besides, how would Farber have gotten into his house? None of this made sense to Martin, but he had to face the fact that he was potentially the last person to see Trisha 'alive' and at some point, some Fed agent was going to snap to that. Simply burying his head in the sand, waiting for the other shoe to drop, hardly seemed like a strategy. While he couldn't figure out the search history right now, he had to deal with something else first. It was a task he could leave to no one but himself. Taking a deep breath to brace himself, he marched down the hallway towards the master bedroom, to tell Lilly that he had to go back to New Mexico, and right away.

11.

As promised, the next afternoon Billy rode in from George Coe's place on a thoroughly enjoyable day in Lincoln County. A few clouds streaked across the deep blue sky, and a slight breeze rustled the tree leaves that would soon fall in earnest, providing a crunchy accompaniment to any who traipsed across them on their daily travails. Hungry after hours in the saddle, he debated stopping at the Ellis Store for a meal, but remembered how insistent Rosita was that she needed him to reach Martin as soon as he was able. Thinking back to his earlier time travel transgressions, Billy knew that in Martin's time, he'd barely be able to turn a corner without some sort of restaurant or eatery being in sight. Having the money to pay for such things was a bit of a challenge, but Billy had always been able to manage such things on the strength of his charms. In any event, there was a trip to take and he decided to get on with it. Spurring his horse towards Rosita's tiny hut, he looped the reins around a post and knocked firmly on the door.

"*Billito*!" Rosita exclaimed, knowing that the boy's presence meant she was closer to reconnecting with Martin than ever, "you are here. You are ready to take the trip, *si*? To see my *Martin*?" Rosita's good spirits buoyed Billy, knowing that he was heading for a meeting with a far from certain outcome. Well aware that he had tried this once, and only come back with the taste of Carl Farber's blood on his fists, he mentally prepared his discussion with Martin about why this time needed to be different.

"Yes Ma'am Rosie," said a chipper Billy Bonney, "I's ready to git on back to ol' Teebsie and give him the good news." Rosita nodded her head in excitement, wanting to send Billy off as quickly as possible.

"Ok then, so you have the book," she asked, "then this is the time to go, no?" Billy smiled at Rosita's impatience, but understood it.

"Yeah, I'm ready." he simply replied. Nodding at Rosita, he opened Sergio Bachaca's book up to the footnotes section that talked about 21st century dates and events. Just before he looked down to read, he stopped to give Rosita one last disclaimer, "Rosie, you kinda know how this works now. I ain't sure when or where I'll wind up. Ain't sure I'll find Teebsie. Ain't sure he'll even listen to me. And hell, who knows, ain't sure I'll ever make it back. Ok? I'm gonna give it my damnedest, but there ain't no guarantees." Rosita's smiling face got serious.

"I know all this *Billito*, truly," she said, "But with you I have hope. Without you I have no hope to ever see my *Martin* again. So please, take the good care of yourself. If *Martin* cannot come to me, I still must have my friend come back, *si?*" A melancholy smile spread across Billy's face as he simply nodded.

"Here I go then…" he said as he began to read the pages of Bachaca's book. That familiar feeling of being pulled away began to take over, and his vision of the inside of Rosita's tiny house began to fade, but something felt, well, off. Billy was like a wagon stuck in the mud, with its team trying its hardest to pull it out, but despite the effort, going nowhere. He could barely make out Rosita's face going from happiness, to surprise, then finally to fear. She could clearly tell this wasn't like their exit from Lincoln, circa 2021, which was almost instantaneous. This was different. This was wrong. Rosita's lips moved as if speaking to Billy, but he couldn't hear a word she said, stuck in the vacuum of time as he seemed to be. His progress was stalled, and he was finding it hard to breathe. The more the pull of time, the less oxygen seemed to be in the room, and shortly he was gasping for breath. Rosita, now in full panic mode, screamed to him, but her voice could not be heard above the din. Billy's eyes began twitching and his eyelids fluttered. His body, although still standing, slumped to the side and to Rosita, he seemed on the verge of collapse. Finally when his head began to loll to the side and he seemed to be losing consciousness, she stepped in quickly and slapped the book from his hands.

Billy's body fell over on the wooden floor, landing awkwardly on his shoulder. "*Billito!*" Rosita screamed as she rushed to the boy, hoping he was still alive. Billy mumbled some unintelligible words as he tried to push his eyes open. Rosita grabbed a cloth and dipped it into a bucket of water on the table. She wrung it out and gently dabbed it at the boy's forehead. The cool water helped The Kid begin to come out of whatever spell had taken hold of him.

"I'm ok Rosie, it's…." Billy's head slumped again, unable to finish his sentence. Rosita stood and slid the boy towards her bed. The movement was enough to rouse Billy again and he was able to get his feet under him.

"Come now, onto the bed to rest *Billito,*" demanded Rosita as she did her best to lift him up to the bottom edge of the bed, "this will make you better." Billy pushed just enough on his heels to slide on the bed and collapse backwards. His eyes now open, he stared at the ceiling, more tired than he could ever remember in his life.

"What happened?" Billy asked, still unsure of why his planned trip to the future failed. Rosita laid the cool cloth on his forehead.

"It was as if you could not go, Chivato," Rosita replied, "and you were stuck in the time." Breathing deeply to compose himself, Billy stared at the ceiling trying to remember anything about the incident.

"That ain't the way it works you know," he was able to croak out, "sposed to just get on with it and be in the other time." Rosita's concerned eyes stared at the young man. She was worried that he might be sick, or even worse, but she couldn't help the disappointment she felt that Billy was not on his way to Martin's right now. "Lemme just lie here for a minute and I'll try again." Rosita reached out to grab Billy's hand, trying to soothe him and let him know it was alright. When she raised her eyes to meet his, she saw the boy was out cold, fast asleep, and would remain that way the rest of the afternoon, all night, and well into the next morning.

12.

"You think we're dead?" asked Kevin incredulously, "Like, for real dead?" Trisha glanced around the silent town, feeling both angry and hopeless at the same time.

"I don't know Kevin," she said, not really focusing on looking at the young man, "but I know we're not alive….not like we were." While for the better part of 2 days Kevin had known something was incredibly amiss, he never considered that he might be dead, locked in some historically preserved purgatory, just waiting for his maker to fly down on angel wings and (hopefully) usher him to the gates of Heaven. That thought, to him, seemed preposterous.

"Slap me," he said, grabbing Trisha's hand and placing it near his face, "hard!" Trisha stood there, looking down her nose at him, wondering if maybe this was some sex game the boy wanted to play before they met their maker.

"Umm, look Kevin…well, I'm not really into…."

"Slap me Trish!" he urged, "let's see if I can feel it. If I can, we're not dead. Maybe it'll wake us up from this nightmare." Without another word, Trisha wound up and smacked the living daylights out of Kevin Barrow, the crack of her hand on his face echoing across the street and back, knowing he was wrong, but hoping against hope he wasn't. "Oww!!" he yelled into the still air, "son of a bitch!" Trisha shook her hand out from the pain, admiring the exact replica of it that she left in an ever deepening crimson on Kevin's cheek. She couldn't help herself but to smile.

"Was it good for you too?" she deadpanned. It took Kevin a few moments to be able to speak, the sting of her slap still growing in intensity before finally, it began to subside.

"Well, that proves it," he mumbled as best as he was able.

"Proves what Kev?"

"Proves we're not dead, and, proves you don't need anyone to protect you. You do just fine on your own." Trisha couldn't help but laugh for the first time in days. Something about releasing that anger allowed her body to ease. Her shoulders relaxed, and her jaw finally slacked. Wherever and whatever this was, she was at least glad she was no longer alone in it.

"Ok then, so what exactly is this?" she asked while gently touching Kevin's cheek to make sure she hadn't broken anything.

"I don't know. Some kind of simulation maybe? I mean, somebody is messing with us, but I can't imagine who it would be?" Kevin said while staring out at a dust devil blowing by in the road.

"What, like the Matrix? C'mon Kevin. Who are we? Who'd go to this much trouble to create something so silly in Lincoln, New Mexico? For us? Besides, that was a movie. This is real. Focus." Kevin, without any other solid possibilities to float, just stared into the street. "I'll bet this all has to do with Martin," Trisha said quietly, "and that whole Rosita thing. He probably brainwashed me or something. Every day, I was feeling less and less like myself. That Sunday, do you remember, I was off? I was barely hanging onto who I was. You saw me out in the stands. Tell me this means something to you Kevin? Tell me you felt something like it too. After all, everyone was crowing about how much you looked like Billy the Kid." Kevin nodded his head slightly, never looking away from the road.

"Yeah, same. That day, I don't know, things were getting to me. Even that Mr. Farber was under my skin. So, you think this is some brainwashing? Some mind control? If that's true, then we're not really here? Where are we Trish?" he asked.

"Hospital maybe? Maybe a padded cell for all I know," she said flatly, "What color straight-jacket would you like?"

"No, I don't buy it," said Kevin firmly, "This isn't how it ends for me, or for you. We're gonna figure this out!" The young man spoke with such conviction that Trisha even began to believe. Kevin had ignored the knowing hunger in his belly for days. Knowing that their escape depended on their ability to stay strong, he decided that a break in the non-action might be in order? "Hey, I've only eaten a couple of protein bars in the last 2 days. Do you have anything to eat at your house?" Kevin asked hopefully.

"Oh…yeah. Of course. Come on, let's walk down there. Maybe we'll even see someone else caught in this freaking rat trap?" Trisha said only half-jokingly. As the pair trudged down Route 380 to the east, each felt the weight of their current existence slowing them down. They passed each historical building, which had been buzzing with life only a few days ago, now silent testimony that they were the only two souls alive in Lincoln, an entire, insignificant town historically preserved for….them.

Struggling with how to ask the question on his mind, Kevin finally spoke, "Trish. I feel, kind of, empty. Do you know what I mean? Like there's some part of me missing. Been feeling it since that day. Does this mean anything to you?" Indeed Trisha did know exactly what Kevin was talking about, being as she'd had that same empty feeling from Sunday morning on. It was as if she was somehow incomplete. While she hadn't put it into words, Kevin's assessment seemed to allow the genie out of the bottle.

"Yes! I feel it too," she said with the enthusiasm of someone who has finally met another soul struggling the same as they were, "but don't worry Kevin. All we need to do is find that missing part and put it back, and I'll bet this nightmare is over."

"Mmm," murmured Kevin, "sounds so simple, doesn't it?" Both Kevin Barrow and Trisha Davis walked on, hoping that it was.

13.

"Now just what in the hell are you doing here Hoss?" bellowed Steve with equal parts anger and amusement. Martin raised his eyes sheepishly, knowing that catching the old cowboy unaware, in his own office no less, was probably not the best ideas. The challenge was, if Steve had known Martin was planning to return to New Mexico, he'd have talked him out of it. Case closed. Steve would have come up with some alternate plan that Martin would have to agree to, but in the end wouldn't keep him from the clutches of the law he was sure was bearing down on him. No, Martin had to be here himself, to make sure that Farber's crappy book would never see the light of day again. If he could just find it and burn it, the whole Trisha Davis and Kevin Barrow thing might just die down along with the smoldering embers.

"Look. Steve, I know, ok?" offered Martin, "we said we'd just stay quiet on this, but I remembered something."

Steve raised his worn boots and plopped his feet heavily on the desk, pushing his hat back and smirking, "Oh, I can't wait to hear this shit. Shoot hombre." Martin sighed and began to tell Steve about Farber's book, the one that would spill the secret that they all wanted kept a secret. "I burned that damn thing Martin, don't you remember? Hell, you drooled all over my shoes when I showed you those last few pages!" Steve seemed to enjoy regaling Martin with his tale of woe. "Now go on and tell me that it was before this damned do over that you orchestrated, and that none of that shit ever happened. Is that what you're trying to tell me?" Martin wagged his head back and forth before Steve even finished the question.

"No, no. That happened, and thanks by the way for reminding me. Farber wrote another book, or shit….Bachaca did. I don't even know anymore Steve, but I do know that there's another copy in that house that Trisha is staying in, and I've got to get it before the Feds or the Sheriff does."

Steve folded his large hands behind his head, lifting his chin before he spoke, "So let me get this straight. You're afraid of some little book dropping a dime on you and your past life, but you're not afraid to come round to Lincoln again and bust into that house? Don't it seem like some of them FBI agents would be keeping an eye on the town Martin?" Martin closed his eyes tightly, not wanting the admit the stupidity of his plan. Of course the feds would be on the lookout for anything strange. The Sheriff would probably be on watch too. Martin hadn't planned on breaking into the house. His hope, if it could even be called that, was that somehow Trisha might wind up back where she belonged, and simply greet him at the door. Of course, if Trisha was back, aside from the obvious "Where the hell have you been?" questions, the investigation would be over and the book would be meaningless. The internet had made it easy to do such things as book last minute, really expensive plane tickets to New Mexico, but it didn't offer much in the way of guidance if you should actually do such things without thinking them through. He'd known the plan was foolhardy, but sitting in New Jersey, waiting for two men in black to show up at his doorstep seemed just as stupid.

"Yeah, ok, sure. So maybe I didn't think things all the way through Steve. This has been a lot, you know? The 5 years, the week in Lincoln, Farber murdering everyone in sight. I'm just looking for a way for this to end." Martin said, both sad and defeated.

"End huh? You know who else wants this shit to end Martin? The parents of that Davis girl and the Barrow kid. They'd really like this shit to end, now wouldn't they?" asked Steve with an accusing tone in his voice, "You ever put yourself in their shoes? Kid goes to work some summer job and all of a sudden they're gone. Vanished into thin air? You and I know what happened to them. Know where they went, but we can't say nothing about that now, can we Martin? Cause if we do, they still don't find their kids and you and I spend the rest of our lives drooling pea soup onto our straightjackets."

Martin's body slumped, and he fell heavily onto an ottoman in the office. With his face in his hands, he imagined the torment that those parents must be facing. It must be a completely helpless feeling to have a child out there, maybe in danger, and beyond your reach, with no one else to care for them.

Like Junior.

"Junior," Martin said aloud, although he didn't mean to.

"Say what now?" asked Steve.

"Junior. My son. I can't find him either." spoke Martin with an emotionless voice. The air went out of the room as Steve and Martin both sat there, lost in their own thoughts. While he could be angry that Martin would risk lighting the flames under the FBI's investigation by going to Lincoln, Steve had to understand that this whole mess weighed much more heavily on Martin than it did on him. Steve hadn't lost his son somewhere in time. He hadn't had a torrid love affair with a woman who was a century and a half old. While Steve had met the real, genuine Billy the Kid, he couldn't claim friendship with the young outlaw. No, Steve had gotten a rare glimpse into a world that he'd never expected, but it was only that…a glimpse. For Martin Teebs, this was all very real and very personal.

"Well shit Martin, I'm sorry. I didn't think about that I guess." Martin just shook his head as if to tell Steve is was ok, but the memory had been planted in his mind and it wouldn't be easy to shake. Forcing himself to focus on the task at hand, Martin sat up straighter.

"Look, I'm going down there. You can come or you can stay here. I don't even have to tell anyone I saw you, whatever you want?" Martin offered. Steve laughed heartily, his chest rising and dipping with the effort.

"You think they don't know you're here Martin? This is the Federal Bureau of Investigation. They knew you were here before you did son. Shit, what's the sense of me sitting here. They might better just question us at the same damn time when they catch up to us." Steve rose from his office chair, grabbed the keys to his truck and began making his way towards the door. Just before he turned the handle, he stepped back and grabbed his gun belt, replete with a single action revolver and 6 rounds in the cylinder. Strapping it around his waist, he looked over at the forlorn Martin, "Get up, let's go."

Martin looked strangely at the gun and asked, "What's that for? You think we're going to shoot it out with the feds?"

"Hell no Martin!" Steve bellowed, "But the last time you took me on one of your little trips, it was to send Billy the Kid back in time. I've finally figured out that when I'm around you, anything can happen. If we somehow wind up in the middle of the damned Lincoln County War, I aim to get in on it." The pun was not lost on Martin.

"Funny, aim, I get it. You should take that act out on the road Steve," he said, "You don't need to worry about that. I don't have the book and I've got no way to get back there. I'm not sure where or when they even went." Steve walked heavily across the wood porch and hopped down into the dirt, two tiny dust devils forming off of his boot heels. He slung himself into his pickup and fired up the engine. Martin walked warily around to the passenger side, now on the lookout for any bland, sensible sedans that could belong to an FBI agent. Seeing nothing he hopped in the truck and announced, "Let's get this over with." As the truck bobbed and bounced down the rut filled driveway Steve turned on the radio to some classic country station that Martin hated. Throwing a spray of gravel up as he accelerated onto Route 380 to the east he popped Martin lightly on the shoulder, "It's like Thelma and Louise all over again, ain't it?" Martin just shook his head and smirked. "Here we come Lincoln, and let's hope that Martin finds exactly what the hell he came looking for this time."

14.

It was nearly mid morning by the time Billy Bonney stirred the next day. Still lying heavily in Rosita's bed, the woman had to check several times during night and morn to make sure her friend was alive. In her 24 years, Rosita had never seen anyone sleep that long or that deeply, Billy stirring nary a time during the night. Finally as the smell of brewing coffee tickled his nose, Billy stirred.

"Where am I?" he asked groggily. Not wanting to startle the boy, Rosita sat at her table, where she'd spent most of the night and talked softly, "You are with me *Billito*, safe. In my home." Billy forced his eyes open wider and tried to push himself up on the bed, a look of confusion pasted on his face, "Rosie? What happened? How long I been out for?" Rosita smiled warmly to let him know he was safe before answering, "For some time. It is the next day, in the morning."

Billy pushed himself higher on the bed and looked around the tiny home. His memories beginning to return, he saw his book lying on the table, easily within Rosita's reach. The entirety of his experience from the day before now aligning in mind, Billy nodded in Rosita's direction. "Dang Rosie, ain't never slept so much in my life," he offered, "Feels like some part of me is still asleep. Can't rightly explain it. Did you spend the whole night sittin on that chair?" With a sigh, Rosita smiled wearily and nodded her head, adjusting herself on the wooden bench. "Oh man, I'm sorry. I didn't mean ta...."

"Is ok," she said, "for what happened yesterday I don't mind that you needed to sleep *Billito*." Billy pushed his legs over the side of the bed, rising on unsteady feet. He shook more awareness into his head and walked over to Bachaca's book. "C'mon Rosie, let's give this another shot. If I ain't rested after all that sleep, I prolly won't never be." Rosita put her hand down firmly on the book, not allowing Billy to pick it up, "No please, it was too much for you. I shall try to go, *Chivato*." Whatever level of sleepiness was still holding onto Billy evaporated at Rosita's words, "No, bad idea! I won't hear of that. That dang near knocked me out cold and you's gonna try to go carrying a baby?" Rosita looked directly at her friend, as she rubbed the tiny life growing in her womb as if to comfort it. She knew Billy was right. Yesterday had scared them both. If Billy was scared after the number of times he's done this time travel trick, then Rosita knew enough to know that she should be also. While her desperation to find Martin was real, finding him only to tell him that she'd lost their child would be more than either of them could bear.

"Ok, you are right. I don't want to put my *bebe* in danger. Before you try again Billito, sit, have some *desayuno, si*? Rosita motioned Billly towards a chair as she rose to pour him a steaming cup of black coffee. Knowing that he probably did need something to give him a bit of energy, Billy plopped down in the chair and grabbed the hot metal cup. "Ok then, maybe I was just tired or something yesterday? That was the damnedest thing. I'm pretty well rested now so it'll be ok I'm sure." Rosita sat quietly at the table, drumming her slender fingers on the worn wood surface. She appeared as if she wanted to say something, but for some reason, was holding back. Billy noticed her discomfort, and didn't allow it to continue, "What is it Rosie?"

With a pained look, Rosita finally asked the question that she'd been avoiding, "Do you think *Martin* loves his Lilly more than he loves me?" The very idea that Martin loved anyone, or anything, more than Rosita seemed preposterous to Billy. He'd seen the man laid bare that night long ago (or far ahead) in Fort Sumner. There was simply no way that he believed his pal could summon up that kind of emotion over Rosita, and then go happily back to his life with Lilly. While Billy didn't understand Martin's choice just a few weeks prior, he also knew there were forces at work in Martin's life that must have made that seem like the right decision. No, Billy decided, Martin did not love Lilly more than he loved Rosita.

"I know that ain't the truth, if you want to know. Know it for a fact Rosie." he said while staring the great beauty directly in her chocolate-colored eyes. The missive calmed Rosita, if even for a moment. Billy took a big sip of coffee and stood up, ready for his journey. "Ok, let's get this started," he blurted out as he picked up the book and stepped back into the middle of the room, "Ain't nothing gonna go wrong, but if I get stuck again, knock this dang book outta my hands, ok?" Rosita pasted on a tight smile and nodded slightly, knowing that if Billy didn't leave this time, he probably never would. Perhaps the book had run out of whatever energy it had to transport Billy and Martin back and forth through time? No matter, Rosita knew that the next 2 minutes would determine the course of her life, and she was tired of waiting for it to happened. As Billy opened the book, Rosita stepped up quickly and kissed him on the cheek, "*Gracias Billito*, for what you do for me and *Martin*."

Billy gently pushed her back as he opened the book to the footnotes section again. The room appeared to get grainy, and Billy felt the familiar pull of time on him. At one moment, he began slipping backwards and feared a repeat of yesterday's outcome, but the slip was momentary and in just a few more seconds, he was gone. Rosita stood, wide eyed at the spectacle, and touched the air where her friend had just stood. Waving it around, she felt nothing, as if he'd never even existed. Suddenly very sleepy herself after a long night of tending to Billy, Rosita sat on the edge of her bed and allowed her head to fall backwards. Sleep came to claim her within seconds and it was long after dark before she finally awakened, hoping against hope that Martin Teebs would soon be on his way to her.

15.

If anyone had cared to ask Lilly Teebs what she felt about the entire Lincoln debacle, they'd either have gotten an earful (or two), or her tight-lipped denial that she cared anything about it. Her brief tryst with Dallas Jones had been the highlight of the trip for her, but she'd quickly moved on from it, remembering how badly her life had spun out of control the last time she thought that he might be a functioning adult human being, versus the 38 year old toddler he turned out to be. No, Lilly didn't lust for Dallas, or Lincoln, or for that matter, even Martin. She'd laid down an ultimatum for Martin on that final day, secretly hoping that he'd take the prize behind door #1, which was his great love, Rosita Luna. She'd never told him this of course, but she put so much pressure on Martin to decide, she foolishly thought she was making it easy on him. She and Martin's relationship had been nearly platonic for years, with only a brief sizzle of sexual activity from time to time. While Lilly and Martin could live out the rest of their natural lives with everything being 'ok', she wanted more than that…for her, and for him.

Natural life, she thought. What in the holy hell was natural about the lives that she and Martin had lived over the past 5 years? Time travel? Infidelity? A black hole that shipped them back 5 years on their timeline, yet cruelly let them remember everything that had happened and that they had lost? Lilly could think of nothing at all natural about that. Her last memories of her previous life were spending time with that movie guy, Michael Roberts, and raising little Austin. They'd forged a nice little life in the very house Lilly as sitting in at the moment. As best Lilly could remember, she was happy, and Austin was too. While Roberts at some point would probably want to move back to New Mexico, this time Lilly might go there with a person she actually saw a future with, rather than the shallow end of the gene pool represented by Dallas Jones.

How did it all end, she tried to recall? How did she go from living and working in Waldwick, New Jersey in her old house, to being back in Lincoln, pounding the green chile enchiladas from Martin's windpipe? What moment did she go from finally achieving a near blissful existence, to forgettable one? In her mind, Lilly believed that there must have been some intense event surrounding her reversal of time. Perhaps she and Michael were wrapped in an amorous embrace, about to tear into each other yet again when she simply vanished from his arms? Was it even worse? Was she dropping off

Austin at school one day and when he turned around to wave goodbye, his mother was gone? The horror of leaving two people she deeply cared about, without an explanation, tore at her. However it happened, Lilly wanted it undone. She'd finally achieved her happiness and only Martin's gluttony stole it from her. She was convinced that that seminal moment of trying to save Martin ripped him from his last world into this one, bringing a number of unwilling participants with him. While she loved Martin, and couldn't imagine letting him choke to death, she wondered….knowing what she knew now, would she still try to save him? Martin himself told Lilly that he was ripped from his seemingly sublime reality when she brought him back to life. A reality that he had finally achieved after tortuous decades trying to remain at the side of his one and only Rosita. Why wasn't Martin more upset about this, she wondered? Why didn't he shove another forkful of enchiladas down his gullet just to choke himself back into Rosita Luna's arms? And again she was faced with a question for which she had no answer: Why, in that final moment, did Martin choose her over Rosita?

The question hung in the air of her empty home, but no answer seemed to be forthcoming. A searing pain began to form behind Lilly's eyeballs as a powerful headache approached. "Great, just fucking great," she said to the still silence of the house, "This is all I need right now." As she padded into the kitchen to retrieve some ibuprofen, before things got too bad, she made a mental inventory. She had Martin, but didn't really want him all that badly. She could have Dallas, but the H.M.S. Dumbass had sailed from port and Lilly wasn't interested in buying another ticket to take that ride. She had found true happiness with Michael Roberts, but in this new reality, Lilly wasn't even sure he existed, and had no idea where to find him?

That left only…Austin. When Martin had told Lilly in his passenger seat confessional that she'd had a son, she was stunned. Lilly didn't feel like a mother, if that was even a thing. She had no sensation that her body had ever given life to another being. Wouldn't she know if she'd grown a human being inside of her? Wouldn't she feel something? That all lasted right up until the car accident where she hit her head, and in an instant, it all came flooding back. Of course she was a mother. Of course she had spent 22 hours in labor bringing him into the world. Of course she cherished that little boy. Of course he was the light of her life. And now, of course he was trapped in a time that she could not reach. It must be a punishment, she thought, to have such acute awareness of something you always wanted, finally had, and quickly lost. Lilly would have traded Martin, Michael Roberts, Dallas Jones, and just about anything else she had if she could just be with her little boy again. Hell, she'd trade Dallas just for someone to tell her that Austin was ok.

Determined, as mothers often are, Lilly vowed to herself that her story was not yet written. She was going to find a way to her son, even if it killed her. When she and Martin finally untangled themselves from this current mess, job number one would be for her to find her little boy, Austin Teebs.

16.

"All of these books are about Billy the Kid? Dang!" exclaimed Kevin as he looked through the palatial library in Rosita's home sitting gig house, "I've got a one room apartment in Capitan and you're living like this?" Trisha narrowed her eyes at him, hoping he didn't forget that they were trapped in, well…hell, at the moment.

"I hardly call what we've been doing for the last few days 'living' Kevin. And besides, the bigger the house, you lonelier you feel when you're all alone in it." Knowing he'd hit a sore spot, Kevin nodded his head in her direction while he continued glancing around the impressive house. Trisha had culled enough ingredients from the refrigerator and pantry to make pancakes, and the aroma wafting through the house brought Kevin to the kitchen, following his nose like a French Bulldog.

"That smells great!" he said, his mouth starting to water, "what can I do to help?" Flipping a few cakes one last time, Trisha made a small stack, put them neatly on a plate, and pushed them across the island towards Kevin, "There, start with those. There's plenty more what these came from." His hunger driving him, Kevin slapped 2 pats of butter on the cakes, then poured a river of maple syrup across the top. He barely allowed it to run down the edges before he hungrily tore into the stack. In what seemed like less than a minute, he was done, using his fork to try to scrape the rest of the syrup to the edge of the plate and into his mouth. Trisha looked over just in time to do a double take. "Well, we are a hungry boy now, aren't we?" she said jokingly.

"I guess so Trish. I think I had 2 protein bars over the past 2 days. Lincoln sure ain't known for its gourmet cuisine." Trisha scooped up another stack of 3 pancakes, reaching over for the plate, and dropped them in the center. Kevin dressed the second batch just as the first, but this time was able to slow down and savor them. Not having much of an appetite, Trisha ran some cold water in the hot pan and watch the tiny bubbles sizzling their way across. "So, what now Trish? I mean, we could stay here but at some point we're gonna run out of food. I mean, we've got to find a way out, right?" asked Kevin between bites of the sweet, sticky mess.

"Yes, we do. I just wish I even knew where to start," she lamented, "Hey Kev, do you think that driving thing of yours was maybe just a dream? Maybe a hallucination? Caused by all that crap on Sunday? Maybe we can drive out of here?"

Kevin wiped some syrup from his lips, "I wondered the same thing. I ain't slept in damn near 3 days now. Thought maybe I was just going crazy. The thing is, I had half a tank of gas when I left Lincoln. The I drove for an hour before turning around, and got back her with just more than a quarter tank. I went out the next day and checked too. I don't think I could have dreamed 4 gallons of gas away." Trisha pressed her eyes close and dropped her head. If she was looking for good news, Kevin's answer wouldn't reveal any. At the heart of all of this, Martin Teebs must have had a part in it. He was the one that poisoned Trisha's mind about this Rosita Luna woman. He'd even convinced Kevin that he looked just like Billy the Kid. If there was some way out of this, Martin must know it. The problem was, Martin, and the rest of the free world, remained hidden from their view and neither of them had any idea how to change that. Trisha walked slowly into the library, retrieving the copies of Carl Farber's two books, The Coward of Lincoln County, and Lincoln County Days. These were the books that solidified that Farber was not the mild mannered school teacher he claimed to be. These were the books that Martin had found, that he claimed proved his existence in the past. These books, or at least Lincoln County Days, told the tragic story of Martin and Rosita. Just looking at them made Trisha's head hurt. She strolled back into the kitchen to find Kevin putting his dish into the sink.

"How the hell did I get myself into this?" she asked herself, but loud enough for Kevin to hear.

"I was gonna ask you the same thing," he said, looking over the two books in her hand, "What's that?" Rosita dropped them onto the countertop with a shrug, "Just some books that Martin and I found. They're by that creep Farber." Trisha looked down again at the grinning face of William H. Bonney on The Coward of Lincoln County, then turned her head to Kevin. "You know, you really do look like Billy the Kid. I guess I never paid attention before." Kevin peeked across the countertop, staring at the tiny photo, "I guess so, huh? And you, you're supposed to look like that Rosita chick, right? Imagine that?"

Trisha laughed a little, relaxing for the first time in days. "Well then look at us. We're like two celebrities. Except we're celebrities in a one horse town with no people in it, and we look like two of them that have been dead for over 100 years!"

Kevin smiled and cocked his head to the side, "Want an autograph? Oh yes, we're famous. Legends in our own mind. Now, if somebody would just come and get us the hell out of here."

Just then, in what sounded like it came from far up the road in the heart of Lincoln, a great metallic crash, accompanied by the sound of breaking glass was heard.

"What the…" said Kevin.

"People!" yelled Trisha as they both ran out of the front door, across the brick path, and make their way up the road to what they hoped would be their salvation.

17.

Billy's arrival in 2021, just outside the visitors center and what was left of Rosita's house, happened much like his departure from the past did. He was 'kind of" there, but then seemed to be slipping back. Finally, shaking his head to clear the fuzz, Billy stood firmly in the year he'd left with Rosita a couple of months ago. Lincoln was bathed in a warm sunshine on this day, while leaves fell from the trees and swirled in a never ending array of patterns. The leaves were an indulgence that wasn't seen nearly as often in Billy's day…being as most of those trees were cut for firewood or lumber. That Lincoln actually had some big shade trees made Billy smile. Standing near the main and only road, he decided that perhaps staying a bit more out of sight might be a good plan. He didn't need any run ins with the locals who'd peg him for either the real Billy, or a hell of a match for him. He walked around the east side of what was Rosita's hut and surveyed the town.

When Billy had been back here in August, he didn't get to see much of Lincoln. His awakening came just before he was to perform (as himself) at that play they had during Old Lincoln Days. The next trip he took was in what Martin had called an ambulance and he wound up in a hospital in Roswell. Coming back to Lincoln, he made it only as far as Rosita's, or was it Trisha's, house before Steve handed him the book and they drifted away. Now, Billy had the time to really look at the place, and to see how closely it matched Lincoln in his own time. Clearly, Rosita's house, and that of her mother Lourdes, had been joined into one bigger building at some point. Peering across the street he saw the familiar turquoise window sashes of the Montano Store. Curious as to what more of the town looked like, Billy removed his hat, adjusted his clothing as best he could to look less like, well, Billy the Kid, and began trekking from building to building, reveling in the fact that Lincoln had somehow been saved…or at least, most of it had. He came to the Torreon, sight of many bitter battles both before and during his time in the tiny town.

"Son of a bitch," he mused to himself, "Somebody really wanted to save this place."

Walking on, Billy came up short when he reached what he recognized as the old Tunstall store. His heart beat a bit more quickly, remembering the times that he'd been there before John's death. Even more, he could almost mark the spot just to the west where he'd first met Martin, by drawing down on him while he laid in the street.

"Dang, sorry Teebsie," Billy said with a smile, "Ain't mean to scare you like that." 'Teebsie', the entire reason Billy was here. Here Billy was walking west when Martin, New Jersey, and maybe the fate of his new baby all rested to the east. Still, Billy rarely had the time in his time or this one to visit Lincoln in peace. He walked a few paces past the store only to find a vacant lot that brought some of the horror of the war back to him. It was from exactly where he was standing, up on the road, that Dolan's men and Dudley's soldiers rained lead on him and his buddies as they desperately tried to escape the burning McSween house. That night, forever etched in his memory, burned at him as hot as the flames from the real fire did. The McSween house was gone, and probably was never rebuilt as best as Billy could tell. Looking at the sun still high in the sky, he continued on past the Wortley Hotel, which looked quite a bit different than he remembered, and finally the imposing two story building of The House. No fond memories of The House remained in Billy's mind, if there ever were some. He'd been forced to kill Olinger, Bell, and another Olinger from there. He'd been shot by Carl Farber just next to the big building. He, Martin, and Steve had been held at gunpoint on the second floor, near Garrett's old office, while Farber murdered that author, Sergio Bachaca. There was simply nothing of this building that Billy wanted to remember, but oddly, he was drawn back to it. As he walked up to the northest corner, he noticed a white stone on the ground, memorializing his killing of Bob Olinger. He glanced up to the window, imagining himself, covered in Bell's blood, thrusting the shotgun through the glass and drawing down on his mortal enemy. Was Olinger scared, Billy wondered? Did he even have time to process what was happening? Looking up at the window, Billy was bathed in a sadness that this place seemed to be married to. For a small instant, he almost felt sorry for Olinger, staring up at the window, ready to meet eternity.

"Hey, look!" said a man walking past the building with his wife, "Look at that guy. He must be some reenactor or something." The man pointed excitedly in Billy's direction as he urged his wife to follow. "Sir, sir?" the man said politely, but urgently, "Is there a show or something? Do we need tickets?" In the midst of his melancholy, Billy had to smile. It was just as Martin said, people were still in love with the legend of The Kid.

"Howdy folks. No, ain't no show that I know about. Sorry bout that." replied Billy. If he expected the man to be disappointed, he was wrong.

"Oh, ok. No problem," said the tourist, "just so great seeing people like yourself keeping history alive!" The man's wife, a pretty blonde who was probably indulging her husband's dream of visiting Lincoln, leaned in and pinched Billy's cheek, "Aren't you the cutest thing!" Billy leaned away from her with a smile, not wanting to give the man reason to think that he was interested.

"Jojo!," the man said in mock surprise, "You can't be pinching 'Billy the Kid's' cheek like that. He's a desperate killer!" Both Jojo and her husband had a laugh as they looked at the harmless boy, dressed as if he existed over a hundred years ago. Just then, the man leaned in and whispered into Billy's ear, "I mean, unless you want her too? I'm just saying, it's ok with me if you know what I mean?"

Taken aback, and not sure about what was being offered, Billy crinkled his eyes and ask, "What? What are you talking about?"

Jojo swatted her husband's shoulder playfully and exclaimed, "Sam, stop that! No cute young boy wants to be with an old woman like me!" The twinkle in her eyes said that she believed, or at least hoped, that she was wrong. Sam leaned in one more time, "Kid, we're staying at that Patron place, ok? Look, here's the key to the casita. Let's say that maybe I go for a stroll about, I don't know…3pm? If you happen to come by at that time, and I'm not there….well, hey…things happen, right?" Sam pasted a big smile on his face, while Jojo looked hopefully at Billy. Unsure of how to answer, Billy motioned Sam in closely.

"You sayin you want me to go belly to belly with your wife here?" he asked incredulously, "and you're just gonna leave me to it?

Sam turned to his wife and then back to Billy, whispering, "Unless you want me to be there? I can watch, take pictures, or maybe you and I can…"

"Whoa there Mister!" Billy shouted, finally understanding the complete offer, "I ain't never been with another man's wife and I ain't starting today. Now if you'll excuse me, I gotta get on with some business." Billy tipped his hat gently in Jojo's direction, "Ma'am." As he walked away, he heard Sam sighed and rationalize to his wife, "Screw him, he didn't even look that much like The Kid anyway. Poser."

Billy shook his head in wonderment of society in 2021. He couldn't imagine anyone in his time even thinking about what he was just offered, but was that true or was he just being naïve? He ambled over to the entrance of the old courthouse. Walking up the stairs, he stepped into the cool interior and was greeted by a kindly woman with the name 'Margie' on her name tag. "Got your ticket son?" she asked, holding her hand out. Billy fumbled around as if he'd misplaced it but after checking each pocket twice he admitted, "No ma'am, I don't." He'd turned the charm on many times in his life to his mother, his teachers, the women of Lincoln, and the pretty *senoritas* who came to *baille* in Fort Sumner. This old woman would be a cinch, "I was just hoping to take a quick look at that window upstairs? That one where Billy the Kid shot that mean old Bob Olinger from? Son of a bitch sure seemed like he deserved it too."

Margie smiled and Billy knew he'd won.

"Of course dear, just as soon as I see your ticket." she replied in a firm but friendly voice. Billy rolled his eyes back in his head, unable to believe that the old woman wouldn't relent.

"You just ain't gonna let me up there, now are you sweetie? I'm just talking a few seconds here." he countered with a wry grin. Margie grinned in return before speaking, "Name's Margie, not sweetie. You might think that putting on some fake old clothes would give you license to go wherever you want in this town, but that's not the way it works '*Billy*'. You see here, we follow the rules, and the rules say that each guest must buy a ticket. You think keeping these buildings in good repair comes free young man?"

Having badly miscalculated the woman, and wanting to end the dress down, Billy shook his head quickly and stepped back to leave.

"No, it does not," Margie continued, "and if I let every single pinched faced little man with no shoulders and big hips in here for free, then I wouldn't have a job anymore. Is that what you want young man? You want an old woman out on the street? You want me to lose my home?"

Billy smiled nervously and backed another step towards the door, "No ma'am, I was just…."

"What you were just doing amounts to wanting to steal something. Is that why you're dressed as Billy the Kid? You want to steal from me?" Margie continued, her head of steam going unabated, "And by the way, you don't even look that much like Billy. He was taller than you…"

"Ok," said Billy turning to walk out the door.

"And more handsome!" Margie yelled after him.

"Yep." said Billy quickly walking across the porch.

"And smarter too, you dumbass!" Margie raged as Billy hopped off the porch and walked quickly out of sight. Walking quickly to the other side of the street, he made his way back towards the Tunstall store.

"What in the hell was her problem?" he asked himself out loud. Breathing out the negative energy, Billy walked under the portal of the store, sat down on the bench, and planned his next move. "Well, I gotta find old Steve to help me, or I gotta find a way to get to the train. Maybe try for Roswell?" he said for his own benefit. Making the 10 mile trek to Capitan would take a few hours. From there, Billy wasn't even sure he could find Steve. He might waste the remainder of the day on a less than sure thing. Likewise, if he got to Roswell and was able to find a train, he had no money to purchase a ticket. In his haste to help Rosita, he'd not done a great job of planning for the eventualities of his trip. Deciding that his best bet was Capitan, Billy rose and started making his way west. He figured that Steve cut a big enough figure in any town he was in to be well known. He'd just have to ask around. Stepping carefully past the spot where the McSween house burned, he noticed a pickup truck rolling lazily down the main road. Billy kept his eyes ahead and stepped lively, trying to make the best time he could. As the truck reached him, the driver's attention was pulled to Billy's side of the road at the last second, and the truck screeched loudly in protest. Unable to stop in time, the truck slammed into the corner of the Tunstall store in a crunch of bent metal and broken glass. Showers of adobe rained upon the windshield. Both airbags had deployed and both driver and passenger slammed into them, the fog of the accident temporarily knocking them both into a mild case of shock.

Billy had never seen a car crash before, and thought for a moment about going back to help. By then, a number of locals had filtered out of their homes and were rushing to the scene. Billy just shook his head, needing to get on with his journey, and double timing it all the way to the west edge of Lincoln. Whomever was in the truck had their own issues to deal with, and Billy couldn't imagine that his presence could help them, or himself, in the slightest.

18.

Martin's face hurt like he'd been smacked by a King Kong-sized hand. His eyes stung from the smoke of the rapidly deploying airbags. In another few seconds his neck began hurting from the whiplash like movement as Steve's truck slammed into the corner of the Tunstall store. Unaware of where he really was, and unsure if he was more hurt than his central nervous system had let on, he sat there for a few more moments, enveloped in the quiet that developed after the crash. Slowly raising his left hand, he reached towards the driver's side of the truck, feeling around to see if Steve has there. Martin hoped he wasn't going to push his fingers into some slimy, oozing stump that used to be part of the big cowboy, as he reached further and further without finding him. As the smoke dissipated, Martin forced his eyes open, the image in front of him profoundly confusing. He clearly saw the Tunstall store in front of him, undamaged by the crash. The two things that tripped him up were that he wasn't in Steve's truck, and Steve wasn't there at all. Sitting on the hard ground and shaking his wits about him, he raised his eyes to scan the area and found that he was completely alone.

"What the hell?" Martin mumbled. He put his hand to his forehead, checking for blood. Not finding anything in disarray other than the pain he felt, Martin struggled to his feet. Looking around, he could see that he was in Lincoln, but not another soul stirred in town. The town looked as it had just a second before the crash. Martin had had an experience like this in the past. Shortly after his final visit to Rosita's grave, he'd been plunged into some version of Lincoln that was similarly lonely and vacant. At the time, Martin assumed he was dead, and that being trapped in the town as a sort of solitary confinement was his hell. He'd walked out onto the street then, and within seconds was astonished to see the beautiful Rosita running to him, a 5 year old version of Junior that Martin had never met holding her hand. That Lincoln had instantly changed, and felt like paradise to Martin, a paradise he was ripped from when Lilly CPR'd him back to life on the floor of the Patron House B&B. Now here was Martin again, in a decidedly less friendly looking version of the town, standing all alone, wondering if this time, death had come for him and succeeded?

"Where the hell is Steve? His truck? People?" Martin wondered aloud, "and if I'm dead, why did Steve get to live?" Immediately Martin castigated himself for the thought. If indeed he was dead, he'd be glad that Steve was alive. Steve could go on. Steve could tell Lilly what happened. Steve could pay for the damage to the Tunstall store that the State was sure to send a bill for. Of course, Martin couldn't be sure that Steve wasn't caught in his own version of solitary Lincoln, or Capitan, or the moon? What if the end, for each of us that hadn't earned a ducat to a meeting with the big guy, was this? A place that you loved in life, but shorn of anyone and anything else that made it so loved? And what if the deceased was a loner? Would their version of purgadise be filled with throngs of annoying people, tearing at and ruining the sanctity of the beloved place. Aside from all of the other fantastical experiences Martin's life had produced, this episode, and the earlier one like it made him wonder aloud;

"Why me?" Wasn't there some better messenger to get right with God than the spectacularly mundane life of Martin Teebs? Shaking his head, Martin decided he could not possibly be the chosen one. It was too much pressure for him to try to save anyone's soul, including his own. Assuming that this was his end, Martin gave himself one last mental inventory and decided he was well enough to walk. He figured the Patron House would be his best bet to bed down for the rest of eternity, being as he'd spent so much time there. Walking to the east a few steps he mused, "Now if only Rosita and my son would come running?"

As if on cue, two people sprinted up the road towards him. The look of relief on their faces was apparent, as if they'd been waiting for Martin to arrive. One was his good friend William H. Bonney, and the other was the most beautiful woman he'd ever know, The Belle of Lincoln, his great love Rosita Luna. Martin smiled, his arms held wide. If he was truly meant to meet eternity, he couldn't think of two better people to meet it with.

19.

Steam hissed from the failing radiator as the sound of a distant siren met Steve's ears. He reached up to adjust his hat, but all he felt was the top of his head. Cracking his eyes open, he could see the billowy remains of his truck's airbags, testimony to the severity of the crash.

"Oh my God! Are you ok?" yelled a kindly blonde named Jojo as she rushed up to the shattered driver's side window, having been visiting Lincoln for the first time with her husband Sam.

"Ummmmmm," Steve groaned as he tried to raise his stiff neck, "what happened?" His eyes slowly began to adjust to the light, and he could see the remains of the roof over the Tunstall Store portal lying across the hood of his truck. Peering further, he noticed there was a significant hole in the adobe outer wall of the store. "Oh shit," he mumbled, "somebody's gonna want some ass for this." Whether from the shock or the actual crash, Steve felt weak and wobbly, even just sitting in the truck. Tilting his head to the side he managed a question, "Hey Martin, you ok?" Drawing a deep breath, Steve noticed that Martin wasn't ok, in fact, he wasn't even in the truck. Shaking the cobwebs away he asked the woman, "Where'd my friend go? Did he get thrown out or something?"

Jojo looked concernedly at Sam, as they'd both been the first ones on the scene, "What friend? You're the only one in the truck?" Steve had seen enough comings and goings to know that he shouldn't press the issue with these strangers. "Do you want to get out Sir? Here, Sam…help him." Jojo commanded as Sam carefully opened the door. Steve took a quick mental inventory that revealed nothing was broken, but most things were incredibly sore, so he slid sideways on the seat and allowed Sam to help him stand. The wailing of sirens grew ever closer as Steve assumed someone had called for an ambulance.

"Lemme just sit on the tailgate and get my bearings here, ok?" he asked what was more of a demand. Sam and Jojo backed off as the current Lincoln County Sheriff arrived on scene. "Yeah, 11-79 in Lincoln. Shit, looks like it's Steve." he said as he slid out of his SUV.

"What in the hell happened cowboy? Ain't been drinking, have you?" asked the Sheriff.

"Shit son, I'd give anything for a drink right now. Might scare this headache away."

"You alright?" the Sheriff inquired, bending down to examine his friend.

"Guess so, just scrambled my brain a little, not that I've got much left to scramble." Sheriff Stone laughed and sat next to Steve on the trucks tailgate as an ambulance rolled quietly towards the crash site.

"So, what the hell happened here? The Tunstall store stands for what, 140 years and you come along and give it some air conditioning?" asked Stone. Steve looked around to make sure no one was close enough to listen, leaning into the Sheriff.

"I saw that Barrow kid. Walking on the side of the road. Just walked out from under the portal and when I swung around to look at him, I skidded into that post." confessed Steve.

"You sure it was him?" asked Stone skeptically, "He ain't been seen in weeks, and today he's just walking down the road in the middle of Lincoln?" Steve paused, as if to make sure he really did see Kevin Barrow, but he was certain he was right.

"I'm sure. I know him too well to be mistaken. Besides, I think Mar….." Steve stopped suddenly, not wanting to mention Martin's name for two reasons. First, Martin was a witness in an ongoing investigation, and second, he seemed to have disappeared at the moment of impact. He'd already slipped up with those tourists and didn't want the idea of him driving around with his imaginary friend getting any more traction.

"Mar?" asked Stone, "what are you talking about?"

Steve took a moment to collect some possible responses, "Margie, over at the courthouse. I'm thinking he musta walked right by there and maybe she seen him too." Relieved that he'd come up with a believable story, Steve leaned back and allowed his head towards the sun, relieving the aching in his neck.

"Alright Stevie boy," said Stone, "let the medics check you out. I'll call Fred with the wrecker, cause you ain't driving this rig anywhere for awhile. I can give you a lift back to town if you need."

Needing to understand where Kevin went, and likewise, Martin, Steve begged off, "Naw, but thanks. I'm just gonna scout around here. I'm sure the m0numemnt folks are going to want to have a word or three with me. I'll just get a ride back later on."

"Suit yourself." said Stone as he sauntered back towards his waiting car. Steve tried to make sense of just where Kevin had come from, and if Trisha might be far behind? How could that kid be walking around Lincoln and not trying to call his parents to let them know he wasn't injured in a ditch, living off of puddle water and grubs? As Steve slid off the tailgate, walking towards the medics, Jojo and Sam approached him.

"Oh, we're so glad you're ok. That was a nasty crash," Sam said with a warm smile, "I heard what you said about needing a ride later. We'd be happy to drive you wherever you need to go."

Steve grinned and nodded his head, "That's mighty friendly of you stranger. If you're still around when I'm done, I might just take you up on that."

Sam winked at Jojo as he reached into his pocket. "Here, this is the key to our casita at the Patron House. Whenever you're ready, come on by. Say…3pm? I might just be out for a walk but Jojo will be there and maybe you two can….." Sam shifted his eyes between Steve and Jojo so his meaning would be clear, or at least clearly implied. Jojo, for her part, lifted her hand to the button farthest north on her shirt and deftly plucked it open, exposing her voluminous cleavage. She slowly allowed her hand to traipse down the length of her torso as she smiled wickedly at Steve.

Instantly awake and clear minded at the offer, Steve barked, "What the holy hell are you talking about Mister? You want me to steamroll your wife while you're out chasing Billy the Kid? Seriously??"

Sam leaned in and said quietly, "Unless you want me to be there? I can watch, take pictures, or maybe you and I can…" Steve shook his head in disapproval and double timed it to the east and away from the sex crazed older couple, never giving Sam the chance to complete his sales pitch. "Crazy ass loons," Steve muttered to himself, "What the hell is this, Lincoln or Las Vegas?"

20.

"Martin!? Oh my God, Martin!!?" yelled Trisha as she and Kevin approached the only other human being moving about in Lincoln. At a flat out sprint, Kevin couldn't keep up the pace and Trisha arrived at the big man first. A trickle of blood, emanating from the side of his head, was running down Martin's cheek and he had a dazed look in his eyes. Trisha came to a stop, staring into the face of the man who had somehow sentenced her to this existence of isolation. Prepared to scream at him, demanding answers, the confused look in his eyes threw her off her game.

"What happened. Are you ok?" she asked, throwing her hands to his shoulders.

Martin looked vacantly around at Lincoln, and towards the Tunstall store as if searching for something only he could see, "Where's Steve? His truck? The crash?" Just then, Kevin arrived on the scene with a concerned look on his face, both for Martin and for himself. He and Trisha had clearly heard a crash replete with breaking glass, yet not a single thing in the town betrayed that it had actually happened.

"We heard a crash! You're with Steve? Where'd he go?" asked Kevin, now turning his head in circles looking for the missing member of their pack. Trisha, unable to resist herself, stepped in and put a hand on Martin's head, trying to find out if his wound was serious. While she knew she would be furious later, at the moment she only felt compassion for the man.

"Hey, you're bleeding. Let's get you to sit down, ok Martin?" she said gently, "I can go back to the house and get you something for the pain."

"No, I'm ok Rosita," said Martin wiping a trickle of blood away from his cheek, "I'm just so happy to see you." Both Kevin and Trisha looked at each other with raised eyes, wondering if the man was in shock, or perhaps had gone mad?

"Martin, come on. Let me take care of you," she said softly, "but I'm not Rosita. Hey! Martin! Look at me. It's me, Trisha. Ok?"

The silence of the town and the complete absence of anyone except Billy and Rosita, coupled with the shock of the accident made Martin freeze on his spot. The name Trisha didn't register with him. Trisha Davis was missing. Had been for weeks. Rosita Luna had somehow come through time, just where and when Martin needed her, and was here in the flesh, standing in front of him. While her modern clothes were distracting, it was clear that he, Billy, and Rosita had somehow crossed the plane of time to once again be together. Martin was almost incredulous that he was being given the chance to right all of his wrongs, one more time. This was not purgatory, this must be the gates to Heaven itself.

"Stop," Martin said with a smile, "don't tease me, my love. Billy, man, good to see you. Can you find Steve? It was a pretty bad crash. Maybe he wandered off to get help?"

Neither of the two young people wanted to speak, unsure of how fragile the man was. Martin, finally clearing his mind and vision, reached out for Rosita and pulled her tightly to him. Trisha wanted to wrestle free but something told her not to break the man any further, and she allowed the embrace. "Mr. Teebs, I think we should get you to the house. I think maybe you have a concussion or something." Kevin announced.

Pulling Rosita in further, Martin inhaled her scent, somehow different than he remembered, but still a luxury rarely afforded to him, "Why are you two talking so funny?" he asked with amusement, "Mr. Teebs? Mr. Teebs was my father, Billy."

With a glance at Kevin, Rosita began leading Martin down the street towards her house. He shuffled along slowly, looking to each side of the street. Something was wrong. In fact, Martin realized that a number of things were dramatically wrong for his reunion with his great love and his great pal. Homes, saloons, and the other buildings of Lincoln circa 1878 were missing. This Lincoln looked exactly like the one he'd just escaped. It was clean, tidied up, and not at all like he remembered. The other cause of concern was that aside from Billy and Rosita, there seemed to be a complete lack of people in town. Not a soul stirred. At this point, Martin would have expected to at least be harassed by some of Dolan's boys. What he wouldn't give to hear Tunstall's accent, or see the dissatisfied look on McSween's face. Hell, even Ham Mills' wife Monica was usually good for a bawdy joke or two. Regrettably for Martin, none of these people were in attendance of his big re-arrival to Lincoln. As the trio approach the visitor's center, Martin instinctively crossed the street to head towards Rosita's tiny house. When he did, the severity of the situation caught up with him. There was no house. No crumbling adobe. No turquoise door. There was no twin house that Rosita's mother Lourdes lived in. All there was, was a large white building where the two homes used to stand, and a very modern looking building behind it, designed to greet tourists and sell them museum tickets. All of it, at once, proved too much for Martin.

"What's going on here? Rosita, what happened to your house?" he said, almost shouting now, "Why is this like this? Billy?" Martin looked at Kevin with desperate eyes, hoping for an answer that would make sense, but Kevin had none and kept quiet. "Rosita!" Martin said, pulling Trisha in closer, "What's happened? Where are we?" Desperation was creeping in Martin's voice as the difference between his reality and expectations frightened him, badly. Trisha slowly pushed herself away, now feeling a deep sadness for Martin, and leading him by the hand.

"Come on Martin, let's go down the road. I'll patch up that cut on your head, ok?" she asked with a tense smile, "Don't worry. I'll take care of you. We'll figure this out." With no other choice, being as turned around as he was, Martin allowed himself to be led away. Kevin walked up and put his small hand on Martin's big shoulder to comfort him. As they pressed on, Martin's vision of the town confirmed his fear and confusion. This was not Lincoln of 1878. This wasn't even Lincoln of 2021, being as there wasn't a single person around but themselves. This was some abomination, created to torment him. He only took comfort that he was here with his friend, and with the woman he loved. They walked slowly to the margin of town, arriving at the path to Trisha's front door.

"Here we are." Trisha said and gently pulled Martin towards the front door.

"Yeah," nodded Kevin, "we'll get you fixed right up Teebsie."

What? Kevin furrowed his brow, wondering where he'd gotten that name from. Trisha cast a confused look in Kevin's direction but led Martin to the front door anyway. Grasping the handle and pushing the door open, she welcomed him into her home, "Come. Let me take care of you, *si Martin*?" Trisha's veins turned to ice water at her words, wondering where in the hell they had come from, who they were meant for, and just who in the hell she really was?

21

One day after Martin left for New Mexico, Lilly sat in his office, surveying the stacks of books that he intended to donate. She'd picked up a few boxes from a friend and was beginning to neatly stack the dozens of Billy the Kid related books in them. While Lilly had met the real Billy only two times, and the boy had spent a night in the guestroom of their house, just downstairs, she knew that Martin had a close connection with him.

"Books," she said half aloud, "What is it about books and Billy the Kid?" According to Martin, one of the first books he'd ever purchased about The Kid had granted him the power of time travel. Martin, in his past life, had written a trilogy of books about his journey with Billy, and his tragic love for Rosita. Lilly had even supplied Billy with a printed version of Martin's final book, Sunset in Sumner, that she hoped would propel The Kid forward (or backwards) in time so that he could meet with Martin one final time. Even now, this new and unimproved version of her husband was off galivanting around New Mexico in search of a book that he was terrified would fall into the wrong hands. The Martin that Lilly had married all those years ago would rather sit back with an barrel of ice cream and watch TV long before he'd ever waste his time picking up a book. What changed? What had brought them all to the precipice they were currently perched on?

Throwing these books away and moving on with his life must be incredibly hard for Martin. Lilly began doing mental calculations and estimated the original cost of these books to be in the thousands, not hundreds of dollars. "What a waste," she mumbled to herself, picking up one of the heavy bound, hardcover tomes. She'd been fascinated when Martin finally came clean with the revelation that he was, in fact, a time traveler. While she wouldn't have even bothered watching such nonsense on TV, knowing it was all fake, Lilly could not deny that a beautiful woman from the past was in love with her husband, and had seemingly come forward from her own time to claim him. On that fateful day in Lincoln, Lilly even saw, as she glanced impatiently over her shoulder, the woman and a young man she assumed was Billy, vanish from sight as they stood next to that big cowboy Steve's pickup truck. That was the morning Martin chose Lilly. But now, it seemed, they were both having second thoughts.

Turning to Martin's computer, Lilly was tempted to logon to Martin's social media accounts. Perhaps he'd somehow found a way to chat with Rosita? Maybe he had some time travel messenger relaying messages back and forth? Lilly hovered over the Facebook icon on the desktop for a few seconds before deciding against it. First, she wasn't sure she even cared anymore. Second, she knew it was a ridiculous thought. That Martin someone had someone traipsing back and forth through time to deliver instant messages to a long dead woman seemed preposterous. Carefully moving the icon over a few other files and folders, she realized there was no smoking gun here. Martin was as plain vanilla as a man could get, and if he wasn't, he was really good at covering his tracks. As she moused over to close his web browser, she decided that one last check of his browsing history couldn't hurt anything. As soon as she looked at it, Lilly realized Martin had been almost a step ahead of her. Swaths of historical browsing had been deleted from his computer, all the way back to July in fact. The first two entries she saw were from July 15, 2021;

Search results for: Kevin Barrow
Search results for: Trisha Davis

Lilly looked ruefully at the entries but was not surprised, after all, she was the one that had made them. She remembered that one day when a weird envelope had arrived in the daily mail. It said only "Teebs" on the outside and didn't have a return address. As far as Lilly could tell, there was no stamp on it, nor had there been, and no cancelled postmark sullied the paper. It was as if the postman had dropped it into their box either on his own, or at the behest of someone else. Remembering back to the scary days after September 11, 2001, when the mails delivered deadly doses of anthrax, Lilly put the strange letter aside while she sorted through the rest of the mail. Finally, she inspected it more closely, hoping it didn't contain some deadly powder that was designed to do both her and Martin in. Finding nothing suspicious (as if the letter wasn't suspicious enough on its own), she gently opened it and removed a sheet of mostly blank paper. In the center, in a non-descript font were typed the names of two people. Kevin Barrow and Trisha Davis. The only other words on the page were typed below the names, "Lincoln, NM."

At the time, Lilly thought it strange, as she and Martin were scheduled to leave for Lincoln in just a few weeks. Perhaps Martin had asked someone where to find another tour guide, or maybe these were friends of his that he'd met in some online Billy the Kid chatroom? Still, why go through the trouble of typing these names out on an otherwise blank sheet of paper, and putting them in an unmarked and unstamped envelope? The entire thing seemed so cloak and dagger to Lilly that it gave her the creeps. Of course, at the time, she was the old Lilly. The Lilly that didn't know about a 5 year rerun of her life. She knew nothing about Lincoln, Rosita, Carl Farber, and Martin's life in the past. After all that had happened just a few weeks ago, she understood how blissfully ignorant she had been. She almost longed to go back to that time, but understood that she knew too much, had seen too much, and that it was impossible.

So, on that day Lilly sat at Martin's computer (as she often did while he was at work) and typed the two names into a search engine. There were a few triathlon race results in Colorado for Barrow, and the Davis girl's Instagram looked like she was living her best life in sun, fun, and sand on the west coast. All in all, nothing seemed out of place with these two kids except for the fact that someone wanted Martin (or perhaps Lilly) to find out more about them. Scrolling through the results, she saw their names listed on the Monument Division's website as working at the Lincoln Historic District. Maybe Martin had requested some contacts for when they arrived? Regardless, Lilly couldn't fathom anything else from the search other than they were two good looking young people who she and Martin might run into while on their trip.

Turning her attention back to the letter, she looked for anything else, any identifying mark that would help determine where it came from. Looking closely, the only other thing she could find was a small smudge of something, grease maybe, on the bottom corner of the page. Lilly instinctively lifted it to her nose and sniffed. Bacon? No, definitely not. Pepperoni? Yeah, that might be it. Inhaling one more time, Lilly was taken by the distinct smell of pizza from the tiny smudge. Whoever the slob was that sent the letter, they could at least have retyped it on a clean sheet, rather than sending along a sample of their dinner with it. Shaking her head at the time, she had slipped the letter back into the envelope and placed it on Martin's desk.

Now in the present, Lilly wondered about the forgotten letter. Why had Martin never mentioned it? Surely, with his fascination for Trisha and Kevin after the fact, he'd have to bring up that someone had mailed him a letter with their names on it, weeks before he ever met them? It just seemed weird that it had never come up. Shaking her head, she looked around the room and rose to fill another box with Martin's now hated books. As she topped off yet another thousand dollars or so of wasted money in a heavy corrugated box, one of the books slipped to the floor. Lilly reached down to retrieve and noticed something under Martin's desk, way in the back, against the wall, awash in dust bunnies. Leaning in closer, Lilly saw that it was the letter! Martin must have knocked it off the back of the desk and never even seen it. No wonder he was surprised by meeting Trisha and Kevin. He had no idea they even existed! Lilly pushed her hand back to the wall and retrieved it, now wondering if it somehow implicated her and Martin in the disappearance of the two young people? While Lilly had no idea what had actually happened to them, she did see Trisha's final transformation into Rosita just after Martin had been shot in Lincoln. At the time it never occurred to her to wonder what had become of her identical twin host? Had this letter been some sort of historical cry for help? Would things have turned out differently if Martin had seen the letter? Was their entire 5 year rewind odyssey courtesy of the fact that Martin Teebs was supposed to do something about these two kids, yet never did.?

Now it made sense to Lilly. Martin's acting like a drooling idiot when they initially saw Trisha, and his fascination with the little pinched face boy, Kevin. Martin was to do something with these people. He was to know about them before he ever arrived in Lincoln. Perhaps he had some time travelers master key that he was supposed to use to send them back to whence they came, long before Carl Farber showed up and the shooting began? Her mind now racing, Lilly understood that her marriage, and her entire life, might be on more solid footing had she simply left that letter for Martin to open. Her actions and his inactions must have set off a chain of events that turned their lives upside down. "Dammit!" she exclaimed in the silent house, "this is my fault??"

Lilly plucked the letter from the envelope one more time, seeing the now familiar names on it. Looking down at the smudge of grease, she again brought the letter to her nose. Pizza, she was sure of it. Pepperoni, most likely. Whatever the letter meant and whomever sent it, it could only cause more problems for her and Martin now. Trying to remember what the punishment might be for destroying evidence in an active investigation, she merely said, "Screw it! Taking one last sniff, she dropped the letter and envelope into the shredder, watching it turn to so many useless pieces, and left Martin's office, cold and vacant, for the balance of the day.

22

July 14, 2021

Sergio Bachaca pushed another slice of pizza past his greedy lips and into his mouth, the grease from a voluminous helping of pepperoni dribbling down his chin. Whenever he visited a new town, he like to ask the locals where he could get the best, most authentic pizza, and there he would frequent as often as possible. On this particular day, he happened upon King Pizza in Paramus, NJ upon the suggestion of a short, balding man who proclaimed he once lived in the town, many years ago. Bachaca counted only 2 slices left from the large pie he'd ordered, plus the one he was currently levering into his mouth. "That little son of a bitch knows his pizza, I'll give him that." he said aloud to the mostly empty restaurant.

With flagging fortunes, Sergio had taken to guerilla marketing for his latent book "The True Life of Billy the Kid." Originally published in 2014, Bachaca's book had initially sold well, but trailed off soon thereafter. With his income and savings in peril, he began writing another book on the rise of the fortunes of Lawrence Murphy, albeit much later than he should have. On the verge of his new book being released, Bachaca wanted to pump sales of his Billy the Kid book in anticipation of his newest readers coming back for a more expensive second helping. As such, his modus operandi was to visit large bookstores pretending to be a Billy the Kid enthusiast. He'd generally schedule his visits to coincide with a replay of Young Guns on local TV. That movie always netted him an audience of middle-aged doughboys who were looking for their first (or next) literary fix of Kid related material. He'd simply show up the next day, generally late in the afternoon, start reading his own book, and then start making recommendations to the newbies about which one they should start with. His first and only recommendation was always his own book. So well did it work that "Serge" as he liked to refer to himself as, could track his publisher's bumps in sales to each town he visited and to each showing of the film. He'd even come to relish the acting job he did, posing as the friendly "hey, I'm just like you" guy in the book section commiserating with all of the other hapless saps who'd never know more than him about Billy the Kid no matter what book they read.

Sitting there, working his way towards the crust, Sergio knew it was going to be a losing effort if his goal was to take down the entire pizza in one sitting. His belly pressed against the cheap polyester shirt he was wearing and there simply wasn't any more space he could rent to push those two slices in. No matter, he procured a box for the leftovers and promised himself a snack when he arrived at his hotel later that evening. Arriving at the bookstore some 10 minutes later, he scoped out the history section and shuffled over, ready to put on his friendly, outgoing persona.

That afternoon was a good one for "Serge". The showing of Young Guns, coupled with a 2 for 1 sale on ice cream meant a lot of these middle class, middle-aged slugs had spent much of the night in front of the TV. By 5pm he counted at least 14 books sold. So much so, he had to alert one of the store's clerks that the shelves needed restocking and that they should place another order from their distributor for the book.

Finally around 5:30 pm, with a few stragglers still scattered about the comfy chairs, a tall, nondescript man warily pushed his way towards the history section. Bachaca readied another book for his dupe just as another man, with a permanent sour look on his face approached from the other direction. Sourpuss seemed to be scanning the room, trying to determine whatever he could from this group of men. The tall guy, looking like he didn't belong *and* didn't want to be there, avoided anyone's eyes as he scanned the shelves for his Young Guns/ Billy the Kid redemption.

"Here!" urged Sergio, "This one is the best. It's by Sergio Bachaca, 'The True Life of Billy the Kid'."

"So, this is a good one huh?" asked the tall guy noncommittally.

"Good? It's the best, most factual account of Billy's life, bar none. I own 3 copies myself," offered Sergio, "I even got one signed by Serge on one of his book tours in Virginia." Being that Bachaca had actually come to New Jersey from a similar stakeout in Virginia, he didn't feel badly about hiding his identity. The tall guy thanked him and decided to purchase the book, leaving 'Serge' fulfilled that he might break his goal of selling 20 copies on this day. "19," he said to himself, scanning the rest of his crowd to see who lucky number 20 might be. Turning around, he saw the sour faced guy again and a nagging feeling took hold, as if a cat was clawing at his neck, and Sergio could barely hold it far enough away to avoid injury. The narrow-faced man looked disdainfully at both Sergio as well as the few guys left who hadn't yet bailed out to return to their suburban nightmare. Something about the look, or maybe it was the guy's eyes, bothered Bachaca and he strolled away to get a better, yet more hidden vantage point. Sergio studied the unhappy man, wondering what his beef was with Billy the Kid. Try as he might, he couldn't place the nagging feeling that he somehow knew this guy, and that missed recollection bothered him. A few minutes later, the sourpuss pasted a gritty grin on his face, apparently finding whatever it was he came to the store for and walked out. Two more of the guys who'd been checking out the book decided they liked it enough to take it to the cashier and Sergio silently pumped his fist like Tiger Woods making a 25-foot birdie putt. "21!" he exclaimed out loud as he figured his work here was done for the day.

Walking towards the front door, he saw the sourpuss talking to someone behind the counter. It rankled Sergio that the man had not left the store minutes ago, and now another faceoff might occur. Peering at the discussion from behind the clearance section, he saw that Sour was actually purchasing a copy of his book! While the man didn't look happy about shelling out the cash for it, Bachaca counted a silent "22" for himself. While Sour waited for his change, he sneered as he flipped carelessly through the pages of the book. It was as if holding it bothered the man, which bothered Sergio even more. He could not shake the bad feelings he had for the guy and wished him to hurry up and leave the store, and Sergio's life, and the planet, forever. After what seemed like an eternity, the guy got his change and shuffled miserably out of the store.

Struck by the diametric differences between the bumbling tall guy and the miserable pinched face one, Sergio got a look, in the span of five minutes, at the breadth of his kingdom…and he didn't like what he saw. With 6 slices of King's Pizza roiling in his stomach, he began to get angry. From know nothing dolts to know it all pricks, was this what he had created? Was his legacy to be a bunch of bland morons, fighting over arcane knowledge of some long gone outlaw on the internet? Would they invoke his name as the keeper of this useless truth, that caused nothing but consternation and ill will? A light had been shown on Bachaca and his Billy the Kid kingdom, and the king did not like what he'd seen. Not sure if it was the pepperoni, or his newfound enlightenment making him ill, he clutched his belly as a bitter bile rose from within.

"You'll pay. You and that dumb tall one," he said to the back of the disappearing, sourpuss man, "And you'll both pay a mighty price. I guarantee it. See you assholes in Hell."

23

Having found nary a trace of Kevin Barrow walking out of Lincoln, Steve walked back a quarter mile or so to The courthouse museum and stepped heavily onto the porch. If you'd asked him this morning what the day might bring, seeing Martin Teebs walk into his office, punching a hole through the historic Tunstall store with his truck, and seeing a boy missing for weeks simply appear and disappear before his eyes would not have been high on his list of prospets. Add to that the disappearance of Martin, at the moment of impact, and an offered threesome by some hayseeds from (probably) Kansas, and Steve's day was complete. The problem was, it was only 3pm and he had no ride back to Capitan, so here in Lincoln he stood, peering through the glass to see if his friend Margie was working.

"Steve! You ok cowboy?" Margie asked, knowing that if he was still standing, he was fine.

"Yeah, I'm ok. Pride might be a bit bruised but that's about it." he replied.

"Now you know, you're gonna have to stomp some mud and make a few adobe bricks to fix that new window you put in the store." Margie said with a laugh. Knowing she was only half kidding and all correct, Steve nodded in her direction with a wry grin.

"Seen anything strange round here today?" he asked, not wanting to raise the alarm on the missing boy if he could help it.

"This is Lincoln. I see strange things every day," Margie said, "Care to be more specific?" Steve huffed a bit, wondering if Margie could be trusted to keep a secret. In her 65 years on the planet, she'd failed to keep even one, regaling everyone who walked into the museum with the latest gossip despite her sworn protestations that she'd take them to the grave. She'd need a casket the size of Texas to hoard all the secrets that never kept anyway. Steve figured that maybe, just maybe, she might be due to keep her word this time.

"Alright look, and keep this to yourself," he said, "I saw….."

Margie cut him off with a serious nod, "I'll take it to the grave Steve, you know me."

"Oh shit, I'm doomed." Steve paused but figured he had no better options, "Well, hell…anyway. I saw that missing Barrow kid when I drove into town. Walking right out there on the damn road. Lost my concentration and plugged the Tunstall store. By the time I looked up he was gone. Not another person said they saw anything. So… did you see him?"

Margie looked around to make sure she wasn't being overheard, probably so that she'd have a bigger audience to spill Steve's secret to later, when he finally left to go home. "You mean that scrunched face little loser?" she said as harmlessly as she could, "Yeah, I saw him. He was trying to get in here without paying. Wanted to go upstairs to that Olinger window. I figured since he didn't work here anymore, he wasn't getting in for free, so I told him to bug off."

"But you know he's been missing, right?" Steve asked urgently, "As in, presumed maybe dead? Why didn't you call someone?"

"The only one I'd have called is the Sheriff to come and arrest that little twit. If he's man enough to try to sneak into my museum, then he should be man enough to show himself and say where he's been. Probably off pulling his little taffy in the woods, you ask me…" Steve raised his eyes in amazement that Margie had not the slightest sense of urgency to report a missing person being found.

"Ok then, did he say anything? Where he's been? Where he was going? Did you see that Davis girl?" Steve asked as calmly as he could.

"You mean the one with the tits?" asked Margie earnestly, holding her hands out a good distance in front of her chest, "I'll bet you'd like to get a piece or two of that, huh Stevie?"

"Oh for Christ sake!" Steve roared, his voice echoing off the adobe walls, "this is serious Margie. This is a federal investigation. Stop joking around!" Looking wounded, Margie looked narrowly at Steve. She was usually the one doing the dressing down but she understood why this particular information might actually be important.

"Look, he didn't say anything other than wanting to go upstairs. I gave him some guff about it and he slid off his rock like a turtle dropping into the Pecos. Not much of a man if you ask me."

"Ok, so where did he go?" asked Steve.

"I guess he went east because you said you saw him by the store? I didn't pay much attention because some older couple came in just then and was asking a lot of questions." Steve was left with zero clues, other than the fact that he'd seen Kevin walking towards the edge of town. The Sheriff would surely find him on the road to Capitan, but if that had happened, Steve hadn't heard a word of it. Deciding that until he could score a ride back to Capitan, he'd walk though Lincoln hoping to find some clues about Trisha Davis, he turned to walk out.

"Hey Steve, wait a second," Margie said just before he reached the door, "Can you watch the place for me for a little while?" She held up a key with a wicked smile. "Got some new friends staying at the Patron place and they invited me to stop by about 3." All Steve could do is slump his shoulders and laugh, wondering where on the invite list he'd actually been for Sam and Jojo's party? As Margie walked out the door, she stopped for a moment and turned around, "Hey, Steve, ummm…what's a threesome anyway?"

24.

Trisha pressed a cool cloth to Martin's head, gently wiping the now dried blood away. A few minutes of sitting in the quiet house had allowed Martin to regain his composure. He remembered the day in this house, less than a month ago, that he and Rosita had made love just about everywhere that could facilitate them, and some places that couldn't. Still confused as to what had happened, he breathed slowly, watching Rosita's worried brown eyes survey him.

"Why are you back here?" Martin asked quietly, "I don't think it's a good idea." Trisha traded a worried glance at Kevin, unsure as to how to respond. Turning to get Martin a glass of water, Trisha retreated while Kevin sat down on a chair near him.

"Martin, man," began Kevin, "I think you might have a concussion. Why don't you lay down there a bit?" A look of concern, and not for a possible concussion, spread across Martin's face, "Why are you talking like that? Since when do you call me Martin? Geez Billy, come on." Trisha glanced over the counter again at Kevin, both thinking the same thing. Martin had either taken a solid blow to the head and temporarily couldn't tell fact from fiction, or he'd come completely unhinged and lost his mind for good. Walking around the counter, she handed him the water glass with a warm smile. Martin smiled back at her shining eyes, transfixed at her beauty. "You take such good care of me my love," he gushed, "I don't know how it happened, but I'm glad I made it back to you Rosita."

"I'm not Rosita, Martin. I'm Trisha."

Martin's eyes registered some syntax error, something that didn't compute. While the entire trip to get to this place had been weird and stressful, it had at least brought him to the precipice of his one true love. To hear her now, in an annoying modern accent, was something Martin just could not accept. "Stop, ok? Please? No more games Rosita." he said, hoping he didn't come off too strong.

"Martin, she's not Rosita. I'm not Billy. You're not in some jacked up time travel game. We're here in Lincoln. Ok man?" Kevin said forcefully. Martin simply looked confused at the moment, as if expecting to lick a chocolate ice cream cone but finding out that while it looked like chocolate, it tasted like vanilla. He just shook his head from side to side, unsure of what to make of it all.

"Martin, Martin!" Trisha said while snapping her fingers to get his attention, "Listen. I'm Trisha. ok? Trisha Davis, remember? You need to snap out of whatever you're in so you can help us." Unwilling to let go of his friend and lover, Martin took a long drink of water and handed it back to Rosita, or….was it Trisha? He took the time to look over both of them closely. On the counter, Farber's 'Coward of Lincoln County' manuscript sat there, defiantly. Martin reached over to pick it up, looking at the photo of Billy on the first page. He held it out, offering the view to Kevin, "Look, it's you." Martin hesitated a bit and then asked sheepishly, "Isn't it?"

Kevin looked as kindly as he could before answering, "No Martin. That's Billy the Kid. I'm Kevin Barrow. This is Trisha Davis, and you are Martin Teebs. For some Godforsaken reason, we're all trapped here in Lincoln, except there doesn't seem to be another person around and we can't get out. Please tell me you understand me Martin. Please tell me that I'm getting through to you, ok?"

The curtain behind Martin's eyes slowly opened, allowing him to see that what Kevin had told him was true. This was not Rosita, and he wasn't talking to his best friend Billy. A cold chill spread throughout his body, making his skin tingle. Breathing more quickly he looked down at the floor, "How the hell did I get here? You two have been missing for weeks, months. Where the hell have you been?"

Trisha snapped her head around to meet Kevin's eyes. Missing for months? It had been no more than 2 or 3 days since the pageant, the shooting, and the release of their historical counterparts. Was Martin's memory that addled that he couldn't account for time. "What do you mean months, Martin?" asked Trisha, "we've only been here like this for a few days. Did you ever even leave New Mexico?" Martin felt the life, and perhaps his sanity, flow back into his body. He braced himself by slapping his own face a couple of times. Fully awake and engaged, he motioned for Trisha to sit down.

"Listen, I don't know what the hell this is, but I've been back in New Jersey for weeks with Lilly. I've even gone back to work. I talked to Steve about your missing iPhone Trisha, and we both agreed that Rosita probably took it when she went back with Billy. I was set to let this all die down, and I remembered that damned book." Kevin picked up Farber's manuscript and held it up, "This one?"

"No, although, that one sucks too, but no. *Lincoln County Days*. That book talks about ME, in the PAST, and sooner or later the FBI was going to come by and find it, and guess whose door they'd come knocking on?" Trisha nodded her head, knowing that Martin was mostly right.

"Well, the good news is I don't think you need to worry about FBI here Martin." offered Trisha with a weak smile.

"Why not?" he shot back.

"Because wherever we are, whenever we are, we seem to be the only ones in Lincoln. We can't even leave here. Kevin tried." Martin looked over at Kevin who was nodding seriously. That would explain a lot, Martin thought to himself. Once again he was trapped in some sort of purgatory, albeit this time with doppelgangers of his friend and lover. One more time Lincoln had bent him over to become not his paradise on earth, but his prison. "How did you get here exactly?" Trisha asked.

"I was with Steve. We were driving into town, hoping to maybe find you two, but needing to get that book out of here. I don't know, Steve was talking to me one minute, and the next thing I knew he was swerving across the road and smashed into the Tunstall store. I bounced off the airbags and hit my head on something, I guess. When I was able to open my eyes, I was all alone. Not another soul in town. Honestly I just figured I was dead, again, but that's another story I guess."

"Wait, what do you mean, dead again?" Kevin asked, narrowing his eyes.

"Forget it, this won't solve anything now. We need to figure out where we are and how to get out of here." Martin replied stiffly.

"No, no Mr. Teebs, I think hearing that you were dead before I met you or something might solve a lot. Please, feel free to share." said Kevin both interested and angry that something so important had been held back from the conversation. Martin glanced at Trisha, unsure of how much to tell the young man. The moment wasn't lost on Kevin, incredulous that he was the only one *not* in on the secret, "What a minute? You KNEW about this Trisha? What? This guy is some kind of friggin ghost and you failed to mention that? In the what, 3 days we've been stuck here you didn't think to tell me that the old dude who fawns over you like you're some 5 dollar a minute webcam girl was, what, dead? Reincarnated? Resurrected? What else am I not in on?"

"Whoa!" yelled Martin, offense clearly taken at the slight to him and the characterization of Trisha. Kevin, as angry as he'd ever been, just glared back at Martin, his fists balled in case the old dude wanted to roll.

Trisha rubbed her eyes while shaking her head, a dull headache beginning to form, "Kev, I'm sorry, ok? I wasn't trying to keep anything from you. It was that night of the dance, at the brewery. Martin told me the whole story. To be honest, I figured most of it was bullshit, but I knew that he believed it. The longer that week went on, the more I got sucked into it. I guess you did too. I just….I don't know…"

Kevin was incensed that something so important had been kept from him. Figuring they all had nothing but time, he pressed the issue, "Ok Martin, since we're here. I mean, we *are* here, right? We're not going anywhere as best as I can tell. Why don't you tell me everything you told her? I'd like to know how you died, how you're here? Tell me about that dying thing the last time, ok? Did you die here, there, somewhere else? How'd it feel to die Martin? You think it'll be any better this time when you take us the fuck with you!" Kevin's voice dripped with sarcastic anger.

"Kevin, stop!" Trisha yelled, loud enough for everyone to sit up and take notice. She then said more softly, "Please…stop." Martin slumped backwards on the couch, now acutely aware of the pain in his head from the bump he took. He knew that Kevin was right, he was owed an explanation. The problem was, Martin didn't have one. As much as he'd like to tell both of them how they got here, and how they'd get out, he didn't have a clue. It was then that Martin began to think he really was dead. If this was some purgatory, or Hell even, wouldn't it be fitting that he'd been placed with people that looked exactly like the two most important people in his world, two people he loved, yet they were not really those people, and they really did hate him? What torture it would be for eternity to pine for Rosita, but watch Trisha sneer at him instead. While he and Billy would have deep conversations about life, Kevin would merely glare at him for the current mess they were in. Whomever designed this hell had done a, well, hell of a job at it. Martin couldn't help but whisper out loud, "Kudos for that you son of a bitch."

"What did you say?" asked Kevin.

Martin turned his head, no longer in apology mode, and replied plainly, "I wasn't talking to you." Martin glanced around the room, and then at Trisha and Kevin, no emotion on his face. He wasn't scared anymore. He wasn't sad. He wasn't sorry. In fact, he wasn't….anything. He felt more like a hollow shell than anything else. No one spoke for a long moment, and finally to break the tension, Trisha slid closer on the couch to check the cut on Martin's head.

"*Martin*, is ok now, *si?*" she asked and immediately froze as did everyone else in the room, "I mean, uh, are you ok?"

"What in the hell was that?" asked Kevin, "You hear that shit Teebsie?"

Once again everyone in the room stopped, eyes glancing nervously at each other. No one wanted to speak first. Like a Mexican standoff, each person glanced first at one, then the other, never allowing their gaze to settle for very long. Each hoping that the other would break the silence and explain what was going on. No one did. The game continued, the trio all standing pat that they would not be the one to speak first. Initially tense, Martin glanced at Kevin and saw a smirk on his face. This caused Martin to smirk which caused a laugh to escape from Trisha, and soon the lot of them were ensconced in a full blown guffaw at the stupidity of their actions. Martin began laughing so hard that tears formed in his eyes, and his gut ached. Kevin slapped his knee hard enough to hurt it as his eyes drained along with his nose. He rose to grab a box of tissues then passed it around to the group, each one grabbing a couple in an attempt to compose themselves. As the laughter receded a calm overtook the group.

"Ok then. That was interesting. Best I can tell, you're not Rosita and you're not Billy, but something weird *is* going on here." spoke Martin with confidence, "Maybe let's go back to that Sunday and see if we can figure out what it is?"

"You mean like, we can wind the clock back or something?" Kevin asked.

"No, well…at least I don't think so. I mean, let's review what happened and see how you all got here. If we can figure that, maybe we can find a way out?"

Trisha hopped up from the couch, "I'll put some coffee on. I feel like this is going to take awhile." Martin reached across the couch to shake Kevin's hand, "I'm sorry man. Really. If I did this, I'll undo it. If I didn't, we'll figure out who did."

Kevin got a rueful grin on his face, happy at least that while they had no answers, they would work together to find some. "No problem Mr. Teebs. I always said I'd come to New Mexico to get some peace and quiet. I guess it doesn't get more quiet than this." Martin couldn't help but nod his head. Trisha returned and plopped down on the sofa next to Martin, "Ok, where do we start?" Martin figured the beginning was probably the best place, so he began to spin his tale of how he'd first met his friend Billy the Kid, and found the love of his life (all of them), Rosita Luna.

Trisha sat close to Martin, warmer feelings than she ever remembered growing for the man. She felt strange, different even. She knew she wasn't Rosita Luna, but in some small way, she began to wish she was.

25.
JULY 14, 2021

Back in his hotel, Sergio Bachaca looked at the small slip of paper that had cost him fifty dollars. At the bookstore, and upon the sour faced man leaving, Sergio approached the cashier just as the young woman headed off for a break. His plan was to get her to review the credit card transaction of the tall dolt, and give Sergio the guy's name. He concocted some sob story about the guy possibly being one of his students in college, and that he had just missed him as he left the store, but wanted to reconnect if only he could remember his name. The cashier politely told him that giving out customer information was against store policy and continued walking away. Catching up to her, he impressed just how important it was to him to reach this particular student upon which the young woman stopped, stared him in the eyes, and asked, "How important is it to you?" with a smirk. Understanding he was about to be shaken down, he reached into his wallet and pulled out a twenty dollar bill.

"Pretty important, young lady." he said with confidence. The woman plucked the twenty from his hands, stuck it inside the neckline of her polo shirt and pushed it down into her bra, "Sure as hell doesn't seem so."

"Come on!" Bachaca replied, "It's one measly name." The young lady smiled, tapped him on the nose with her index finger, and said, "Actually, it's two. First, and last." She tilted her head and beckoned the portly man to challenge her.

"Alright," he grumbled, fishing into his wallet for another twenty. He held it up, just out of her reach, "Now, the name please?" Not to be outdone, the woman held her hand out, palm up, waiting for it to be greased, "Payments are due in advance unless otherwise agreed to by both parties." she mocked. Bachaca rolled his eyes and slapped the bill down into the girl's palm.

"Let's go," he said impatiently as they walked to the front of the store. Logging into her computer, the woman scrolled down until she got the name. "Well?" he asked.

"Yes, got it right here," she said as she checked her watch, "You know, I've missed 5 minutes of my break already. Have I told you how much I really love my break time?"

Laughing and smiling at the older man, she simply stood and waited for him to reach into his wallet one more time.

"Oh for crying out loud!" he snapped, reaching into his wallet, "Look, all I've got left is a ten." The young woman accepted the negotiated price, slipped the bill into her pocket, and barked out the name, "Martin Teebs. Waldwick, New Jersey. Good?" As she started to walk away, Bachaca stepped towards her, "Wait, I need the other guy's name too. That last one with the pinched face. A deal's a deal." Reviewing the transactions, the girl saw the one Sergio was talking about.

"Sorry, he paid with cash. No idea who he is." Bachaca threw his head back in frustration.

"Who who is?" said a younger boy, also about to head off on his break.

"That angry looking dude who bought the Billy the Kid book. This guy wants to know his name," said the young lady, motioning with her thumb at Bachaca.

"You mean Mr. Farber?"

An ice cold chill shot through Sergio's veins. "What?" he asked seriously.

"Yeah, he teaches history over at Waldwick High. Real pain in the ass." the boy continued.

"Did you say Farber?" Bachaca asked slowly, as if he didn't want the answer to be yes.

"Yeah," said the boy, "Carl Farber. Dude's off the reservation though. I'd stand clear. Plus he's really got some hard on for Billy the Kid, whoever that is?" With that, the boy and girl walked off towards the back of the store. Bachaca stood there, shaking a wave of vertigo from his head, trying to remain in control.

"Carl Farber," he said quietly, holding onto the wall and glancing out at the parking lot, "you've got to be fucking kidding me."

26.

Making his way out of Lincoln, Billy retreated to the Bonito Creek, hoping that it would afford him some cover as he made his way to Capitan. With a 10-mile hike in front of him, unless he could steal a horse, he paced himself on the journey. The car crash had shaken him up a bit, and the sight of some vehicles speeding by with blue and red lights flashing, added to his confusion of what was going on. His plan, as thin as it seemed, was to make his way to Capitan and ask around to find Steve. He'd known enough of the old cowboy from their time in the hospital to understand that he could probably count on him for some help. If Steve had one of those iPhone things that Rosita had brought back to Lincoln, he might even be able to get a message to Martin about Rosita's pregnancy? In any event, this journey was significantly shorter than trying to reach New Jersey and find Martin on his own.

From the angle of the sun, and knowing it was mid Fall, Billly estimated that he had a few hours of daylight left as he reached Fort Stanton road. Intimately familiar with the area in his own time, he marveled at how little it had changed in the intervening 140 years. He could just see that pompous ass Dudley, astride his mount, leading his troops into Lincoln to "save women and children". Billy wondered briefly if Dudley might too have been gifted the talent of time travel? If he had, Billy would be glad to march up to Stanton right now and punch the Colonel square in his bulbous nose. "Save women and children my ass," he muttered to the trees rimming the Bonito, "more like save Dolan's boys from getting their ass handed to them."

Spying more of the flashing lights vehicles up on the road, Billy picked his way along the riverbank, scarcely noticing that at least one of those 'cars' was turning off the road and was headed towards him. Too late, he saw a vehicle some 50 yards away, the driver looking straight at him. While Billy had run from the law a number of times, he usually had a horse, a couple of guns, and Pat Garrett never showed up in one of these car things. He decided that playing it cool was the best option he had at the moment. As the car rolled to a stop, a man that Billy figured for some type of law enforcement stepped out and put on a hat very much like the one that Steve always wore. The man had some sort of firearm on his hip, but it looked about as different from a Colt as peas did from carrots.

"Howdy," said the man in a friendly voice, "Names Delbert Stone, Lincoln County Sheriff."

"Not again," Billy said quietly while laughing to himself.

"What's that son? Not again what?" asked Stone.

Billy smirked and turned his palms up, "Aw, nothing. I like the Lincoln County Sheriff's office. Every last one of you guys. Might could say me and your department's got a long history together." Stone scrunched his eyes up, wondering exactly what the young man meant.

"Your name Kevin Barrow son?" Stone asked in a mild tone, not wanting to scare the boy into retreat. Billy didn't have to feign looking confused.

"Say what now? Barrow? No, I ain't him if that's who you're looking for." Stone adjusted his sunglasses in the late afternoon light, "You ain't in trouble son. I'm sure you know, there's a lot of people that want to see you safe. Why don't we take a ride back to Lincoln and talk about it?" Billy had been arrested enough times to know that the Sheriff wasn't really asking him. Still, Billy was unarmed and didn't have a mount. Sheriff Stone had a gun (or three) and one of these cars that seemed like it could chase Billy to eternity and back.

"Supposing I ain't interested?" Billy asked, wanting to understand his options.

"Look, Kevin. I'm not going to arrest you for being a young man who wanted to get away from things for awhile. I just need to know where you've been for the past month or so. I need to find the Davis girl too. Is she with you? Have you seen her?"

Still unaware of who Kevin was, and not knowing any Davis girl, Billy understood what while he was technically free to go, he most likely shouldn't. "How about we do this another time? I'm on my way to Capitan to meet old Steve. Got a favor I need him to do for me." Billy said.

Stone pulled his aviator sunglasses from his face in surprise, "Steve? You kidding me? Hell son, he's in Lincoln right now. Crashed his damn truck into the Tunstall store when he saw you walking along the road. He'd be happy to see me bring you in." Something about the way Stone said 'bring you in' didn't set well with Billy, but if it was true that Steve was the one crashing into the Tunstall store, Billy would get to him a lot quicker by getting a ride from the Sheriff.

"Look, I ain't the guy that you're looking for, but if you can bring me over to old Steve, then I'm happy to get the ride."

Stone slipped on his glasses and motioned Billy around to the other side. Sliding into the seat, Billy was met with the aroma of something, beef maybe, that was probably part of the Sheriff's lunch. Pulling a white bag from the back seat, Stone apologized, "Sorry about that, was just eating my lunch when the call came in about Steve. Hamburger." stone offered. Billy glanced down at the console and noticed two small packets of salt, which he surreptitiously slipped into his hand when the Sheriff wasn't looking. As the car bumped and swerved its way up the hill, Stone picked up something that Billy didn't recognize, but the Sheriff appeared to want to talk into it. Reaching the road, Stone carefully slowed down, lest a car came screaming around the blind corner to his left. Billy waited for the Sheriff to head to Lincoln but instead, just as he began to talk into the device, he turned right towards Capitan.

"Hey Gil, I've got a….." Stone began, "Ahhh!!!" The Sheriff's car lurched along the road as the salt Billy had thrown into his eyes worked its way in deeper. "What the hell did you do that for?!" Stone screamed, temporarily blinded. Billy pulled the latch and pressed hard on the door, tumbling out and rolling down the embankment. Stone had the sense about him to press on the brakes, searching blindly for the mic for his radio. Billy gained his feet and sprinted to the Bonito, assuming that the Sheriff would be floating rounds at him any moment. All he could hear however, was Stone's voice cussing in the distance as he reached the creek. "Why the hell are you running?!" the Sheriff screamed as his voice receded from Billy's ears. Knowing his options were few, Billy ran for a minute towards Lincoln but realized that he'd be found before he ever reached it. He closed his eyes tightly and grimaced, pulling Bachaca's book from his waistband.

"Shit, I'm sorry Rosie…..I'm sorry!" he yelled as he opened the book, and vanished into thin air, quickly on his way back to the time he had worked so hard to escape from.

27.

JULY 14, 2021

Slipping his key card into the slot, Sergio Bachaca walked quietly into the air conditioned business center of his hotel. Over his final two slices of cold pizza, he'd decided what he was going to do. He'd spent the last 5 hours furiously writing something, as if possessed. Now, it was time to make it all worthwhile. He'd remembered, through a grainy sepia memory in his brain, going to a puppet show as a child. The kids around him laughed and rolled around on the floor with glee. Even then, Sergio was so much smarter than them, or so he believed. How could they not see the strings? How could they not see the occasional dip into reality of the puppet master's hand? Couldn't they tell that sometimes Mr. Beasley's voice didn't change to Ms. Terpitiller's when it was supposed to? At that young age, Sergio decided that it wasn't the puppet's fault if the show sucked, it was all on the puppet master.

Sliding into one of the leather office chairs, he clicked open a new document and hit 'enter' until he was halfway down the page. Without any forethought, he simply typed.

Kevin Barrow
Trisha Davis
Lincoln, NM

And hit the 'print' button. Finding a small stack of fresh envelopes, he fed one into the printer and typed: 'Teebs' on the front of it.

"This should do it," he said to no one in the tiny room. Grabbing the letter from the printer, he pushed his greasy thumb down hard enough to leave a trace of his dinner behind. Once in the envelope, Bachaca's oily lips licked the glue and he pushed the whole thing down firmly to seal it. It had been easy enough to find a listing and address for Martin and Lilly Teebs online and Sergio knew right where the letter needed to go. Rather than delay his plan any longer, or risk some stupid, lazy postal employee losing his masterpiece, Sergio decided that the next day, he'd wait for the postman to make his regular delivery to the Teebs house, and then he'd slip through in his wake to drop his letter in the box as well.

"Dupes," he said out loud as he glanced at the letter, "ruining the legacy I've built. Embarrassing real historians with your nonsense? You'll get every single thing you deserve, and more." His malevolent laugh filled the room. In a last fit of megalomania, he rose from the chair and proclaimed loudly to no one, "You will NOT be my legacy!"

He wearily shuffled from the business center to return to his room, noticing the time. 11:57pm, July 14, 2021. This, is when it all began.

The next day, Bachaca would make good on his plan. His writings that night, and the accompanying letter that would prompt a search for the two young people, would unleash a torrent of pain, aguish, death, love, and utter despair. As the clock ticked past midnight, he sat among the discarded soda cans and greasy paper plates, his empire of pain now complete. In a ratty wife beater shirt, threadbare boxer shorts, and high black socks he looked nothing like the master of puppets he had sworn to become, yet somehow, that's exactly what he was.

Martin Teebs would realize his destiny, only to have it snatched from his hapless grasp time and again. Carl Farber, well…he'd finally get what he should have gotten as a child. Finally, Sergio would get to finish the job he started. The thought warmed him as he slipped under the covers. "You have no idea what's coming. No idea of what I'm capable of. Tonight is yours, but tomorrow, and every day thereafter…..everything that you are, belongs to me." Bachaca closed his eyes, his hatred and madness burning a hole in the night. In mere moments he was fast asleep. When he awoke, the world, and history, would never be the same, ever again.

28.

Through his stinging tears, Sheriff Stone headed back to Lincoln as fast as his cruiser would take him. He'd never completed the call to dispatch about what he was up to, an event that would prove fortuitous for him. His goal now, as he scanned the terrain along the Bonito, was to find the punk that had thrown salt in his eyes, and to catch up with Steve, whom had been labeled as somehow being involved in all of this. Stone knew that he wasn't likely to find the young man, who'd by now understood he wasn't going to get a friendly ride to see his buddy Steve. The best bet for Stone would be to find Steve and have a discussion about just what the hell was going on.

Rolling into town, it didn't take long to find the big cowboy, chatting in animated fashion with Margie, the older woman who worked at the courthouse museum. Stone pulled up sharply on the dirt, rolling down the passenger window.

"Hey! Steve! Get in, we need to talk." is all the Sheriff said, expecting that anyone on the receiving end of that speech would comply.

"Well," Steve started to Margie, "Looks like ol Stone's got his ass hairs up about something. I gotta git. Glad you enjoyed that, uh…thing you just did." Margie smiled as she hadn't in over 20 years and returned to the museum. Plodding down the two steps to the street, Steve peered into the car, seeing Stone's bright red, tearing eyes. "What in the hell? You ain't gonna tell me you missed me so much you're crying about it!" Steve joked.

"Get the hell in the car. Now." Stone said in a voice that didn't expect to be trifled with. "Oh shit," replied Steve as he jumped into the car. Throwing up a shower of dirt and gravel, Sheriff Stone made a U turn and pulled quickly into the vacant pageant grounds, the site of the new famous gunfight between Carl Farber and, well, everybody.

"What the fuck are you not telling me!?" Stone roared.

"Ok Hoss, you've got me at a disadvantage," replied Steve calmly, "Just what are we talking about here?"

"You send me off looking for that little prick Barrow," said the Sheriff, "So I find him.

No problem. He's walking along the creek, hiding. Says he's trying to get to Capitan to find you. Sound familiar?" A fragment of an idea hit Steve in that moment, but not enough to make him confess anything.

"No, actually it doesn't," Steve lied, "what's he want with me?"

"That's what I'd like to know? We come up the hill from the river and I'm going to in-process him at the office. After that, I'll bring him to you. No problem right? That little son of a bitch got some salt from my lunch bag and throws it in my eyes! Could have killed us both if I drive head first into an eastbound semi!"

"Salt, huh?" Steve pondered, "you don't say?"

"I do say Steve!"

"So, where's the kid now?" Steve asked innocently.

"That's what I'd like know. I told him you were back here in Lincoln so I'm assuming he's headed this way. This time you're going to help me get him and I might just run both of you to jail for obstructing justice."

In the back of his mind, Steve already knew the truth. Hiking out of sight along the Bonito? Throwing salt in a cop's eyes? Being evasive and escaping while completely unarmed? That wasn't the M.O. of Kevin Barrow. That was Billy Bonney. Whatever the reason, and however he'd managed it, The Kid had seen fit to cross time to find Steve. What for, he wondered? Martin had been explicit that Billy should not come to find him, and that he wasn't going back in time anymore. Of course, that plan worked really well until just a few hours ago and Steve crashed Martin right out of his truck, and out of Lincoln on his way to, well…somewhere? Every single time Martin Teebs showed his face in Lincoln, something weird happened and this time proved no different. Steve's sixth sense told him that Billy was already gone, not going to risk being picked up again by the law and detained so far from his own time. He could just imagine The Kid down along the riverbank, in the trees, opening up that damned old book and releasing himself all the way back to 1878, or whatever time he'd come from. While he couldn't tell Delbert Stone the truth, he could offer him a sound warning.

"Delbert, that kid ain't never gonna be found. If I was you, I'd just forget that this entire thing happened, cause you won't ever prove a word of it."

"Is that so?" taunted Stone.

"Yeah son, that's so." Steve replied calmly.

"So, I find a boy missing for what, 6 weeks, and I'm not supposed to say anything? I just call the search off? That's your advice Steve? You've gotta be able to do better than that? You wore the badge. You know that shit will never fly with me."

Steve pondered for a moment before answering, "You didn't find half what you think you did Delbert. Can't explain it better than that. If that kid don't wanna be found, he won't be…guaranteed. Right now it's as if he never existed. You can't reach him, and I sure as hell can't either."

Sheriff Delbert Stone sat there with red stinging eyes, staring at his friend. For whatever reason, Steve's words had power, and an underlying truth. As distasteful as believing he'd been had by a guy with a packet of salt was, he sensed that somehow Steve was right. He knew the big cowboy wasn't telling him everything, but he also sensed that knowing everything in a case like this might not be the best thing. He glared at Steve for what seemed like an hour before he finally put the car into gear and drove them both silently back to Capitan.

29.

Kevin Barrow sat on his side of the couch, mouth draped open, aghast. For the previous 2 hours he'd either been party to a madman, or one of the most incredible stories that he'd ever heard.

"And that's how we wound up here, at least, I think so." said Martin. Kevin looked up to Trisha, hoping that she'd surprise him with some "gotcha!" Candid Camera moment, but her serious look said otherwise. No one spoke for at least a minute, trying to absorb their place in this intricate ballet.

"So, you…believe this really happened?" Kevin asked, although neither Trisha nor Martin knew who he was asking it of, "Five years of your life, all over again? Martin, I admit whatever the hell is going on here is weird, but time travel? Billy the Kid comes back to life? You're in love with….her, or Rosita, or whoever she is? C'mon man…I'm doing my best to keep up here."

Martin sighed, knowing if he were on the receiving end of the same story, he'd think the teller just as crazy as Kevin now did. For a split second, and for the millionth time, Martin had to question again:

Did all of this *really* happen, or had he gone mad and just thought it did?

Trisha leaned closer to him, her arm pressing up to his, and the jolt it sent through his body made him jump. "I'm sorry Martin," she said absent mindedly, "Sorry…."

"You believe this, don't you Trisha?" Kevin asked, pointing directly at her.
"Look, at first I thought it was nuts too," she replied, looking apologetically at Martin, "but I started feeling something. Not like I was Rosita or anything, but like she was some piece of me, you know? Didn't you feel anything Kevin?"
Kevin swallowed hard and glanced around the room, uncomfortable with being put on the spot. While he wanted to say no and dismiss the entire thing, he didn't think that a lie would help matters any. Before he even spoke, the look on his face told Martin and Trisha all they needed to know.

"I guess, that time I saw Mr. Farber sleeping outside the courthouse, I don't know…," he began, "I just had this hate burning up in me for him. I mean, he was a nice guy to me. Why am I hating on him? The look on his face made me sick. I'll tell you the truth, I was happy to throw him out of Lincoln that night. I was even hoping a little that he would challenge me. I felt like…..shit, felt like…I would have killed him if he did." Kevin looked down at the floor, unable to face Martin and Trisha. "And," he continued, "the thought of killing him? Made me happy. What's that all about?"

With no answer forthcoming, Kevin continued, "And yeah, the pageant and all. I felt kind of, in control maybe? Like I knew what I was doing? I felt like I was in the NFL and they sent me to play against a high school football team. Like I was that much better than everyone else. Like I knew that much more than them. I can't explain it any better than that." Martin just stared at the boy, nodding solemnly.

"What about this 5 year thing?" Kevin asked, "If your story is true, we weren't part of that, right? I mean, you lived this whole life, died in, whenever it was, and then you wound up back here in 2021, right? Where were we for those 5 years? You never even heard of Trisha Davis and Kevin Barrow at first, right?"

"That's right Kevin, I didn't," Martin slowly replied, "I wish I had more answers for you, but I'd just be guessing. As far as I know, it was just me, Lilly, Steve, Farber, Billy, and Rosita that knew anything about it…that felt it. I guess the rest of the world just went on like nothing happened. I guess for you, nothing did happen." A heaviness hung in the air as the room again went silent. Finding out he was the host for some murderous outlaw would have been enough to ruin Kevin's day, but now being stuck in a place he didn't want to be, with seemingly no opportunity for parole was too much.

"I need to go for a walk," he stated, rising from the sofa, "Alone, if you don't mind." It wasn't a question, but a statement and neither Martin nor Trisha even tried to object. "If I suddenly find some other people out there, I'll tell them where to find you." he said matter of factly, as if he'd take the first chance to leave without even coming back for them. With that, Kevin walked out the front door, closing it gently behind him.

"He'll be alright, it's just a lot right now." Martin said.

Trisha turned to Martin, looking him deeply in his eyes, "You lied."

"What?" asked Martin, confused, "What did I lie about?"

"About those 5 years Martin. That was a lie, wasn't it?"

"No," Martin protested, "It's true, why would I lie about something like that?"

"It wasn't 5 years Martin, you said so yourself." The look in Martin's eyes told Trisha that he didn't understand. "Just now, you said you died much later. You were in your 80's, right? Martin, that's a hell of a lot longer than 5 years. You were an old man in Fort Sumner, walking down to my…..to Rosita's grave every night. Did you make all that up?" asked Trisha, knowing that he hadn't.

"Of course I didn't," Martin said.

"Right, and that's why you didn't live just 5 years over. You spent half of your life in pain, broken, alone. You spent every single day pining for the woman you loved and she was gone. You said it yourself Martin, you wished for death just to escape the pain, didn't you Martin?" Trisha's voice was rising in urgency with each word. A few tears began to stream down Martin's cheeks as he barely nodded his assent.

"The one great love, that the world wishes for, and you had it! And then Rosita killed herself, right in front of you Martin! You couldn't stop her, could you? She couldn't bear for you to see her so broken Martin, am I right!? She took her own life just so you didn't have to see, every God damned day, what you created! Isn't that right Martin!?" Trisha was practically screaming now.

Martin's lower lip quivered, unable to respond.

"And now I learn you had a chance to do it all over with her? Lilly told you to make a choice? You could have lived out your days making that woman happy in a time you so much better suited for than this one? And you chose Lilly!? What the fuck were you thinking Martin?!" Trisha was so enraged that before she could stop herself, she swung her right hand and hit Martin across his face as hard as she could. The sting in her hand, coupled with the satisfaction of having said what she did, allowed the anger to drain completely away from Trisha. Martin, shocked at how quickly things had escalated, and how hard Trisha had hit him, remembered back to a day in his current timeline, that hadn't even happened yet. He remembered his first meeting with Billy and Rosita, when he'd let slip that he was married. Rosita had hauled off and hit him as hard as he'd ever been hit….until just now.

Holding the burning skin of his cheek, he knew, had always known. He looked back at Trisha and said the only thing he could, "It's you."

30.

Within a millisecond, Billy opened his eyes and stood on the exact spot he'd just been standing on 143 years in the future. The hum of modern society, scarce as it was in Lincoln County, had completely disappeared and Billy knew he was back. Still, he was miles up the creek from Lincoln and it was getting late in the day. He knew enough people and ranchers on the outskirts of town that he could probably get a meal and a bed, but he also knew that Rosita would be waiting for him to return, either with Martin, or with news that he was on his way. That he wouldn't be able to do that made Billy both sad and frustrated. For the best part of 2 hours he picked his way along the Bonito, finally looking across the road at the imposing figure of The House.

What would he tell Rosita? The truth seemed like the best option, but the truth was that Billy allowed the law to scare him out of 2021. For a young man who'd lived the kind of life that Billy had, that was not something he wanted to advertise. When he thought back on the Sheriff, he realized that he'd panicked, which was totally unlike him. It was as if some small piece of him was gone, and whatever replaced it made him act like a scared schoolboy. "Damn it!" Billy castigated himself, "Should have just gone with it. Sheriff didn't know what he had anyway."

With the sun failing in the western sky, Billy walked down the dirt road towards Rosita's house. As he passed the Tunstall store, he could see Sam Corbett flitting to and fro, stocking shelves by oil lamp. Somewhere inside, or at least nearby, John Tunstall would be preparing for dinner, maybe at the house of Alexander and Susan McSween? Jimmy Dolan was probably 5 shots deep into his depression over the financial ruin his business was quickly falling in, and Sheriff Brady, who in this time held the office that Delbert Stone did in 2021, probably wasn't far behind. Billy reached into his waistband and retrieved Martin's book. How it possessed the properties to allow him to skip through time amazed Billy. He was careful to stay on the chapters dealing with his own time, lest he slingshot back to Martin's Lincoln and be run down by one of those giant 'semis' as he'd heard Steve once call them. Billy already knew who wrote it, as he'd seen the man's demise right in front of his eyes on the top floor of the courthouse. Carl Farber, who might have been planning to kill all of them, dropped a dime of a shot right between Sergio Bachaca's eyes when the portly man admitted he'd been the one driving this time travel train of insanity. Billy wondered though, why didn't it end there? If Bachaca was some sort of wizard, once he was dead, didn't his powers die with him? What would be the point of Billy, Martin, and Rosita still being held captive to the whim of Father Time when the man who invented the machine was gone?

With many questions, and no answers forthcoming, Billy walked off towards Rosita's house. Martin would know what to do here. He'd have some sane and sound advice that would just *make sense*. He'd have some of the answers that Billy sought, but of course, he was nowhere around. Billy did wonder for a half second what Steve had been doing in Lincoln, and if Martin had been any part of it. Since Sheriff Stone didn't mention a middle-aged nobody as being part of the crash, Billy assumed that Martin was not.

Back in old Lincoln far faster than he intended to be, Billy took a deep breath as he walked up the step to Rosita's portal. He knocked gingerly on the door and heard shuffling behind it. The distinctive click of a Colt revolver cocking brought him to attention just as the door cracked open?

"Who is there?" Rosita asked into the gloaming.

"It's me Rosie, don't shoot or nothing." Billy said loudly enough so his voice could not be mistaken. Rosita quickly released the hammer on her Colt and swung the door open, surprised to be seeing her friend so soon.

"*Billito!*" she said excitedly, "Are you with *Martin*?" Her eyes peered into the twilight, hoping to catch a glimpse of Martin's large figure.

"Un, no Rosie, no. Not yet. Can I come in?" Rosita smiled tensely knowing that Billy's arrival back on the same day he left probably didn't mean he brought good news.

"Of course, *si*, of course," she said while beckoning him inside, "Sit *Chivato*, are you hungry?" While Billy hadn't eaten a thing since early this morning, plus the fact that he'd traveled over 280 years back and forth, he decided to forego his hunger and get right down to the business at hand.

"No, thanks Rosie. I'll git something to eat later," he began, "So, I made it to, well... whatever that year was, I guess. It all kinda looked the same so I'm pretty sure I was in the same year as we was the last time."

"*Martin*! Did you text the message to him on the eye phone?" Rosita asked urgently.

"Well, no. I didn't really get the chance Rosie. Things went south kinda quick. See, I was looking around Lincoln, you know, to see if there was someone that could help me reach Steve."

"Mr. Steve, yes. He helps you?"

"No, cause I didn't exactly find him." Billy said, trying to keep from being interrupted.

"Well then, who helps you that you are here so quickly?"

"I was walking, and I think maybe Steve saw me, and he cra…."

"You said Mr. Steve did not help you? I don't understand *Billito*?" Rosita said with confusion.

Wanting to tell the story truthfully, Billy said more firmly, "Rosie, lemme tell you what happened, ok? Lemme just tell the whole thing then I'll answer your questions, ok?"

"*Si Billito*, this is what I have been doing, with the telling of the story." Rosita said in the way that only a woman can, to make a man feel like they are speaking two different languages.

"Alright, so Steve is in his truck and I guess he sees me. You remember that big old truck we was in coming from the hospital? That one. So I guess he was distracted and drove that thing right into the front of Tunstall's place. Course, it ain't John's no more in that time, but, well.." Rosita's eyes widened but she didn't speak. "So, I didn't even know it was Steve, as I was walking towards Capitan to find him, thinking he might just know how to get in touch with Teebsie. I got as far as the turnoff to Stanton and the Sheriff found me. Came on down and picked me up." Rosita wanted to ask why, but remembered Billy's offer to answer all questions later. "See, you remember, I don't know…who we 'were'? Those kids that look a lot like us? I was that Kevin kid and you figured you were Trisha? Well, they's missing now. For weeks. Don't know where they got off to. Anyway, the Sheriff thinks I'm Kevin and puts me in the car. Tells me he'll drive me to see Steve who's still in Lincoln. Cept, he doesn't drive towards Lincoln, he turns to Capitan and I figure he's gonna arrest me or something." Rosita looked seriously at her friend, having no idea his trip would be so challenging right from the start. "I threw some salt in his eyes and jumped right outta that truck and ran me down to the Bonito. Now I know, he's got deputies all over the place and I ain't gonna get far, so before they can get me, I open this dang book and come back here." Billy took a deep breath, waiting for Rosita's reaction, which didn't seem forthcoming so he added, "I'm sorry Rosie. I failed. Seemed like I couldn't do no good being in jail, people thinking I'm some missing kid." Billy waited for something. Anything. Tears, anger, happiness that he friend wasn't hurt. But all he got was nothing. Rosita's eyes were glazed over as if looking at some faraway object only she could see. "Umm, Rosie. You ok?" Billy asked gently.

Without changing her expression, she carefully asked a question, "So the Trisha, she is gone? *Desaparecida*?"

"That's what he told me Rosie."

"Where do they go *Billito*? I feel in Lincoln when Martin comes to see me that she is gone, but now I feel like I'm missing her. *Entiende*?"

Billy wished he didn't understand, but the events of the day made him believe otherwise. He had not a clue how some kid from 2021 who worked in a museum could house his spirit, or was it his body? But regardless, it seems to have happened. When Billy stepped out of the shell of Kevin Barrow, he left something behind, or perhaps Kevin left something of himself with Billy? At the moment, Billy wasn't even sure that Kevin or Trisha were real people and existed before Martin had happened upon the scene, but he sensed they were. Somehow connected to their modern day counterparts, Billy could only admit, "Yeah, I get it. I kind of feel it too."

"Do you think *Martin* knows of this?" Rosita asked, "And that he tries to find them?" The one thing Billy was sure of was that Martin only loved Rosita, and not some discounted version of her. He didn't believe for a moment that Martin would go searching for the missing young people because to Martin, they were not his friend and lover.

"No Rosie, I don't think so. Teebsie wouldn't spend no time trying to find someone who ain't you. If he ever sees them again, I'll bet it'd be a complete accident."

"So what to do now *Chivato*? Wait until *Martin* has some accident and winds up here? Wait until the *bebe* comes and needs its father? Or maybe *Martin* will find the Trisha and this will be good enough for him to live with her in his own time?"

Billy shook his head sadly, trying to wipe Rosita's fears away, "No Rosie, if Teebsie finds Trisha, the only thing he's gonna ask her is how he can get back to you, just as fast as possible."

31.

"Can I kiss you?" Martin asked, quivering at the very thought.

"I'm not Rosita" Trisha replied calmly

"That's fine, but may I kiss you?" he asked again.

"Why Martin? I'm not the woman you love."

"You have no idea who you are. I do." he countered.

"I'm not in love with you Martin" Trisha said firmly.

"I'm not asking you to be. I just want to kiss you." he replied, his body trembling with anxiety.

Trisha sat on the sofa, unsure of what to do next. On one hand she knew kissing Martin Teebs was a bad idea. It could lead to all sorts of unwanted entanglements and drama for however long it took them to get out of their current predicament. On the other hand, well…she wanted to, although she had no idea why. Some small part of her urged her hands to grab his face and pull him to her. The tiny, yet powerful message she was receiving was as clear as day; 'this is the man you belong with'. Try as she might to tamp the urgency down, it came back stronger each time. Then she wondered, was Martin trying to test her? Or maybe he was trying to test himself?

"You want to do this so you can prove that you only love Rosita, don't you?" she asked.

Martin glanced around, realizing the question had an obvious answer, and one that Trisha didn't even suspect.

"Yes, that's exactly it," he replied, "and Rosita is the only one I love." Martin stared straight at Trisha, his glance never wavering. This moment had put them on a line which could not be straddled forever. They'd both need to pick one side or the other if they were ever to achieve their destiny. The words that Martin spoke touched Trisha in a way she'd never before felt. During her last days before the pageant, she had become envious of her historical doppelganger, wondering if she herself would ever have a ma[n] pine for her the way Martin did for Rosita. Yet here she was, faced with exactly what she hoped for, and for some reason she could not abandon her reason.

"You're not in love with me Martin. You know that. You're scared, and sad, and you'[re] trying to convince yourself that I'm someone that I'm really not."

"Why did you hit me?" he asked gently, bringing his hand to his still stinging cheek.

"Because you fucked up Martin. You brought me into this little world of yours, telling m[e] how much I…..Rosita meant to you. You had a chance to leave your old life behind a[nd] you ran off with Lilly? You had everything you said you ever wanted at your fingertips a[nd] you walked…no, ran away from it."

"But, why did you hit me? All of that stuff is true, but it doesn't explain why Trisha Dav[is] hit Martin Teebs?" Martin said, unwilling to allow his glance to move from Trisha's dee[p] brown eyes.

"What do you want me to say Martin?" Trisha said with some sense of urgency, almost a[s] if she was trapped.

"Just tell me the truth Trisha."

"What's the truth Martin?" she asked, getting more emotional as a tear formed in her eye[.]

"You know what the truth is. You just won't allow yourself to believe it." Martin repli[ed] as he reached out to take her hand. The connection of their skin touching was too much f[or] Trisha and she lunged forward, grabbing Martin's head and pulling herself to it. Their li[ps] finally met, breaking the suspense that had been building for hours. Trisha closed her ey[es] tightly, not wanting to see the crime she was committing with a married man, who ha[p]pened to be in love not with his wife, and not even with herself. The warmth she felt as s[he] pressed her body to Martin's was a welcome relief from the sterile coldness of the aba[n]doned town she was serving her sentence in. Forgetting everything that said she shouldn[']t be doing this, she wrapped her arms around Martin and pulled him to her as she lay ba[ck] on the sofa. The full weight of him on her, she felt the need for more. She needed Mart[in] to want every ounce of her. To want her, and her alone. She needed this man to spend t[he] rest of his days knowing that there was only one, great true love for each of us, and he had found it in her.

And then, in a moment, she didn't.

A sudden chill swept through the room, dousing their passion. Martin must have felt it too as his movements became less urgent and quickly stopped altogether. He pushed himself up from Trisha, helping her sit up.

"What was that?" she asked, as if placing all of the blame on Martin. He exhaled, trying to make sense of what had just taken place. Failing to come up with an answer, he just shook his head and remained silent. "I told you Martin, I'm not Rosita. Do you believe me now?" Martin sadly looked at the beautiful woman, unsure of how to make the point he knew to be true.

"You felt it, right? I know you did Trisha. Even if it was just for a moment." Even though Trisha understood exactly what Martin was saying, she lied, "No, I didn't feel anything." Somehow, the lie was the release of Martin's tension. He knew that Trisha had felt the same connection, the same urgency as him. He smiled warmly at her.

"Oh, is this funny now Martin?" she asked, a slight smile spreading across her own face.

"No, it's not funny. It's wonderful. It's confusing. It's familiar. I know you felt what I did, and I know you felt it go away. I did too," Martin confessed, "And now I know exactly what happened in Lincoln 6 weeks a……I mean a few days ago."

"Ok then, please, explain it to me?"

"Trisha, you didn't see it. You weren't in that courthouse when that author was shot. I know everything happened so fast after that, how could you know?" Martin began, "That guy, Sergio Bachaca, admitted that he'd been writing this, I don't know…story? Play? I'm not sure what to call it. This all sounds incredibly ridiculous and hard to believe, but that guy, the one that Farber killed, is the one responsible for all of this."

While Trisha had no idea that anyone had been killed in the courthouse, due to her transformation to Rosita when Martin was shot, each word of Martin's story rang true. "Ok, so how does any of that involve me? And tell me, did this really happen? Is this really happening now? Are we even real human beings or is this some kind of, what, simulation?"

Martin pondered the question before answering, "I don't think it's a simulation. It's real. It has to be, no? Don't you feel real?" Trisha smiled and felt her arms, deciding that they did in fact feel real. "Somehow this guy, this Sergio Bachaca, decided to pick on me, and on Farber I guess. I have no idea why?"

"Did you ever meet him before that night when he did the talk? Maybe he and Farber had a past?" Trisha offered.

"I never met the man before in my life," Martin said firmly, "and if I did, I sure don't remember it. I don't know, maybe he and Farber have some connection?"

"Ok then, but why you Martin? Why does this Bachaca, start messing with you, if it's Farber he wants? Hell, why am I involved? Because I put him on the spot with some question about Rosita?"

"I don't know why he picked me. He and Farber had words in the courthouse and Farber shot him, right between the eyes. This probably should have ended right then, but for some reason, here we are. It's like maybe he wrote more of the story, and we just haven't lived it out yet?" Trisha shrugged her shoulders, able to offer nothing that would explain Martin's confusion. "But here we are. I lived a long life before I ever got involved in this Billy the Kid world. I can't imagine I was just born to be some pawn in a crazy author's game. I should hate the guy, I know, but without him I'd never have met Billy, never fallen in love with Rosita. How can I hate that?"

"I can hate it Martin. What did I get out of all of this? You're telling me some crazy ass old man wrote me into his script and I'm supposed to just accept it? You got a long life with a house, a car, a wife….and I got to wind up here, trapped for who knows how long? I can definitely hate this Martin, and I do."

Martin nodded his head sadly, feeling worse for Trisha than he ever could for himself, "I know. And you're right."

"So what was that shit a few minutes ago? I felt it, ok? Yes. Hell, I felt it a couple of days ago when I just wanted you to want me like you want Rosita. Did that guy write this part, or did you Martin? You're an author after all, aren't you?"

"No! Trisha, I wouldn't do that. I wouldn't mess with someone's life just because I could."

Trisha pursed her lips into a tight smile, "Really? Are you sure Martin?" Unaware of what she was referring to, Martin shook his head earnestly, "Of course I'm sure!"

"Let's ask Michael Roberts about that, shall we? You remember Michael Roberts, right? You told me the whole story. You made up some bullshit name to hide behind and stole Roberts' picture off the internet? Ruined his career? Made a mockery of the guy. Just because you could, right Martin?"

No, wait…" stammered Martin, "I can exp…"

"Wrote him right into your little web Martin, didn't you? And now you want to push all the blame to some author who I've never even heard of until he shows up in Lincoln for his little lecture?"

"Trisha, listen…."

"Listen nothing Martin. I know that this thing was all preordained. I can see that someone was pulling the strings the entire time. The only question I really have is, was it Sergio Ba-whatever the hell his name was, or Martin Teebs? Was it, and is it, you?"

The lights began flickering in the room, or at least Martin thought they had, and a cold chill shot down his spine. Trisha's words had power, and in some way, he felt like they contained at least some truth. Had he done this? Was there some other version of Martin Teebs, gleefully sitting at a computer right now, conjuring up his next words, his next thought? He'd convinced himself that after Sunset in Sumner, his story was over. His life had gone on, yes, but he had nothing but experiences to show for it, or so he believed.

"It was not me. I didn't do this." Martin said, although he wished his words were more convincing.

"You sure about that?" Trisha shot back.

The accusation in her eyes dared Martin to speak, but instead he got up and walked around the room. Trisha followed him with her gaze. Finally, Martin shook his head and walked towards the library. He needed a moment away from the tension, from the accusations, and from the confusion that was Trisha Davis. He glanced back to make sure he wasn't followed and walked slowly around the room. This place, this was the entire reason he had come back to New Mexico, to get that damned 'Lincoln County Days' book by Farber. Now, Martin looked around at the bulging shelves, full of books, photos, manuscripts, and magazines, and wished the entire place never existed.

He heard stirring in the other room, and the water running in the sink. Trisha had shown no proclivity to follow him so Martin gazed upon the thousands of items, all somehow related to Billy the Kid. Walking up to a small table next to a reading chair, Martin found the offender he'd come to recover. The horribly printed book that Carl Farber had written just to fuck with him years ago. Martin picked it up, knowing all the horrors it contained. Tempted to read about Farber's gruesome ending in Fort Sumner again, he decided the better of it and dropped the book back on the table. There'd be no FBI coming to this version of Lincoln to find evidence. Hell, if they did, Martin would parade the book around, even putting it in the little plastic evidence bag himself. Anything to get out of this nightmare. He imagined himself thrusting his hands out in front of him, just waiting for someone to click the cuffs on. At least he'd be free of this prison, even if on the way to another one. At least he wouldn't have to face the accusing stare of Trisha, and probably Kevin, whenever he got back. At very least, he'd know that his life would go on, even if behind the walls of some tiny cell in some forgotten place on the edge of nowhere. Martin decided, he wanted this over with. He wanted to give Trisha a piece of his mind, scolding her for ever thinking he had something to do with this. In short, he wanted to be free.

Martin stood up with a start, so much so that he knocked the wobbly table over, the copy of 'Lincoln County Days' crashing to the floor. As Martin bent over to retrieve it he came up short with the image of the Pals tombstone in Fort Sumner on the cover of a book. There was an inscription on the tombstone that Martin didn't even need to read to know what it said;

ROSITA LUNA TEEBS
BORN 1852 DIED 1881
REST IN PEACE, MY LOVE

The book was titled 'Bonney & Teebs: The Lost Years' and was authored by Michael Anthony Giudicissi, the man Martin had created, but didn't even exist. The shock that went through Martin could have derailed a freight train. "I didn't write this," he mumbled to himself, reaching out to grab the book. Already knowing the entire story it contained, Martin lifted the book from the shelf, only to have another book behind it be revealed. The cover of this book shocked him even more. It was an illustration of Rosita, dressed in modern clothes, holding a rose, and standing in front of the old courthouse. Martin's breath came in short bursts. The title did nothing to assuage his fear and confusion, 'One Week in Lincoln' also written by Michael Anthony Giudicissi. Martin's trembling hand touched the cover gently, the fear of what was happening beginning to accelerate from within. Of course, Martin knew every word of what must be in the book. He'd lived the entire experience only weeks ago, or days…in Trisha and Kevin's timeline. Even if he'd been in some sort of trance, how could he possibly have written and published a book so quickly? The paperback staring him in the face told him that somehow, he had, or at minimum, someone substantially more powerful was pulling the strings. As he lifted the book to open it up, he saw a space behind where it appeared one more book might be missing. Martin rubbed his eyes and swallowed hard in his parched throat. Just when he was about to give up wondering what the blank shelf space could have held, he heard footsteps stopping at the doorway and looked up to see Trisha standing there, "Looking for this?" she said plainly.

She stood there, defiantly, holding another book with an image of the Fort Sumner grave having been exhumed, as a red sky blazed behind it. Martin could barely make out the title, '4 Empty Graves'. Just before he blacked out, his vision zeroed in on the name of the author:

Martin Teebs.

32.

Steve walked across the creaky porch to his office, ready to put the events of the day behind him. That would have proven easier had a small rental car belonging to Martin Teebs not been sitting in the dusty driveway. Sinking down into his chair, Steve wondered exactly what to do next. Nothing, came to mind as a possible strategy. He could just wait this entire weird experience out and wait for the next card to be dealt. Searching for Martin didn't seem like a great idea as Steve knew not where nor when the man had gone. He was now sure that it was not Kevin Barrow, but Billy Bonney that had come looking for him today, although the young man seemed to have vanished, and Steve had no way to reach him either. Unless the ghost of some outlaw from over a century ago returned, Steve was stuck exactly where he'd been since sending Billy and Rosita back to their own time; nowhere. He hadn't a clue how this time travel thing worked, and didn't know if the people doing it were any better versed either. Reaching into his desk drawer for a bottle of hooch that was reserved for just these types of occasions, he poured himself two finger's worth and raised the glass to his lips. As he did, as if on cue, the phone rang.

"Yep," Steve answered, not really caring who was on the other end of the line.

"This is Steve? The detective, right?" asked the tentative voice.

"Yep, go for Steve little lady."

"Steve, it's uh…Lilly Teebs," said the voice on the other end.

"Well, ain't the circle just complete then?" Steve answered in a bemused voice, "What can I do for you little lady?"

Lilly gained some confidence, and maybe the slightest hint of anger, "What the hell does that mean?" Steve just laughed in return before speaking, "With the day I've had, well, let's just say this call ain't a surprise."

"Fine then," Lilly shot back, "I haven't been able to reach Martin all day. He said he'd be with you, or at least stop to see you. Have you seen him?" Alone in his office, Steve tilted his head in amusement and looked at the ceiling, "Oh yeah, I've seen him, then didn't see him, then…well, who knows what's next?"

"Look," stated Lilly impatiently, "I'm not interested in throwing cowpies, or guess how many teeth your mama has left, or whatever other games you country hicks might be playing with me and Martin. I want to know where he is! Did he get that stupid book he was looking for?"

"You're a pistol, ain't ya," Steve replied, "I like that. In any event, I'm not sure if Martin got the book cause of the fact that we were in a crash in my truck in Lincoln."

"Oh my God!" exclaimed Lilly.

"Easy now, weren't that big of a deal except when I looked over in the passenger seat, he was gone. Kinda like he comes and goes them other times. Don't waste your breath Missy asking me to where, cause I ain't got the faintest damned idea." There was a silence on the other end of the phone as Lilly breathed slowly and deeply.

"So, you're telling me that you lost my husband. Do I have that right Steve?"

"Haha! Well I hadn't looked at it exactly like that, but yes….I guess I probably did. Guilty as charged."

"Ok…" Lilly said slowly, "So, what's your plan to find him?"

"Well, that's what I was just sitting here drinking about and thinking about, now that you ask." replied Steve with a soft chuckle.

Lilly was incensed by the big cowboy's attitude, and she didn't hold back from letting him know, "Well Stevie boy, I suggest you start doing a whole lot more thinking and a lot less drinking and figure this out. Because if not, I'll just place a call to the Sheriff of your little Podunk county and let him know that my husband was last seen with ex-mayor of fucking Mayberry, or Micanopy, or whatever that hick town is that you call home, and now he's missing. Then you can deal directly with the authorities. Is that clear?"

Steve laughed so heartily into the phone that Lilly thought he'd perhaps gone mad, "I saved you the trouble Mrs. Teebs, and set with the Sheriff for a long spell today to tell him exactly what happened. Hell, it was him that dropped me off at home. If you're gonna threaten someone, at least make sure that what you're planning to do is an actual threat." More laughter followed as Lilly stewed.

"Screw off hayseed, just find my husband and send him home…NOW!" Lilly yelled as she banged down the phone.

Steve smiled and reached for his glass, deciding to add another two finger's worth just for all of his trouble. "Makes ya wonder, just why Martin disappeared, and why maybe he ain't going home?"

33.

The day was mild and Kevin was in no mood to head back to the insane asylum that Trisha's house had become. Listening to Martin's long-winded story of his life, and then his do-over at life didn't help Kevin's mindset, or optimism of being released from this prison at all. While he had spent the entire summer here, Kevin rarely had time to enjoy the sights. Working the various buildings, and then maintaining them, took most of his available hours, and he spent the rest chasing the scarcity of young women who were interested in coming to the town made famous by Billy the Kid.

In any other setting, Lincoln on this day would have been considered peaceful. Birds chirped, squirrels played in the trees, and the occasional deer would peek it's head up from the grass where they lazily laid. The one downside was the complete lack of people, and to Kevin, that gave the town a creepy feel. He'd tried driving out of town to Capitan and that hadn't worked. He wondered if heading east to Roswell might prove more successful. Of course, with now only a quarter tank of gas, he might make it into the middle of some netherworld, and then get stuck. If so, where would he be? Would it be better off to be alone in some halfway house between Lincoln and Hell, or should he stay here and watch the rest of his life drift by while Martin and Trisha swooned over each other?

Walking farther to the west, drawn as if by some force, he passed the Tunstall store, and then a vacant lot. Just beyond, he knew from the signs, had stood the McSween house. It burned on July 19, 1878 and was never rebuilt. Kevin had a visceral reaction to the place, not wanting to loiter any longer than he had to. The margins of that empty field felt like a lost cemetery, where men had died where they stood, which of course Kevin knew to be true from the many tourists he'd talked to over the summer. Every time, every damn time one of those middle-aged Billy fanboys met him they remarked how much he looked like Billy. It always rankled him because, from what he'd heard, the tintype of The Kid was always considered a 'bad' picture of him. Kevin himself had looked at it many times, with Billy's pinched face, narrow eyes, and filmy chin and thought, "they think I look like that?" to himself. Some of the tourists that came through town proclaimed a character named "Brushy Bill" Roberts was actually the kid and had shared photos of the man in his younger days. Looking at the smooth, swarthy face, jet black hair, and strong dimpled chin Kevin couldn't understand how anyone could compare the tintype of Billy with photos of this man and conclude they were the same person? "If I had to choose, I'd rather look like Brushy than that old tintype." Kevin said out loud as he walked past the now defunct McSween house.

A sudden craving for oysters hit the young man as he walked, strange since Kevin couldn't remember a time he'd ever had them, nor did he even know what they might taste like. "Oysters?" has asked of himself, "What they hell is that about?" Shaking the weird déjà vu from his head he took a few more steps before blurting out, "Haven't had any good ones since Cullum's anyway."

What?

Just the tiniest sliver of a memory had hit Kevin, of an old oyster house on this spot. How could he know that? Was it even true? How the hell did he have a taste for a food he'd never before eaten? The place brought back some uneasy feelings as well, as if Kevin had made a deal with someone, and quickly reneged on it. He contemplated turning back to the house, but the thought of Trisha making dove eyes at Martin gave Kevin cause to retch. Screw it, he thought, and continued along the road, inexorably drawn towards the courthouse.

The events of the past Sunday were still a blur to him, being as he couldn't remember much more than getting ready for the 2nd show. Trisha's crazy notion that they were somehow connected to Rosita and Billy, two people that died well over a century ago, made no sense to Kevin, but then again, did any of this make any sense? Reaching the courthouse, he decided to walk around outside, through the sets of the escape reenactment. The place looked like someone's house who'd thrown a rager the night before, and they just went to sleep when it finally ended, figuring they'd clean it up the next day. Garbage was strewn along the dirt field while some ragged flags flapped gently in the breeze. In the middle of the field still stood some police line "Do Not Cross" tape around an area that had been greatly disturbed. Peering closer, Kevin could even see some dark lumps of dirt, crusted over by what he assumed was blood. Martin and Trisha had told him enough to fill in the blanks of what happened on that day, past the point of Kevin's faded memory.

There was no enlightenment from this place and Kevin decided to turn back to the house, a mile to the east. Turning towards the courthouse where he'd spent the first two nights of this nightmare, he remembered leaving his car keys on the 2nd floor. While the car, parked patiently across the street, wouldn't get him out of Lincoln, it could save him the walk back to the house. Maybe, if his two roommates made things sickening enough, he'd try a suicide mission by driving towards Roswell with his foot planted on the floor, and the outcome be damned?

Trudging up the balcony steps, he stopped at the top and surveyed his kingdom. "Ha," he laughed to himself, "This is it? This is my great accomplishment in life?" Being the prince of a one-mile-long town with no people in the middle of nowhere wasn't much to brag about, and there wasn't anyone to brag to even if Kevin wanted to. Opening the door to the courthouse, he walked inside towards the little cot he'd been sleeping on that was supposed to be from the time of The Kid. On the table next to it he saw the wrappers of the two protein bars he'd eaten, and nothing else. Where did he put his keys? He checked the floor and quickly walked the rest of the upper floor with no success. While it wasn't a great loss, not being able to drive a car that couldn't take you anywhere anyway, he still wanted to have the car at the ready in the event the spell that was holding him in Lincoln temporarily broke. Kevin shrugged at no one, figuring the keys would turn up sooner or later, and walked out onto the balcony. Just before he hit the first step down towards the street he was shocked to see the figure of a pudgy man standing across the street, as if waiting for him. His excitement getting the better of him, Kevin quickly hustled down the stairs towards the man, hoping he didn't disappear. As he approached, the familiarity of the guy struck him. He knew this man? He'd seen him before, on a spot not far from where they were now. What in the hell was going on that he suddenly appeared after two days of total isolation?

Kevin skidded to a stop in front of him, panting from the rapid effort. The man, dressed in a cheap polyester shirt and pair of jeans showed almost no emotion as the boy approached him. For a long moment, neither one spoke until Kevin was unable to control himself any longer.

"You? You did all this? I thought you were dead?"

The man just smirked and waved his hands down the length of his body to show that he most definitely wasn't dead. Kevin's glare could cut glass, but didn't seem to bother the man, who put his hand on Kevin's shoulder and guided him east, towards Trisha's house, "Come on son, we've got a lot to talk about."

Kevin, irked by the man's calm, swatted his hand away and snapped back, "Don't call me son, dude, my name is Kevin!" to which the man responded, "Don't call me dude, Kevin, my name is Sergio."

34.

Three days later, Billy rode into Lincoln from the Coe Ranch. While his work with Tunstall hadn't started in earnest, Billy knew he'd be needed soon. The Coes seemed to enjoy having him around and offered the boy a bunk for the coming winter months. While Billy wondered just what the next few months would hold for him, he gratefully accepted the offer knowing he'd at least have a warm place to prepare for the coming war. The sun blazed in a spectacularly blue sky on this day, warming up beyond what one would expect of the New Mexico fall season in the high valley. People moved about the town doing this and that, and Lincoln seemed nothing more than a peaceful village existing in the middle of almost nowhere. As his mare trotted towards Rosita's house, he spied her mother Lourdes, shaking out laundry on the porch. He was familiar with the woman, having met her several times.

"Hola Mrs. Luna!" said Billy with good cheer, "Is Rosie around?"

The pretty woman, even in her later years, smiled at the boy, "*Si, como no Billito*. She is just at the Wortley at this minute." Billy only wanted to check in on Rosita, not knowing if she had divulged her pregnancy to her mother yet. Deciding that he shouldn't mention a word of it, he nudged the bay mare closer to the porch and leaned out of the saddle, "Mrs. Luna, you sure are a pretty woman. If I was to get a vote, I'd say there should be two Belles of Lincoln, you and Rosie. It's clear ta me where she gets her beauty from." The beautiful woman blushed at the compliment, "*Oh Chivato, me halagas demasiado*!" Billy smiled and tipped his hat, trotting off towards the Wortley.

Rosita was soaked in sweat, the heat of the kitchen coupled with the unusually warm day making her skin glisten. With no current orders to fill, she called into the dining room, "*Samuel*, I shall be just outside for a moment." Stepping onto the back porch she wiped the sweat from her brow and walked towards the front of the hotel to hopefully catch whatever faint breeze might be blowing.

"Heya Rosie!" Billy said cheerfully as he slid from the saddle, "How's that baby comin along?" Rosita glared at Billy with a quick shake of her head, but with good feelings, that he shouldn't mention anything of the sort where people might overhear. It was already enough that she was pregnant again, but by the same man who was noticeably absent yet again would be more scandal than Rosita was willing to bear. Sensing his mistake, Billy quickly added, "Sorry Rosie, sorry."

"Is ok *Chivato*," she said, glancing up and down the road, "I see you are not with *Martin*, so I think he hasn't come to me?" Billy winced a little bit, hoping that every future conversation with his friend didn't start with an assessment of Martin Teebs' absence.

"Well, I was kinda hoping I'd find him here with you Rosie, but no, I ain't seen him." No words were spoken for a moment as a breeze finally did blow in and cool Rosita, if only temporarily. "Hey Rosie, I been meaning to talk to you about something."

Rosita peeked into the dining room, seeing that there were no patrons waiting on their lunch order to be filled, "*Si Billito*, then this is such time to talk."

Billy looked more carefully around, making sure no one was ease dropping on what would be considered lunacy, "Them kids that we, I don't know, came from? I been thinking about em." Rosita raised her eyes in interest, but said nothing. "I know you felt it too, but it's like some piece of me was kinda left behind when we came back here. Can't explain it better than that, but I ain't all here, you know?"
Indeed Rosita did know exactly what Billy was talking about as she'd wrestled with the same feelings over the past weeks.

"*Si*, I feel this too." she said simply.

"So, you think that's us? You think that there's two of us, each, I mean? You think maybe we's here in Lincoln now, but we're still there in Lincoln then? That make any sense?"

Rosita knew without question that Trisha did not exist in Lincoln in the year she and Martin last made love. From the hospital, Martin had sent her a message asking what had happened to Trisha and Rosita said that she was gone, and only Rosita remained. That thought had nagged at her though. Where did the woman go? Where did that boy Kevin, who looked so much like Billy, wind up? Was it that she and Billy were just pretending to be someone else? No, she decided, it couldn't be that. Rosita was on the edge of reality while Trisha was in charge. Rosita existed, but so did Trisha. It had taken the better part of a week, Martin's tearful confessions, and the brutally violent end to the pageant to finally release her from Trisha's identity.

"This is not so *Billito*, the Kevin and Trisha, yes…are part of who we are, I think. I can no explain this better, but they are not in the time that we were in. This I know, because when I ran to *Martin* when he was shot by that Farber, Trisha was all gone."

Billy had no choice but to defer to Rosita's beliefs as he didn't have any different experience to go on, "Ok, so they aren't there. Where'd they go? I can still feel some piece of me missing, you know?"

Rosita swallowed hard, not wanting to burden Billy with the notion that she was missing two pieces of herself, Trisha and Martin. "I do not know where they go *Billito*, but it is somewhere like this," she said waving her hand around Lincoln, "after all, we don't know anything else. Where would we leave to?" Billy glanced around the peaceful town, which would erupt in war in just a few months and wondered, if he had the chance, would he abandon Lincoln for calmer and greener pastures? He had one more question to ask, that he wasn't sure he wanted the answer to.

"Who did this to us Rosie? I mean, this ain't natural. You know that. Somebody musta wanted this to happen real bad."

Rosita pressed her eyes closed, as if trying to erase a thought that had illegally intruded into her mind. She shook her head back and forth, hoping it might recede, but to no avail. Pursing her lips, she opened her eyes and straightened her shoulders before she spoke.

"This I would like to know too *Chivato*, but I'm afraid to find out the answer."

Billy confused look was met with a dead stare from the pretty woman, "Wait, you don't mean…..?"

"*Si. Martin* shows me the books before we leave that Lincoln. The books that he writes. He says it was to tell his story, but now I wonder if it was all not to tell the story, but to create one?"

Billy had seen Martin's books, or at least the ones that went through the horrific night in Fort Sumner. He couldn't believe that his friend would do something so controlling, so damaging, and so hurtful to them all. Billy felt a genuine connection with the man. Could it all be a lie? Was Billy being moved around like the chess pieces he used to command when playing the game as a boy in Silver City? Was Martin Teebs the man who'd spun this web that they were all caught in? Billy shook his head no even as his mind told him it could be possible. Rosita looked sadly on as Billy was only able to mutter a single word.

"Teebsie?"

35.

"Wha..", stammered Martin as he gazed upon the book, "What is this? I didn't write this!"

"Oh," said Trisha disdainfully, "I guess it's some other Martin Teebs who travels through time and is friends with Billy the Kid? Sound about right to you Martin?" Martin's head snapped to and fro around the room like a trapped animal. He was woefully underprepared for this conversation, only having discovered seconds ago 3 more books that purported to be written by him.

"No, of course not! That's not what I'm saying," he shouted back, trying to gain control of the situation, "Look, it even says my name on it. I never used my own name in those other books. This is a setup!"

Trisha mused as she looked at the cover of "4 Empty Graves", at least admiring the artwork, even as she currently despised the author. "I've got to hand it to you Martin, at least you finally found some balls and put your real name on the cover. No more hiding, huh?"

"Listen Trisha, I don't know what the hell is happening here, but this isn't me. 10 minutes ago you were kissing me like the Titanic was going down. You felt something, even briefly. You know me, and you know that I couldn't have done this."

"The Titanic, Martin?" she replied with a laugh, "Don't flatter yourself over one kiss. It wasn't even that great, to be honest."

Martin painfully closed his eyes, wishing to be released from the nightmare this entire trip to New Mexico had become. Still, he was curious. While he couldn't be sure, that Bonney & Teebs book seemed like it picked up somewhere around when Martin was a much older man in his first life? The "One Week in Lincoln" book was pretty self evident. It must have covered the week during the pageant that he, Trisha, and Kevin had lived through only months (or days) ago. What Martin couldn't reconcile was this last book that Trisha still held menacingly, as if a weapon. The book even had a number 5 on it that was crossed out and replaced with a 4. What did that mean? Where were there 4 empty graves? And the cover image gave Martin the chills. Had someone actually gone and dug up Rosita's grave in the old post cemetery in Sumner? The thought made him shudder. If they had, his only wish at the moment was that they had somehow found him lying next to her, for all eternity. Was the big discovery in that book that the world now had conclusive proof that Billy didn't die in 1881? Was that the reason Martin was brought back to this place, to bear witness to the fact that he'd fucked up history so completely that it could never be rectified? The cascading thoughts and fears made Martin simply want to scream.

In his previous go at life, Martin had lived to be an old man, living fearfully that someday the big secret would be revealed. Someday, someone was going to discover exactly what was in that grave and that he was responsible for all of it. Now that day had apparently arrived, greeted not by angry masses, but by a deep look of unhappiness from Trisha Davis. If Martin was to be persecuted for his crime, it appeared that Trisha would be judge, jury, and executioner. He wondered how all of the keyboard warriors who'd panned his first book 'Back to Billy', would feel now? They eviscerated him for his 'fake' story of Billy living to be a sad old man in Magdalena. Whatever this last book held, it seemed to defy the generally accepted account of the demise of one Billy Bonney.

"Can I see that please?" he asked, reaching out for the mysterious book, "Because I didn't write it and I have no idea what's in it, regardless of what you think."

Trisha adjusted her posture in the doorway, sliding her hip to the side and smirking at Martin in a way that Rosita sometimes did. Holding the book out in front of her, she allowed Martin to take it while saying, "Oh, I know you didn't write this Martin. I have no doubts about that." Now clearly even more confused, Martin opened the book to the title page, with his name clearly printed on it. Fanning the pages in a quick scan to see what was in it, he was stunned.

He saw, nothing.

The book was empty. Empty as in, not a word of print on the 300 or so pages inside of it. Martin stared at the pages flipping before him, wondering what this was supposed to be? "Is this a joke? Who did this? Did you?" he asked accusingly, point the book towards Trisha.

Now calm and interested to see what Martin's story would be, she answered, "Me? Um, no Martin. I had nothing to do with this, other than coming back here after that shit show up the street and finding these books. The better question is, what did you have to do with them, and why is this last one blank?" Martin flicked through the pages once again, making sure he hadn't missed some important message in them.

"Look Trisha, I've told you, I don't know anything about these. Sure, ok…I guess they're about my life, but I stopped writing after Sunset in Sumner. That whole thing with the publisher and critics? Never again. I swore, never again. So there's no way I was writing more of these, and certainly no way I was going to publish a book with blank pages. Who does that?"

The question hung in the air for a moment before Trisha added, "Well, that's the question now, isn't it?" Martin took the 3 books and walked towards the living room, Trisha grudgingly moving out of the way to allow him to pass. He sat and began to flip through 'Bonney & Teebs', the parts that he was in, at least, were perfectly accurate. Picking up 'One Week in Lincoln' he examined the cover again, finally holding it up to Trisha, "This is you, you know?"

"Yes, thank you Martin," Trisha said curtly, "That's very helpful. Never had that outfit by the way, although it is super cute." The remark caught Martin off guard and his shoulders jumped while he laughed. Trisha's comment seemed to dissipate the tension in the room and she sat down on the other end of the couch. "So, are you going to read it? You think it's accurate? How would somebody know to write a book about something that happened a couple of days ago? What, are we being spied on?"

Martin's mind wandered to the characters he'd spent a week in Lincoln with. Trisha seemed honest enough and Martin didn't believe she had anything to do with the book. Kevin never struck Martin as much of an author either. He was left with a few choices. Steve, Farber, and Brandon. Steve didn't seem like the type to shy away from controversy, and Martin was certain the big cowboy would have told him had he been writing a book. Brandon similarly had a lot going on that probably would have prevented him from scribbling an entire book out in 2 days. That left only one man, Carl Farber. It wouldn't be the first time that Farber used his writing skills to mess with Martin and company. First Lincoln County Days, then The Coward of Lincoln County. The problem was, until that last few minutes of the pageant when everything turned bad, Carl

Farber was….ok. He wasn't the sleazy bastard that had raped Rosita, killed Bachaca, and laid Steve's head open. He was just a normal, decent guy. Why would a normal guy go writing a book, in 2 days no less, about people he barely knew? It struck Martin that he had lived some 6 weeks after leaving New Mexico, yet Trisha was convinced it had only been a couple of days. Wherever, and whenever Farber went, could his timeline had a similar curve? If he was somehow alive, could Farber be months into the future, giving him plenty of time to write these books? None of it made sense to Martin as he flipped through One Week in Lincoln. Everything described in the book, as least the things Martin took part in, were accurate. It creeped him out a little bit that someone had been documenting his entire trip without his knowledge. Finally having enough of the mental gymnastics, Martin placed the books on the coffee table and met Trisha's eyes.

"Hey, I'm sorry…about all of this. You know?" Trisha looked carefully at him, but said nothing. "I mean, I'm not sure how this all happened, and maybe I did have something to do with it. If I did, I'm sorry. It wasn't on purpose. Even if I had nothing to do with it, I'm still sorry, ok?"

"You know, before I met you Martin, I was perfectly happy," Trisha said matter of fact-ly, "Job, school, friends. Just a girl whiling away the summer in some mountain town. Life was good." Martin lowered his head, but raised his eyes to see what she might say next. "And one day, this guy…this, Martin Teebs stumbles into my courthouse and calls me Rosita. And from that day on, my life has been more or less miserable. So yeah, you're responsible for some of this Martin. Maybe all of it? If you hadn't come to Lincoln, you'd never have seen me, and I'd be back in LA right now getting ready to finish my masters. I guess what I'm saying is, I accept your apology, because I'm not sure you know any more than I do what's going on, but if we ever get out of this, just do me a favor and stay out of my life, ok?"

Martin was stung a bit by the beauty that he'd been passionately kissing just minutes ago, but decided that Trisha was right. Martin's original time travels involved him, and of course it affected Lilly, but he never brought anyone else into it, until Billy showed up on his doorstep. Now he'd dragged two innocent kids into this depravity and he wanted nothing more than to release them.
"That's a deal. Really. The one thing I can't promise is that Rosita won't follow you. You're some piece of her Trisha. I felt it. You felt it. You think that's just going to go

away when I head back to New Jersey? Everything inside me tells me it won't."

Trisha considered Martin's point for a moment before asking, "Kevin too? He's going back to Colorado with Billy the Kid on his shoulder? This is a life sentence?"

Everything inside Martin told him the answer was yes. "Yeah, I'm pretty sure."

"Well aren't we all just burdened then Martin Teebs? You, me, Kevin? We get the distinct pleasure of carrying around some ghost for the rest of our days. I'll tell you what, if that's true, I'm going to find the son of a bitch that did this, if it's the last thing I do!"

Just then, the door swung open to reveal a surprised looking Kevin Barrow standing side by side with another man. The portly man in the polyester shirt said simply:

"It won't be the last thing you do Trisha, and I'm the son of a bitch you're looking for."

36.

"You. You're….dead." stammered Martin, as if he'd seen a ghost.

Sergio Bachaca ran his hands up and down his body, "Well, it appears that I'm not, eh Mr. Teebs?" Spying the copy of 4 Empty Graves on the coffee table, he continued, "Ah, I see you've found my little treasures? So nice to have your story memorialized in writing now, isn't it?" Trisha glared at the short man, her anger at Martin temporarily redirected. For his part, Kevin seemed unsure what was to happen next.

"I saw it. Up in the courthouse. Farber shot you, right between the eyes. How the….?"

"Come now Martin. Didn't you get a do over? As I remember, you died as well, a broken old man, and got another chance at life. Would you deny me the same privilege?" Without being invited, Bachaca moved into the house further, allowing Kevin to shut the door behind him, "It seems we might be here for awhile, no? Might we at least get comfortable?" With that, he plopped down heavily on the sofa and waited for the others to do likewise. That no one did was not a surprise to the man. They were angry at being trapped in some uninhabited version of Lincoln and they all wanted just one thing. Out. "Well then, at least I'm comfortable. Join me whenever your defenses lower enough to allow it." Bachaca blew out a big stream of air and looked hopefully around the room. These people were not his enemies, although they probably saw themselves as such. He knew there were questions and he'd come to provide answers. "Well, it's a quiet bunch here today. Kevin? You had some words with me at the courthouse. What would you like to discuss?" Kevin just shook his head, unwilling, or perhaps unable to speak. Martin's face was an array of angry, frustrated, and confused looks, but he too didn't say a word.

"Ok then porky, where in the hell are we and how do we get out of here?" demanded Trisha.

Bachaca smiled greatly at the beautiful woman, "Name calling? Come now Trisha, you're cut from stronger cloth than that. I've personally seen to it."

"So, you did do all of this? Freak. Where'd you get that shirt anyway? I thought K-Mart went out of business years ago?"

"Ha ha," laughed Sergio, "I understand. You want answers. You want freedom, you want to get on with the lives that you were living before this…..thing all happened. Correct?"

Martin finally found his voice, "Yeah, that's right."

"Well, I fear to tell you that that is not possible. Those lives, as you knew them, are gone. Dear Trisha and Kevin, you were here for a very specific purpose, don't you know? Having fulfilled that purpose, there's simply not enough of you to go back and live as you did."

"What the hell does that mean?" asked Kevin sharply.

"Oh dear boy, I believe you know exactly what that means. Some piece of you is gone, no? Some part of who Kevin Barrow is has been left behind….about 140 years or so behind. I'm certain you feel it. And you too, fair Trisha."

"You mean, kind of like you left your hair and looks behind all those years ago?" taunted Trisha.

"Look, this bickering won't get us anywhere, I'm quite sure of it. I've come here for a very specific purpose, but if you have questions, I'll answer them as best I can."

"Fine," said Martin, "then tell me about this book. 4 Empty Graves. You put my name on it. And you filled it with blank pages. What's that all about?" Bachaca nodded his head as he looked around the room, glad that they'd finally have some productive conversation.

"Right then Martin," he began, "Well, good Sir, that book has blank pages because that part of your story has yet to be written. I do believe, against all doubt, that when you find out what your ending is like, you will want to write it down. Call it a bit of wishful thinking on my part."

"These other ones? What about them? How in the hell could you, or me, or….whoever, write this 'One Week in Lincoln' book when it just happened?" Martin asked with some sense of urgency.

"Martin, some of us write retroactively, like you do. Others, however, write proactively, as I do. Those words were in that book long before you ever ran from Rosita to Lilly just outside this front door here." The memory of that day, still very fresh in Martin's mind, made him visibly wince, a fact which did not escape the portly author.

"Second thoughts?" Bachaca asked, "Totally natural Martin, with such a great beauty like Rosita, or like Trisha here."

"Why are you doing this?" Trisha asked flatly.

"Dear lady, that is a fair and honest question," Bachaca began, as if going to launch into a long soliloquy, "I spent a good portion of my life studying the human brain. Quite an organ, if I do say so myself. Some 30 plus years, studying it from the inside out. Mostly my own, and mostly in isolation."

"So you're some kind of psychiatrist?" Trisha countered.

"Well…hmmm, not so much. I did however spend a lot of time examining what the mind was capable of. I found that in my studies, one could use the power of the mind to alter their current reality. You could, for instance, will yourself to be on a warm sandy beach even in the midst of a freezing winter."

"You realize you sounds nuts, right?" said Trisha, "Will yourself onto a beach? Ummm, I don't think so Serge. Maybe it was you who needed the psychiatrist?" Bachaca looked wistfully away at a memory only he could see. When he spoke, it was with the honesty of a man who wanted to have all the answers, but knew he did not.

"Maybe so?" he replied, "Perhaps everyone can use someone to talk to now and then?"

Martin, unwilling to believe this portly madman had any mental health training, asked, "Tell me where was it that you studied again?" Bachaca raised a tight smile before replying, "Various institutions around the tri state area."

Martin gazed at Trisha and Kevin, finally asking the question he knew was on everyone's mind, "Why us? If you're really doing this thing, why are you doing it to us?"

"So, full circle?" Bachaca replied, "Ok then, here's your answers. When we first met Martin, I saw something in you. A need, if you will, for information, for fact, for a different kind of life than you'd been living up until then."

"What? Last week? You had this great epiphany a week ago at the brewery and all of this shit happened?"

Bachaca smiled like a person who knew a secret that would turn the conversation on its ear, because that's exactly what he had. "A week ago Martin? Come now, our history goes back farther than that. Think!" Martin narrowed his eyes as if the man was crazy, which everyone in the room but Bachaca considered a distinct possibility. "What are you talking about?" Martin asked, "I met you last week here in Lincoln. Where and when else do you think we met?"

Bachaca stood up and smoothed out his horrid shirt, tucking it more deeply into his pants, "You really don't remember, do you?" Martin just stared at him with blank eyes. "The bookstore. Back in Paramus, New Jersey Martin. Right? You do remember now?"

Martin tested his memory from 90 days ago, or was it 40 years? He vaguely remembered walking in and buying Bachaca's book after it had been pressed on him by…
…"You!" Martin shrieked, "You were there! You made me buy your book."

"Made you? That sounds rather strong, doesn't it Martin? I believe I merely suggested it."

"But you never looked anything like the picture on the back cover. That was some…." Martin's voice trailed off, unsure of how to say the quiet part out loud.

"Good looking guy, Martin? You can say it. Later in life, and after many trials and tribulations, my looks have been robbed from me. Tis far easier to sell a book from a good looking author than from….well, me."

"Well that seems dishonest." Martin said which prompted a huge laughing roar from

Bachaca. "Dishonest? You might want to ask Michael Roberts about that Martin!" Martin hung his head ruefully, unable to argue the point.

"So what the hell was that? You go to bookstores posing as someone else and recommend people buy your book? Who devised this great marketing strategy?"

"Everyone's got to eat Martin. When the sales of my book slumped, I had to do something and got little help from my publisher. I devised my 'book store drop in' to coincide with every showing of Young Guns that I could. It worked quite well too, as you saw in your case."

"Ok, fine. So, you picked me for this game you're playing. Why?" Martin demanded.

Both Trisha and Kevin leaned in closer, hoping to glean something that would explain the absolute cluster that their lives had become.

"It wasn't really you, at first anyway. There were any number of people that purchased my book that day. To be honest, I didn't even plan to go any further down this path until I saw Carl. Something about that man and his attitude set my blood to boiling."

"Farber?!" Martin exclaimed. How did Farber enter into all this when Martin hadn't even met him until arriving in Lincoln that first time.

"Why yes, Martin," Bachaca explained, "He was there too. I would have thought you'd noticed him?"

"No!" shouted Martin, unwilling to believe that he and Farber had anymore of a past than he realized, "I'd have recognized that pinched face little loser anywhere."

"Well, you didn't this time, now did you Martin? He stood just off to the side, probably seeing how many people would buy a Billy the Kid book after a showing of Young Guns. If memory serves, he was working on his 'Coward of Lincoln County' book at the time. To me, the dichotomy of your wide-eyed innocence and his jaded hatred for Billy was all I needed in order to make my decision."

Martin racked his brain, trying to remember if he'd actually seen Farber there? He did have a fleeting memory of some guy giving him a dirty look, which finally chased Martin out of the store after buying Bachaca's book. "Make your decision about what?" he asked accusingly.

"To make my decision to take control of your life Martin. I could not let my legacy be the two diametric ends that you and Carl represented. I had spent years of my life studying and researching fair Billy, to give the world a true treatise of the young man's life. His importance to American history cannot be overstated. You, and well, Carl represented the two shallow ends of the study of Mr. Bonney. The truth is, I couldn't stand the both of you, for you're both wrong when it comes to The Kid. So yes Martin, I intervened in your dull, boring life. Yours, and hers," he said pointing to Trisha, "and his, among others." Bachaca finished his missive with a hand towards Kevin.

"Others. Like Farber?" Martin asked angrily, "You created that madman?"

"I have the power to create nothing Martin, I can merely accentuate it. If Carl Farber is a madman, then he was such a long time ago before I ever got involved."

37.

Billy spent a restless night in Lincoln, rising early to head back to the Coes. His discomfort was caused by the notion that perhaps his friend, Martin Teebs, had been the person behind all of this absurdity in their lives. On one hand, Billy couldn't believe it. Martin was so incredibly torn up by his comings and goings with Rosita, he couldn't imagine any person creating that personal hell, and then inserting himself into it. On the other hand, Billy wondered who else might have a hand in this? Carl Farber was one idea that came to mind, but Billy never viewed Farber as smart enough to pull off something so substantial. Was it Steve? Again, Billy had gotten good feelings from the man and just couldn't see any sort of payoff for him by weaving this strange and painful trip. The only other person that it could be, and Billy had heard him say it while he was bleeding out in the courthouse, was Sergio Bachaca. On the surface, Bachaca was a normal guy, writing books about the Lincoln County War, and hoping to line his pocket with a little coin in the process. On the other hand, Bachaca had admitted that he was the one driving Farber to more and more desperate deeds, and had written him into this nightmare.

Why though?

Did Bachaca have a personal vendetta against Martin, Rosita, and Billy? How could he? Until that day in the courthouse, Billy had never even met him. Maybe he had some beef with Farber, but it made no sense to admit it with a Colt pointed at your head and no way to defend yourself. Farber had pressed his advantage and shot the man right between the eyes anyway. If Sergio Bachaca was the man driving the rollercoaster that they were all on, with his departure, the entire thing was on a free fall that might never end.

"Great, just great," muttered Billy to himself, "Can't help Rosie, can't help Teebsie, can't seem to help anybody."

As Billy trotted through the east edge of town, 3 horsemen approached him, heading into Lincoln. From a distance he could easily make out the form of Jesse Evans, and as they approached he found himself staring at Buck Morton and Frank Baker. The hair on the back of his neck bristled, already knowing the horror that these 3 men would create in just a few months. Billy had lived through the Lincoln County War once already and he also knew what untimely and violent end Morton and Baker would meet. That thought warmed him, even as he knew that these men hadn't done anything yet, and that Billy would have to reserve his anger for a more appropriate time in the future.

"Kid," said Evans, nodding to Billy.

"What are you boys headed off for? Something no good I 'spose?" Billy said, exposing his buck toothed grin.

Baker laughed, but Buck Morton did not. He looked at Billy with the narrow eyes of someone who'd like to put an end to the person in front of him.

"You're lining up with the wrong side here Billy, you know that don't cha?" asked Morton, not allowing Billy to answer as he continued, "Cause you don't think that Dolan's gonna go down without a fight? It's gonna get ugly, and when it does, there ain't gonna be no going back, and no switching sides."

"Thanks for the history lesson Buck, preciate it." said Billy to a perplexed looking Buck Morton.

"Look Kid, you wanna ride with the winning team? Go on up the House and talk to Jimmy. He'll get you right on the payroll, then you won't have to worry about somebody dropping a slug in you." announced Frank Baker with as much friendliness as you can when talking about someone's impending demise.

Billy grinned again. That these men thought enough of him to try to get him to defect to Dolan's mob meant they were afraid of him. While he didn't much care whether or not he inspired fear in people, it was a welcoming thought that they knew he'd be a formidable opponent. "Well, I think I'd just gonna stay with old George and Frank Coe this winter and see how this all shakes out. You know, there really don't need to be no bloodshed over this. Lincoln's gotta be big enough for a couple of stores, ain't it?"

Jesse grinned, clearly in the lead of his little gaggle of 3, "Kid, you know this ain't about no store. It ain't about no beef contracts. Hell it ain't even about that bank that your boy Tunstall is opening with Chisum."

"Alright, I'll bite. What is it about Jesse?"

"Dang son, you been in the territory long enough to know that the Ring controls everything. They say jump, Dolan asks how high? They say move one Englishman along no matter what it takes, and we do it. What the hell you want with some damn Englishman anyway? You's Irish, so's Dolan and Murphy. If you wanna fight, fight for the people that you got something in common with."

Billy sat there, wondering how the war would have turned out if he would have taken Jesse's advice? While he didn't seriously consider it, maybe aligning himself with Dolan's crew would stop the bloodshed? Maybe by his presence on team Dolan, the rest of Billy's friends might have backed down and encouraged Tunstall to head to California? As soon as the thought formed in his mind, he knew it was silly. Brewer, Scurlock, Bowdre, Herrera, Folliard, and more were real warriors. They weren't about to get scared off by an 18 year old boy. "Well, I 'spose I'll stick with what I'm doing Jesse. Hopefully it won't come off to a fight. We's square no matter what, ain't we?" Bill said while staring directly into Jesse's eyes.

"Yeah Kid, we're square. You earned at least that." replied Evans.

"We ain't," interrupted Buck Morton, brandishing his razor sharp Bowie knife, "ain't square at all. You line up against me, you best prepare to meet your maker. I'm gonna make it through whatever happens. You ain't Kid."

Billy couldn't help but chuckle, knowing the outcome and untimely upcoming end to Morton's life, "That so? Don't bet money you need on that Buck. I gotta good feeling you're wrong."

Morton growled back in Billy's direction. Unable to resist the urge to pile on, Billy added, "Hey, you and old Frank ought to file a claim on that piece of ground up in Blackwater Canyon. Something tells me you boys'll be spending a lot of time up there."

Morton and Baker looked confused by Billy's remark, but Jesse looked concerned. "Anyway, we best get up the road Kid, don't want to miss out." said Jesse.

"Miss out on what?" Billy inquired, in the event his services might be needed in Lincoln awhile longer.

"Some photographer named Tomlinson. Taking photos, 4 for a buck. Thought we might just get ours taken and send em to our families. You want to tag along?" asked Jesse.

"Nah, I gotta git. You boys make sure you don't break the lens now!" Billy joked.

"Right," said Jesse as the 3 men spurred their mounts towards town, "Hell, I might just tell old Tomlinson that my name's Billy Bonney. You know, just to throw people off track!"

Billy shrugged and watched the men ride off. Knowing he had to get moving, he rode off towards the east for a few minutes before he stopped. He'd always hated that picture of himself that was taken in front of Beaver Smith's place. It might be good to have a good photo of himself in the future. Since he was about to become some sort of legend, he wanted to put the best face he could for future generations. Checking the sun, he knew he'd have an extra hour or so in town and could still make it back to the ranch before nightfall. Turning his mare back towards town, Billy gave her a light nudge. "C'mon girl. Let's go git a picture my Momma would have been proud of."

38.

"We want out, that's it, ok?" Kevin demanded of Bachaca, "how do we get out of this…thing?"

"I imagine you would young Sir," said Bachaca nobly, "but it's not that easy."
Trisha, fuming at Bachaca's circular answers, stepped in, "Listen asshole. Enough! Ok? We don't leave here, you don't leave here? You want to stay in this little hell you've created for us? Get comfortable old man. Go ahead and take your shoes off."

Bachaca sighed sadly, unable to make these people see that he was helping them, although it didn't feel like it at the time. "My dear Trisha, I'm not here because I have to be, I'm here because I want to be. I can leave anytime I like. Honestly, Martin can as well." Martin was struck by the words. If he had some magic escape button, why didn't he know about it?

Trisha looked suspiciously at Martin, "Is this true? What are you still doing here then? Was this just to get into my pants Martin?"

"No! I didn't….we didn't….no!" Martin said defensively, "I don't know what's he's talking about."

"I suspect that's true Martin. You'll figure it out sooner or later however. When you really want to go, you will." offered Bachaca.

"And us?" asked Trisha

"Ah well, with these time travels, things get messy, don't you know?" began Bachaca, "You do one thing, and it throws another thing off…and so on, and so on. I never meant for you to be trapped here, of course, but I needed a vehicle to bring both Billy and Rosita back into the story. The book, that famous copy that's caused so much of this, wasn't back in the 1870's. I needed something…or should I say someone, to transport them back to Martin's time."

"So we're some kind of, what, pack mules or something? Ferrying people back and forth through time?" Kevin spat out. Bachaca seemed sad at the accusation, as if he'd wished he'd never started this game, "No dear boy, you're so much more than that. Please believe me."

Trisha stared at Martin, wondering why he didn't just leave, assuming Sergio's words were true? A lump caught in her throat, thinking about once again being trapped in the vacant town with just Kevin and her own mind for company. The truth was, she admitted to herself, she didn't want Martin to leave. If he was, she wanted to go with him. Bachaca's admission that she and Rosita were one in the same stung her deep down in her soul, and despite her desire to the contrary, she knew it was true.

"Every story must resolve, my friends. I'm afraid yours hasn't reached that point yet. Martin, had you simply left with Rosita that morning, we most likely would not be here. Your story would have been resolved and life could have gone on as normal."

"What about Farber?" Martin asked, "Nothing would be resolved as long as he's…. well, wherever he is."

Bachaca sighed mightily, knowing that what Martin had said was true, "Yes, an unfortunate turn of events with the shooting of me, and all that came after. That copy of Sunset in Sumner should never have been there. It was mostly for Kevin's edification, you know. That it fell into the hands of Carl Farber was most unfortunate. It allowed him an escape to some time or place that we're not aware of. But you see Martin, you had your book. You had your Billy and your Rosita. You had it all, in fact. going back to 1877 with them would have ended your story, or at least the part I've been involved in. You'd be where you'd be and Carl would as well, never the twain shall meet, eh? By running towards Lilly it was you who created this mess. I was certain, beyond any doubt, that when you finally got what you wanted, you'd take it. I certainly underestimated you Mr. Teebs."

Martin was incensed, as if Bachaca was laying the blame for this entire cluster on him, and he didn't hold back, "Are you kidding me? You want to make this my fault? You self serving, fat little fuck! I walked into a God damned bookstore to buy a book on Billy the Kid, and you and your 'mind control' or whatever the hell it is, conjured this all up. I didn't ask for this! I didn't want this! I'd have been happy going home, reading a book about Billy, and calling it a day!"

"Would you? Are you certain about that Martin?" Bachaca asked simply.

"Yes!" Martin yelled, his now beet red face leaning closer to the Bachaca's.

"Be that as it may Martin, but we have an unresolved issue with Mr. Farber. Until that threat is abated, I'm sorry, but your story is not done, and these young people are not going anywhere." The air seemed to go out of the room, and Bachaca, tired of sitting, rose and walked toward the large picture window at the front of the house. A deep seated anger spread across Kevin's face. Instinctively he reached to his hip for a Colt, but of course, none was there. The author pulled the curtains aside, looking sadly out at his empire of nothingness. Trisha walked over to Martin, finally understanding that he hadn't caused this. She put her arm around him as a conciliatory gesture. Sensing the anger building in the room, especially from Kevin, Bachaca played what might be his final card. "Lest you think about doing something, lady and gentlemen, you should know something important, I think." Not knowing what it could be, and tired of the author's games, Martin spat back, "What?"

"My appearance here is not what you think. Not for the reasons you think. Seeing you all has been a great pleasure, of course, but I arrived in this Lincoln for a completely different purpose." Seeing that he had his audience on the edge of their proverbial seats, he continued, "Martin, I've written 2 more books, and came here to hide them, maybe forever? If something should happen to me, those books will determine the course of your life in my absence. Based on our cooperation here today, I'd say that having me around and alive gives you a better chance to achieve your happily ever after, no?"

Martin glared at Bachaca, "Where are the books? What are they?"

Bachaca rolled his head with a smile, "If I told you where they were, they would not be hidden, now would they? Let's say that someone might search a lifetime and not find them? Of course, you've had two lifetimes so if push comes to shove, perhaps you will? As far as what the books are? Well, that's simple. The first is called 'The Martin Teebs Chronicles'. It lays out what the rest of your days will be like, providing I'm not around to intervene." Bachaca smiled broadly, almost daring Martin to ask about the 2nd book. When he didn't, Sergio continued, "The other book, and one I think you all might be interested in, is called 'The Curious Life & Times of Carl Farber'. I'm my own worst critic, but I think that one has best seller potential!"

Bacaha's smugness finally proved too much for Kevin. "Arrrggh!!!" he screamed as he launched himself, sprinting across the room towards the author. In the last moment, Bachaca turned to the young man, eyes in confusion that his play hadn't worked, and with a great crash they both went violently through the plate glass window landing heavily outside.

"Kevin!" screamed Trisha as she and Martin ran to the shattered window. When they looked outside, they saw Kevin, unconscious, laying on his stomach, and Sergio Bachaca, gone, as if he'd never been there at all.

39.

Billy wasn't 5 minutes into riding back towards Lincoln when he heard what sounded like a scream and shattering glass. There were no buildings nearby so the sound caught him off guard. He recognized the area as being where he and Rosita had returned to Lincoln a few weeks prior, just outside of Trisha's house in the year 2021. Trotting off the road a bit, he saw some movement in the tall grass as someone, or something was struggling to get off the ground. Just in case, Billy lifted his Colt from its holster and shouted, "Who's that?" Hearing only the sound of someone's lungs trying to suck in air, he rode further into the grass and saw the prostrate figure of a man roiling about. "Hey, hombre. You ok?" Billy asked.

The man pushed himself to his knees, his back still to Billy. Immediately on alert after seeing the man's modern clothing, Billy barked, "Turn round. Slow. Now." in a voice that said he should not be trifled with.

Sergio Bachaca slowly turned towards the familiar voice, finally looking Billy in the eyes. The immediate recognition of who he was, was evident on the young man's face. "You? You're that chunky author. You're 'sposed to be dead."

Exasperated that no one could look past the size of his belt, Bachaca wheezed, "Don't you people have anything to worry about other than my waistline?!" Billy just laughed and slipped the Colt back into his holster.

"What are you doing round here, dead man?" Billy asked seriously, "I saw that shell split your forehead open."

"Indeed William, it did," Bachaca replied, "But you must know that you and your friend Martin got a second chance, and as such, I've written myself one as well." The admission was all Billy needed to hear to know that Martin was not responsible for their tumultuous lives, nor was Farber. It was this guy. Sergio Bachaca was public enemy #1.

"So it's you." Billy said with conviction, "You did all this, every damn bit of it!" With that, Billy pulled his Colt again, cocked it, and prepared to send the man to eternity, once and for all. Bachaca held his arms up quickly, waving his hands in Billy's direction.

"Not so fast, not so fast, that is, if you ever want to be done with this?" said Bachaca with some urgency in his voice. Not one to be fast talked by a failing author, Billy kept the Colt trained on the man. "Talk, if you want to see the sunrise tomorrow." Bachaca, having bought himself a brief respite, took a few deep breaths to steady himself.

"I've just come from seeing your friend Martin. Based on what I revealed to him, I doubt he'd want you to harm me Billy."

"Teebsie? Where'd you see him? He's here?!" asked Billy, the vision of a reunion between Martin and Rosita dancing in his head. Bachaca had the boy where he wanted him, so he rose from his knees and dusted his pants off. He took a moment to straighten himself up before replying, "Not here, per se, Billy. In Lincoln, yes…but an entirely different Lincoln than you've ever seen."

"Keep talking…." demanded Billy as he wagged the barrel of the Colt in Bachaca's direction.

"Well, kudos to you fine Sir, or your other half as it were. Your missing piece, that Kevin Barrow fellow, is the one who sent me here. I was beginning to wonder if he, or you, had the fortitude to do it?"

"You mean Teebsie is with that Kevin kid?"

"Why yes, and Trisha too. Does that surprise you Billy?"

"He coulda been here if he chose to. Why'd he wind up with them?"

"Ah, I guess you could say it was a happy accident," Bachaca surmised, but upon thinking it through he wanted to edit his answer, "Maybe not so happy, but an accident nevertheless." Billy received the information skeptically. This man, this coward, as Billy judged him, might be saying anything at all to save his own skin. Telling Billy that he had some portal back to his friend, and to those two kids, was just the kind of lie that might do it.

"What if I don't believe you? Seems you can't prove any of this."

"Then you'll pull the trigger and send me again, mind you, to that inky blackness that is the great beyond." waxed Bachaca poetically.

"Fine," taunted Billy, "Then let's us just get this over with." Billy raised the Colt again, his anger rising at the smugness of the man. Dramatically, Bachaca threw his arms open as if waiting to greet St. Peter. The gesture surpised Billy enough for him to hesitate, a moment that Bachaca took advantage of.

"When that bullet enters my cerebral cortex, it will be over for me. But have no doubts young man, it'll be over for you, Martin, and Rosita too. I've written all of your futures in two books that I've hidden in Lincoln. Should I not be around to change them, you'll live out every single day of the rest of your insignificant life just as I have determined. You see, William, as long as I'm here, you have a chance for happiness. For peace. For love. When I'm gone, you have none of those. So then, blast away, and enjoy what's left of your life, if you can." Bachaca smiled mightily, almost as if he'd gone mad. The man was asking for death, but with a catch. Billy knew by now that Martin didn't just happen upon Lincoln that first time. He knew that his meeting, and his life with Martin Teebs was preordained. If this psychopath was the one who was responsible, Billy decided to keep him around for a little big longer. He slowly released the hammer and holstered his Colt, a calm look spreading over Bachaca's face.

"Excellent then. So now we understand each other?"

"How do I find Teebsie? I gotta talk to him. Rosie's pr…."

"Pregnant, yes, I know Billy. How could I not?"

"I think the man deserves to know that he's got another baby coming. Why ain't you just bring me to him?"

"That's easier said than done. I don't have the mechanism to do it right now." Billy struggled to understand how this time travel worked for Bachaca? If he was the guy driving the agenda, shouldn't he have the power to skip back and forth as he saw fit? Reaching into his saddlebag, Billy retrieved the well worn copy of the author's book.

While it had seen better days, Billy knew it still held some magic, for he'd used it just days prior to arrive in the year 2021.

"What about this? Won't this work?

Bachaca seemed immensely pleased that the book still existed, like a proud father looking at his newborn baby for the 10th time. "You've got it? Good. I was hopeful that someone trustworthy still did. Alas, for where Martin is right now, that book will not get you there." Billy narrowed his eyes, wondering how badly the man was screwing with him? He looked over the cover of the ragged book and slipped it back into his saddlebag.

"Well, what in the hell is it good for then?" Billy asked. Bachaca paced back and forth on the high desert ground, now in his element.

"Wonderful question young Sir," he said with gusto, "I think you've only scratched the surface of what that book might do for you."

Warily, Billy asked, "Like what?"

"Well, any number of things, of course. The greatest of which goes back to your conversation with Martin back in the Tunstall store, which now seems like eons ago, does it not?"

"What conversation?" asked Billy. If he'd had one, it escaped him amongst all of the other drama and commotion that had happened since that time.

"Why, the one about your dear sweet mother Catherine. Do you remember? In fact, it was just after you'd found that book of mine." Bachaca said wistfully as if he was daydreaming of a pleasant memory. The conversation coming back to Billy, he simply nodded his head. This was the moment he'd screwed up, royally. Had he just handed Martin his book back, his entire world, his entire life, could have been completely different. Sure, he'd have been killed in Sumner by Pat Garrett in 1881, but he would have died free, unrestrained by some madman author. He could have avoided a long, guilt laden life of watching his friends die, doing nothing more about it than silently marking the pages at each loss. The memories of the bad times came like a torrent, and

Billy could not escape them.

"What about it? You think I shoulda gave it back to him?" Billy asked sadly.

"Not at all! You were given the keys to the kingdom William. What man could rightfully turn down the plan of his future? You talked to Martin about your mother. About how you'd move heaven and earth to save her if you could only go back in time. Is it becoming clearer now?" A wave of revelation washed over Billy, as the conversation's bits and pieces came back to him. Could this book allow him to go back and fix his mother? Save her life? What kind of life would Billy have had if she hadn't passed? The possibilities seemed hopeful, optimistic even. If Billy truly was a man of his word, he'd ride this book all the way back to Wichita so that he could change the course of his mother's life…and by proxy, his own.

"You're telling me I can get there with this? This whole time I coulda saved my mother and I didn't know?"

"It appears so Billy," Bachaca stated, "as always, open to those footnotes of the time, and I expect you'll be whisked away to it."

"Tell me the truth, did you already write what's gonna happen if I do? Save me the trip if you did, cause I ain't got time for more tragedy."

"I did not." Bachaca lied.

"Alright, let's go," said Billy, waving his hand up the road towards Lincoln, "I'm gonna put you up with some friends of mine, make sure you don't cause no more trouble. You'll be safe as a kitten if you just stick to what they tell ya." Knowing that he had no options, Bachaca trudged out to the road and began the walk to town. Passing the Montano Store, Billy saw Evans, Baker, and Morton, just having finished up with their photos. The photographer, Tomlinson, was about to pack up when Billy Bonney rode up, "Need a photo sir. For my ma." Tomlinson wearily looked at his equipment and decided he had time for one more photo. Dropping a one dollar coin on the table, Billy dismounted his bay mare and stood deathly still, remembering how a slight bob of his chin in the other photo ruined his image for all time. Tomlinson fetched and finished the plate, pleased with the outcome. He used a pair of snips to separate the 4 images, handing them carefully to the young man. Billy took one and handed it to Bachaca, whose ridiculous clothes were already attracting too much attention. "Might as well have one after what you done." Billy said.

Tomlinson began packing his gear up when Billy mounted his bay mare. "Looks good sir, my Momma is sure gonna like it." The photographer nodded in appreciation and as an afterthought, called after the young man, "What'd you say your name was?"

Billy, already shepherding Bachaca towards the Tunstall store, called back, "Names Billy. Billy Bonney. I 'spect some people call me Billy the Kid." Tomlinson was tired and not in a mood to be trifled with. He looked at the photo he had taken just a few minutes ago of a tiny man on a poor horse with the Montano store in the background. While he swore one of his friends had called him Jesse, the slight man presented that his name was Billy the Kid. Keeping one of the images at the man's request, Tomlinson had scratched the words "Billy the Kid" onto the back of the image. If this new guy was pretending to be Billy the Kid as well, the photographer didn't want to know about it. "Stupid punks." Tomlinson complained to no one, and tossed the picture of Jesse Evans into a box, with the photographer's own inscription about to set off a decades long search for another verified photo of one William H. Bonney, alias Billy the Kid.

40.

"Ohh…my ribs," Kevin groaned, lying in one of the home's 6 bedrooms, "That hurts like a mother."

Trisha looked at the young man, concerned, while Martin's expression conveyed something more of disgust. If Kevin truly was some piece of Billy, it had to be a very, very small piece. "Well, that's what flying through a plate glass window will do now, won't it?" Martin asked sarcastically. Kevin gave a few more groans and whimpers as he positioned himself on the bed, hoping to find a way to relieve the fire in his ribcage.

"Sorry Teebsie," he began, "I just saw red is all. That smug son of a bitch thinking he's calling all the shots didn't set well with me." Kevin looked up at Martin and asked quizzically, "Teebsie? Where'd that come from?"

"It's what Billy calls me. Don't worry about it."

Trisha stood by as the young man rolled back and forth, adjusting himself to find a comfortable spot, "Ok, so we have another problem. Or you do Martin. Or Farber does, or….I don't know, maybe we all do?. Those books that he wrote. He said he hid them somewhere here in Lincoln. If he's gone, then that's what happens to us, whatever he wrote?"

A look of concern spread across Martin's face. He wanted to dress Kevin down for the foolhardy stunt, knowing that they'd now be at the mercy of whatever and wherever Bachaca hid his writing. The boy was in so much pain however, that Martin didn't have the heart. "Look Trisha, he didn't say anything about you and Kevin. He just said it was me and Farber. Whatever the fallout is, I'll deal with it."

Trisha's eyes narrowed, unhappy that her concerns were being dismissed, "Look Martin, look around! In case you haven't noticed, what happens to you, happens to all of us. You think that we're going to be somehow immune to the rest of your life story? Come on. We're past that. We're all in this, like it or not!" Martin reached down and pulled a blanket up over Kevin and motioned for Trisha to follow him out of the room. Out in the living room, their conversation continued.

"I know, whatever that bastard did is affecting you too. I'm sorry Trisha. Really. The time travel, that was enough in itself. To find out someone has the power to write your future into existence is scary." Trisha took a deep breath, happy at least that Martin hadn't again dismissed her concerns. "Let's make sure Kevin is situated. Get him something for the pain? Maybe you and I can go out exploring. I know it's a longshot, but maybe we'll just find the damn books and put this thing to rest once and for all?" The pain of the previous days, the week in Lincoln with Martin and Lilly, and the arrival of Sergio Bachaca all proved too much for Trisha and she broke down crying, in great guttural sobs. All of the tension she'd been holding onto hitched a ride on her tears and began to pool on the kitchen floor. "Oh my God!" she cried, "Am I ever going to see my family again?" With her face buried in her hands, Martin didn't even think twice. This was his woman, or at least part of her, and she needed him. He walked over and gently wrapped her in his arms. It felt….right. Immediately he could feel Trisha yield to him, as if she wished for and needed the contact as well. Her crying continued unabated, with Martin doing nothing other than holding her through the episode.

"I can't do this Martin," she stammered, "I have a life, friends, school, my family. I've got to get out of here. Please, please! Help me get out of here?" When Trisha looked up through her tear stained eyes, it was as if Rosita had taken over. Martin had looked deeply into those eyes so many times, often knowing exactly what to say to make the moment right. This time was no different.

"I promise you. We're getting out of here."

"But if Bachaca is dead? The window?"

"If he's dead, he still wrote something else for us, right? He wouldn't write another book that would just keep us where we already are. We're getting out of here. Look at me Trisha. We. Are. Getting. Out of here…" The confidence in Martin's voice immediately soothed the young woman, who nodded her head as she dabbed at her eyes.

"Ok, let me get something for Kevin and we'll go look," she said genuinely, "Thank you Martin. I lov…." Trisha stopped short of saying something that she really didn't mean. She wasn't even sure why it was a thought.

"No you don't," chided Martin, "but Rosita does and she's probably making you say it to make me feel better." After securing some meds for Kevin, along with water and more blankets, they set off towards the front door. Just before walking out Martin heard Kevin call out, "Hey Martin. I couldn't find my car keys up in the courthouse. Could you look please? Could you maybe bring my car back here?"

"Will do Kevin. Get some rest now," replied Martin as they walked out the door.

Back in his bed, Kevin nodded and moaned to himself, "Thanks Teebsie, you old son of a gun."

41.

After securing Bachaca with his buddies Charlie Bowdre and Doc Scurlock in the Tunstall Store, Billy quickly rode off, making for Silver City at double quick pace. Both Charlie and Doc looked suspiciously at the strangely dressed man before asking Billy what he wanted done with him?

"Just keep him here and keep him alive till I get back. That's all. Don't care how you do it neither. Hell, saw a hole in the floor of the store and throw him under there for all I care." The worried look in Bachaca's eyes didn't faze the men as they rustled him onto the portal and into the store. Satisfied that Bachaca would still be in Lincoln when he returned, Billy set his sights on a reunion with his beloved mother. The biggest issue he had was that he didn't know precisely when or where his mother contracted tuberculosis. There certainly was no mention of it in the book, and people who had the latent variety of the disease could have it for years, decades even, before showing symptoms. There was no reliable way for Billy to try to project back in time and save his mother from the infection. He decided he'd try for Spring of '73, when he and his family first arrived in Silver City, and at a point where his mother was still healthy enough to work and take care of the family. Billy reasoned that he could talk to his mother, and maybe she would have some idea when she was infected? If so, he could try to somehow move farther back in time and prevent the whole ghastly episode from ever happening in the first place? As shaky a plan as it seemed, it was better than no plan at all.

The journey from Lincoln to Silver City was not a short one, covering over 200 miles. Billy's best efforts would land him there in 3 days, 4 if weather or rogues intervened. Along the way he had nothing but time to think of the almost unbelievability that his life had become. He tried to imagine what his mother would think if he explained this his best friend was a time traveling salesman from the year 2021? What would Catherine's reaction be when Billy told her he'd traveled to the year 2060, just to see his friend Teebsie, as an old man on the verge of death? For that matter, could he even relay to his mother that he himself had lived to be an old man in Magdalena? Would Catherine want to know about grandchildren? Billy had a pang of regret that he would not be able to let his mother know that even in absentia, she had finally become a grandmother.

A deep melancholy overtook Billy as he made his way to the west. Was this even a good idea? He hadn't become a successful rancher or farmer. Billy would never go on to teach school. He would not serve his district faithfully as a local politician. What would he tell his mother if she asked what had become of him?

Trying to force his thoughts elsewhere, Billy focused on Joe, his younger brother. He hadn't seen Joe for a couple of years (or almost 200, depending on how you were counting), and Billy felt bad about it. Perhaps he could find a way to bring Joe into his life? While Billy had never had the time to find out what happened to his brother, he was sure the funny, happy little boy that he remembered in Silver City had made good with his life. Maybe, thought Billy, it's just better to leave well enough alone?

By the end of the 3rd day, Billy was still hours away from reaching his destination. Being careful in these parts, lest the Arizona Rangers still had a warrant out for the killing of Cahill and might not mind riding over the border to enforce it, he bedded down in a rocky canyon. At sunrise he'd make his way into Silver City. Without using Bachaca's book, Billy intended to see if he could find Joe in their current, native time. Sure, his brother would be surprised to see him, but maybe they could have the time to catch up before Billy attempted a time travel infused elixir to save his mother? As far as William Antrim was concerned, Billy had already decided he didn't give a damn where the man was, or whether he was alive or dead. The absentee stepfather had farmed his stepsons out once Catherine died and did little to help them, or maintain a relationship, since. Billy's dislike for the man didn't rise to the level of being a killing offense, but he offered a silent warning to the cosmos to warn Antrim to steer clear of Silver City, at least for the next few days.

Gaining a restless sleep, and excited to see his dear mother again, Billy woke just as the first rays of light colored the eastern sky. Not bothering with any food or drink save for a few sips of water, he gathered his belongings, saddled his mare, and began slowly picking his way into town. By the time the sun had cast enough warmth for Billy to stop shivering, he was there, looking down upon the town he'd spent perhaps the roughest time of his life in. From his vantage point, he could see townspeople stirring. While more trees than he remembered clouded his view of the old Antrim home, he knew exactly where it was. There was no point aiming for it in current day, being as William Antrim had thrown the boys to the proverbial wolves and headed to mine the Mogollon Rim. Billy would have to tread carefully, no matter what, as Sheriff Whitehall or his successor would have warrants out for him. Billy wasn't much scared of a charge of stealing butter or clothes, but being detained, even for a day might give someone enough time to tip off the authorities in Camp Grant that 'Kid Antrim' was under lock and key in Silver, and they should come and string him up before he escaped yet again. "I didn't come here to kill nobody." Billy said aloud, as if to reinforce to himself what he expected to accomplish.

Trotting down the hill, he saw the glances of a few people, not unaccustomed to seeing a well-armed man ride through town. Still, Billy felt the glances lingered for a moment longer than they needed to, and began to wonder if this was still a good idea? Facing Sheriff Whitehall and his deputies in 1873 was a no brainer to Billy. He knew more about them than they did about him. Facing whoever might be in charge in 1877, and not knowing what their predilection towards a teenage outlaw might be, seemed like less of a sure thing. Cautiously, Billy pressed on, trotting down Main street towards the site of his old home. When the old place came into view, the Kid was unprepared for the torrent of memories that would accompany it. His eyes immediately stung with bitter tears, reliving a months long ordeal of watching his mother die, while his stepfather made excuse after excuse as to why he couldn't be there. Even from his current vantage point, some one hundred feet away, the smell of death carried on the breeze, like a wicked poison that you can't help but to taste. Billy knew this to be a creation of his own mind, his mother having passed and been forgotten some 3 years earlier, but it was as real as the sting of a scorpion. A few people noticed the boy in distress, but said nothing and moved on about their morning. Unable to resist, Billy spurred the mare closer to the house, just to see if someone there might know where he could find his brother Joe. As if on cue, the door cracked as someone reached for a bucket outside. The bucket had been left just out of reach however, and the person who wanted it had no choice but to open the door all the way. Not expecting any visitors this early in the morning, the man wore a long nightshirt and only stockinged feet. Sensing he was being watched, he looked up.

"What?" the man said incredulously.

"Chauncey?" Billy replied, more surprised than his host.

"Oh Henry? That you? What in the hell?" muttered Chauncey Truesdell to the young man on the horse, "What are you doing here?" Billy swallowed hard, trying to make sense of the young man before him. When last he'd seen Chauncey, he was but a pudgy boy, with curly locks adorning his round head. Now, before him stood a man with broad, powerful shoulders, a chiseled face, and standing, as best Billy could guess, almost six feet tall.

Forgetting the potential danger in his surroundings, Billy slid from the mare and walked towards his old friend, "Chauncey? What in the hell they done to ya? They took that little boy away and stuck a man in his place." Chauncey, use to these same missives as his body raged quickly through puberty, smiled and stuck his hand out towards Billy.

"Dang Henry, never expected to see you around here again. Ain't safe for you, I don't think." Remembering where and when he was, Billy nodded and looked towards his old house. "I'm renting it now. Working for Garner selling hardware but I'm gonna open my own place soon, soon's I get the money together." Billy smiled slightly, thankful that at least his old home was in good hands. "C'mon Henry, get inside. Not everyone here is your friend you know." Tying the mare up to a post, Billy followed Chauncey into the familiar home.

Staring at him and shaking his head, Chauncey still could not believe that his old childhood friend had come back to Silver City…and for what? Stoking up the fire, he used tongs to grab the coffee pot, offering some to Billy.

"Coffee? Did you ever get in the habit?"

Billy smiled and nodded, "Yeah, ain't we all after we ain't kids no more?"

Chauncey poured a steaming cup for Henry and slid it across the table to him. "Ok Henry, what are you doing here? I know this isn't some social call." he asked, looking directly into Billy's eyes.

"Well, you wouldn't understand the half of it, but for now I's just hoping to find Joe. You know where he's at?"

"Joe's gone. Left last spring. He waited for you to come get him, but eventually I guess he just got tired of waiting."

"Where'd he go?" Billy asked, surprised that this part of his plan wasn't going to work as easily as he imagined.

"Colorado, I think. Got in trouble here, stealing. Mostly food. Got to being a pretty good gambler though. You know how a gambler goes, right Henry? Can't stay in one place too long, unless you're losing. Then they love you. Then they roll out the welcome mat. Till you're out of money that is. Then you're yesterday's news."

"Where abouts in Colorado?"

"Don't know. Really don't know Henry."

Billy contemplated asking about Antrim, but quickly realized that he didn't want to know. As if reading his mind, Chauncey offered, "Uncle Bill ain't been around for a year. Mighta checked on Joe once or twice since you left, but that was it. Guy wasn't never cut out to be a father. He'd drop off a leg of mutton or a loaf of bread for Joe and get to thinking he was Daddy Warbucks or something." Billy contemplated the point quietly, realizing that kids might come along with a marriage, but the skills to parent them isn't an automatic. He decided that it was probably better that Antrim was gone, lest his ineptitude screw up him and his brother even worse.

"Got word that you killed a man Billy. Just back in August. That true?" asked Chauncey seriously.

Billy's eyes went slack as he looked around the room, trying to avoid his friend's gaze. "Yeah," he answered in an emotionless voice, "Cahill. Windy Cahill they called him. Up Camp Grant way. Big, mean bully. Always picking on me. Always beating on me. Some point you have enough, see? Some point, it's too much talk and not enough action. Reached that point."

"You killed him. You murdered a man Henry."

"Damn right I did Chauncey. I'd do it again every day if I could. Some people don't get what's comin to em in this life, but he did," Billy paused for a moment, "He did…" Chauncey took in the chilling news as it spread through the warm cabin. He'd never known a killer. Never shook hands with a man that had taken another man's life. Despite Billy's protestations of how much Cahill deserved it, Chauncey could not shake the unsettling feeling that he no longer knew who Henry McCarty was.

"Hope they buried that piece of shit under a chunk of pissed on soapstone. Hope the inscription wears off so nobody can't never find him. Hope no one ever visits that grave and tries to make a hero of him. They do? They put up some marker to his life? I'll come back from the grave and haunt every fucking last one of them."

Chauncey was quiet, a question burning in his mind, and one that he wasn't sure he wanted the answer to. "Ummm, what's it like? I mean, killing a man. How does it feel?" he finally asked. Billy sat on the chair, rocking a bit from side to side. Being as he'd already lived thru the Lincoln County War and its aftermath, he had killed a fair share of men, although Chauncey believed the total to be only one. Billy wished he did't have so much information to answer the question with. The fact that he did, meant that meeting his mother now, after all he'd endured, would surely be the heartbreak that would kill her if somehow the consumption didn't. "Feels like nothing Chauncey. See, you don't kill people you care for, you only kill them that need killing. If it gets to the point of having to shoot somebody, you ain't got a thing left to care about when it comes to them. That's the best way I can explain it anyway." The room got and stayed quiet for a few long moments, the thought of death and murder on both of their minds.

"What are you going to do now? Head for Colorado? You can't stay around here Henry." offered Chauncey, hoping that the impromptu meeting would soon end. Billy thought about it. What would he do now? Should he explain what really had gone on in his life to Chauncey Truesdell? Could a young man who'd barely ever left the confines of Silver City have the capacity to understand the time and torment that Billy have lived through? No, he decided, better to leave his friend where he was, and not try to bring him to where Billy was going.

"Don't know Chauncey. I got some business in Lincoln to take care of. Left an old friend there, you know. Maybe I'll become a writer? Always loved reading stories, maybe that'll help me write them?"

"Do you know any writers Billy? Anyone that could help you along?" asked Chauncey

Billy grinned but managed to stifle his laugh. Did he know any writers? Teebsie, Farber, Bachaca? They all wrote their way into his life, and now they were all so intertwined, he might never break free? "You could say I know some guys that like to spin a tale or two," Billy said mysteriously, "Yeah, guess I know some people that could help me. I got me a few real doozies that I'd like to tell. But hey, Chauncey, I didn't mean to come and take up your morning. It was good seeing you. Glad you're doing well. Don't expect I'll be around this way again, so you go on and live yourself a good life, see?"

Chauncey was glad to be let off the hook, not knowing what the punishment would be for aiding and abetting a felon. He rose to shake Billy's hand and opened up the front door. "Thanks for stopping by Henry. You could still lead a good life. You still have a chance. Pray for forgiveness, and I'll pray for you as well. Take care." Billy nodded and eased out of the door, walking towards his mare. For what was to come next, he needed to be out of sight, so he slid into the saddle and reined her around toward the treeline. As Billy became smaller and smaller in the distance, Chauncey watched from the doorway, finally saying to himself, "I'm glad his mother's not around to see this. She wouldn't believe what her boy turned out to be."

42.

Martin and Trisha walked quietly out to the main road. As expected, the town was ghostly silent, as it had been for their entire current stay. Martin surveyed the landscape and asked Trisha, "So, should we get Kevin's car first, or do you want to jump in and start searching?" He noticed that she seemed more relieved than at any time in recent memory, which could only be a good thing.

"You know Martin, what I'd really like?" she asked suspensefully, "is for you to point out where everything happened with you and Rosita. Please? I've heard so much about her. I might even kind of, be her. I want the visual to go along with the love story. What do you say?" Martin was puzzled. Just moments ago Trisha was inconsolable, sobbing that she had to get back to her previous life, and now she wanted to stop and smell the time travel roses?

"Uh, sure. I mean, we have stuff to do and I know you want to…."

"Stop Martin. We're here. We're going to find a way out of here, you said so yourself, right? So, let's take a few more minutes and show me the sights of Lincoln, NM." Martin could only giggle and shrug his shoulders, but he had to agree. There seemed to be no accounting of time in this abyss they were in. Why not show Trisha the places where Martin had wooed and won the love of his life?

"Alright then, Miss Davis," he said in mock formality, "Let us begin here at what we call our 'east end' of town." Martin held his arm out for Trisha to take as if he was escorting her down the aisle, as they headed towards the cemetery on the margin of Lincoln. "Now, I won't be able to go in chronological order, mind you, because we'd be bouncing back and forth all day, but I'll do my best to keep the timelines straight." As they approached the gravel road to the cemetery, Martin winced for just a moment, and not only for himself. Knowing that this was part of Rosita's history, he pressed on. "So, here we are at Lincoln's main cemetery. We're not here to revisit any old friends, although there are many, but this spot, apparently just days ago, was the first, and hopefully last meeting of Lilly Teebs and Rosita Luna."

Trisha glanced upwards, trying to determine if Martin was making some kind of joke, but his serious expression seemed not to. "I'm not sure how much of this you remember Trisha, but it was that day. The day I got shot. You were, or maybe, Rosita was, walking back to your house. Lilly came driving by and picked her, you, both of….. listen, I'm just going to refer to Rosita separately than you, ok? Anyway Lilly picked her up. I know Rosita was scared and didn't know how badly Billy and I were hurt. From what I heard later Lilly really laid down the law and told Rosita she was never to see me again." Trisha's anger sparked as if Lilly had been talking to her.

"Is that so? Now Lilly is calling the shots?"

"No, I didn't say that. I only said that's what she told Rosita that day. Obviously, by the next day she'd kind of changed her mind." Not wanting to relieve even a fraction of Rosita's sadness, Trisha grabbed Martin's hand and dragged him toward the west and into Lincoln proper. "Ok, I get it. Keep the tour moving Martin, right?" he asked to Trisha's mischievous grin, "Ok, onward!" They passed Trisha's current house which gave Martin no cause to pause. As he remembered Lincoln, this was vacant ground back in 1878. With the turquoise blue doors of the Montano Store in the distance, Martin gathered his knowledge for the highlight reel spinning in his head. "Well, you already know that this big building was Rosita's house. Hers was the one on the right and her mother Lourdes lived in this other one. Somebody wanted to have a bigger building so they just came along and put a roof between them, built some walls, and called it all one house. Kind of sad to me, every time I walk by it. But if I go inside, it's like I'm right back in 1878 with her all over again."

Trisha squeezed Martin's hand, hoping her warmth might help him ward off the chill of sorrow he felt. "So in there, you two had, you know…." she said shyly.

"We made love in that tiny house. A number of times. Yes. Each time better than the time before. That's not just words, that's a fact." Martin said fondly.

Reflecting back on Farber's Lincoln County Days book, Trisha knew something else had happened here. Something horrific. Something so brutal that she could not bring herself to even discuss it. Martin must have sensed her uneasiness and offered, "Yes… that happened here too. I can't even….." his voice trailed off as tears welled up in his eyes, but he was determined to go on, "I wasn't there. I should have been. This thing would all have been over if I was. You and Kevin would never have been a part of it." Trisha allowed a few of her tears to mix with Martin's, responding, "You couldn't be, right? You told me that Martin. Farber hit you in the face and knocked you out. That sent you back to our time. How can you beat yourself up over that?"

"I should have tried harder. I should have tried until I dropped dead. After what happened, I was as good as dead anyway."

"But then you'd be gone, Martin, and Rosita would have been left here alone." As soon as the words passed her lips she regretted them, knowing already what Martin's answer would be.

"And so she was. Alone. Right up until….." Martin's eyes were vacant as the brutal image of July 14, 1881 played out in front of them like his own personal cinema. Even his tears dried up, having nothing left of emotion to say on the matter.

"Hey! Hey!" Trisha insisted, "You had happy times too. Somewhere right around here. You told me, when you first met Junior?" Martin's face immediately softened, relishing the pleasant vision of Rosita and Junior running to him. The fact that he was already dead not seemingly fazing him a bit.

"Yes, that's right. I was just a little farther back. It was kind of like this. Totally alone and deadly quiet until I heard her voice pierce the silence. She came from there. They must have been playing outside. It's funny, I'd never met Junior, well not that I knew of at that time, but I instantly recognized him. Most handsome damn boy I'd ever seen." Trisha dropped Martin's hand and jogged up the road a bit.

"So she was here?" she yelled.

Martin waved her back with both hands, "No, a little farther I think!" Trisha jogged back a few steps, waving her arms for Martin to confirm her position. He wagged his head from side to side, trying to remember. If everything that had happened to him was true, this took place less than 2 weeks ago! "Two weeks ago, I was dead?" he said aloud. The enormity of it hit him like a sled full of bricks. He'd been dead, as confirmed by Rosita, in the time it takes to play 2 weeks of the NFL season. Everything that had happened since, although he couldn't explain it, had been fit into a tiny slice of time, capped now by walking hand in hand with Rosita's stand in, measuring the distance of his memories. The thought of it was proving too much for Martin, standing there trying to blink the dizziness away. Trisha noticed his dismay and began running towards him.

"*Martin! Martin!*" she yelled in a voice not her own, closing the distance to Martin's shocked eyes. He stood at attention, unsure of what was happening as she launched herself into his arms upon arrival. Without a second thought they both tumbled to the ground, lips locked in a lusty reunion over a century in the making. Martin closed his eyes and let her thick hair wash over him like a wave. He quickly slid his hands to her hips, pulling her closer to him, that they might never again part. The connection was back, and so was Ro…..

"Hey, stop. I'm sorry Martin," Trisha said, looking embarrassed, "I shouldn't have done that. I don't know what that was?" Martin let his head fall back against the asphalt, knowing in the final second that it was not what he'd hoped.

"I know, I know," he said with a rueful smile, "it wasn't like the Titanic going down." Trisha still would not move her hips from him however, keeping him pinned down, "It wasn't, but hey, it was kind of like the Andrea Doria this time, if that makes it any better?" Martin laughed again as Trisha allowed him up. "You know, actually, it does make it better." he said with a smile. They both got a good laugh as they dusted themselves off and continued walking up the road.

"There's one thing more I wanna see, ok? I want to see where you and Rosita first met." Trisha said with a gleam in her eye.

"Ah!" Martin said, rubbing his chin with his thumb and forefinger as if a university professor, "back to the scene of the crime. Ok. This one I know well." They walked on easily, any remaining tensions now gone. Martin assumed that Trisha wanted to know where he and Rosita first met, not the first time he met Rosita. To recount that might invite another hard slap in the face that he wasn't prepared to be party to. Also, while his own timeline was mightily screwed up, Rosita's was heretofore not. Martin decided that the first genuine meeting between himself and the Belle of Lincoln happened near the Wortley where Rosita had been headed for work. In the scant distance between the hotel and the House, Martin had found his paradise, although it didn't seem so at the time. Still with a ways to walk, Martin decided to play tour guide to his time with Trisha, rather than Rosita.

"You remember the dance, yes?" he asked her, "You and Jane were up there making fun of me."

"We were not!" protested Trisha with a laugh, "I thought you were cute. We were drunk so who knows what we were laughing about."

"Ok then," Martin replied, letting her off the hook, "then we went and talked back on the deck. That's when you found out how crazy I was, huh?"

"Oh Martin," Trisha said with a dismissive wave of her hand, "I didn't need you to tell me any of that stuff to know you were crazy." They both had a good laugh at the joke as they passed the Tunstall store and the site of the old McSween house.

"Hey Trisha, don't these old buildings mean anything to you? I mean, do you remember anything from back then when you see them?" Trisha stared at the Tunstall store as if trying to get it to speak to her. Every time she looked at the buildings in town she was left with the same nagging feeling.

Nothing. No connection whatsoever.

"I don't Martin. That's why I question this whole 'piece of me' thing. Wouldn't I have some recollection of the place I lived? I mean, these buildings were key to the whole Lincoln County War, right? I was there? That lawyer's house? Didn't it burn up? Why don't I remember it?"

"I don't know," Martin said honestly, "Maybe Bachaca is full of shit? Maybe we're just 3 normal people that got talked into this stupid idea and just have to figure a way out. Maybe there's no Billy, no Rosita, none of it. This is all probably just one big, sick joke."

Trisha reached out once again for Martin's hand, "You don't believe that Martin." she said softly.

Looking deeply into her eyes, trying to find Rosita, he replied, "No, I don't." They walked on a few paces until Martin found the spot he'd been looking for. "Here! Here's where it happened," he said pointing to a nondescript spot in the road, "So I'm pissed. I'm stuck in some time I don't know. I can't find Rosita although I'm assuming we're in love. Billy almost shot me in the head, and it's getting darker and colder by the minute. I'm thinking this is the most stupid idea I've ever had and I finally decide 'that's it!' I'm going to march back to the courthouse where I came from and find a way to leave this time forever. I spin around and take one step, and boom!, I knock Rosita right down in the street."

Trisha laughed and clapped her fingers at Martin's reenactment, "Smooth, Martin. Was she impressed?"

"Ha! No she was not. She might have even called me something bad in Spanish, but I didn't understand it. Anyway, she yells at me for being clumsy and starts to walk away. Luckily I was able to smooth things over just a bit before she ran off to the Wortley for work."

"Every love story has a great beginning Martin, except for yours!" joked Trisha as she walk towards the man, "Thanks for sharing. Really. It makes this all somehow more... complete."

Martin sighed, "You bet. Should we go see if we can find Kevin's keys and those damn books?" The two explorers headed towards the courthouse, hoping to find both the keys to a car, and the ones that would unlock their future.

43.

Trotting off of Main Street towards a more private area in the trees, Billy contemplated the conversation with his boyhood friend. Joe was gone, although Billy assumed he'd be able to track him down in Colorado if he wanted. While Chauncey didn't specifically say that any Arizona law had been looking for him, it was a safe bet that they'd alerted the sheriff in Billy's last known place of residence to be on the lookout for him. Billy had a little surprise in store for anyone looking to slap a set of shackles on him today though, they'd be trying to arrest someone that had just jumped back some 4 years. Sure, Billy would be in the exact same spot just a few minutes from now, but in time, Windy Cahill would yet to be mustered out of the Army in Arizona, and Billy would be guilty of nothing but bad feelings for the bully. Ready to get on with it, he pulled Bachaca's book from his saddlebag. As the memory of his mother was too painful, Billy had read that section only one time, and certainly with no intent of ever visiting it again. Today however, today was different. Peeling the pages apart, he found the section he was looking for. Just as the fuzzy exit started, Billy noticed the 1874 date of his mother's death and then in a flash, he was gone.

In what seemed only a blink of an eye to him, Billy looked around at the sparsely covered ground, with more scrub timber than the trees that had been here just seconds ago. He hoped his exit hadn't frightened his mare too badly, but she was well enough concealed that she shouldn't raise notice. With a gust of optimism blowing in the breeze, he began to march off towards the same house he'd just come from. It looked more dilapidated than Billy had remembered, but assumed his childhood memories were just more fond than finite. Getting some 50 feet from the front door, he was stopped cold in his tracks. The unbearably familiar hacking of a dying consumptive patient sliced through the thick timber walls. Between each one, a groan or gurgling sound was heard, as Catherine lay dying in her bed, racked with pain, and with apparently no one to comfort or care for her. The blood drained from Billy's face, unable to believe he'd miscalculated so badly. Should he stop, go back and try again to land in an earlier time? The thought itself was repulsive to Billy, being that his mother, the woman who bore him life, lay dying and in pain just a few feet away. The sense of urgency to see, and care for his mother overwhelmed him, and he sprinted for the door.

"Who's that?" Catherine cried out upon hearing the door creak open, "Clara?"

Billy's heart hit the floor. His once jolly, beautiful, full of life mother was unrecognizable. Her strong frame now just draped with ashen colored skin, flecks of blood and tissue splattered about, not caring whether they landed on Catherine, the bed, or the floor. His lips trembling, he opened his mouth to speak, but he could push no words out.

"Clara?" Catherine grunted and then wheezed, "Who's there?"

Suddenly, nothing mattered anymore to Billy. Not Martin, Rosita, Maria, or anyone or anything in his life. He'd been transported back here, on a mission of mercy, but wound up landing on death's doorstep with only a ticket to watch the show one more time. He tried to regain his composure and softly walked towards the bed.

"Ma," he said while stifling a sob, "It's me…Henry." Whether from the unexpected news, or perhaps it was simply time for Catherine's lungs to try to expel their demons again, she rattled off on a coughing jag for what seemed to be a minute. Blood flowing from her lips, her face etched in pain, Billy looked to the heavens for some guidance on what to do. Feeling completely helpless, he realized that this was not a life, this was death just having its way with you until it grew bored of the game and allowed you to expire.

"Easy Ma, I'm here," he whispered, placing his cool hand upon her burning forehead. For the moment, Billy thought she'd passed out, or perhaps died because she didn't stir at all. Forcing open her eyes, she looked in the space where Billy's voice came from, but she could see nothing. Thankfully, so she could not see her son's face, Catherine's sight had been robbed from her in her final moments.

"Why?" was the only word she could push from her grizzled lungs.

"Ma, it's me. Henry. I'm here to take care of you." he said incredulously.

Catherine had to breathe in three or four times, just to load her lungs with enough air to speak. She reached a bony, sputum covered hand to Billy's knee, gripping it as tightly as she was able to get his attention. He leaned in, not wanting to miss any instruction he might get.

"Leave," she hissed as her head fell back on the pillow, pushing him away with her hand as best she could. Unable to believe what he'd heard, he leaned in again and asked her, "What Ma? what?"

"Get….hh….out….hh"

As if a hammer had fallen from the heavens and hit him squarely on the head, Billy was floored. He remembered his first time through this, that his mother would send him and Joe away, not wanting her boys to carry the horrific image of her dying for the rest of their days. Still, Billy always snuck back, always sat with his mother, and she always let him stay until she tried to send him away again. This….this was different.

"I'm not leaving Ma. I love you. I…."Billy broke down into tears, burying his eyes in the stained bedclothes.

Catherine shook her head, which wasn't difficult since her entire body was shaking anyway, and pushed at Billy's head, "not…..ag…..hh….again….not again."

Again? What did she mean?

"Ma please!" Billy begged, "I can help you. I'm here to save you!"

Catherine's lungs rattled badly as the woman approached death. Billy must have somehow been transported back on the very day of her demise. It's true, he hadn't been with her at the moment of her passing the first time, having been sent away by Clara Truesdell, but this time he was intent on saving his mother, or ushering her as peacefully as possible to the other side. It was clear that nothing had changed in his absence as William Antrim was again noticeably absent.

"No….book….saves…hhrrg…me." Catherine forced out.

What!? Catherine knew about Billy's book? How could she? How could anyone from this time in his life? Was he set up? Billy quickly vowed that if Sergio Bachaca had any hand in this, he'd get a matching hole in his skull to join the one that Carl Farber had given him.

With his mother's life rapidly coming to an end, Billy felt the walls closing in on him.

He curled up in a fetal position next to his dying mother, her coughs, rattles, and pained groans the only sound in the room. Billy began wailing as if a little boy, only wanting to be put safe in his mothers arms. But this boy was not little and his mother's arms could no longer reach him.

"Save….hh….your…."

Billy sniffed to regain his composure and turned his head towards his mother, "Save my what Ma? Brother?"

"your….hhrgg….self"

Billy froze. His mother knew. She knew everything.

He laid there, listening to the sound of her failing breath, totally defeated, and completely alone. What was he here for? What was the lesson? Why did Bachaca send him on a mission that he already knew was doomed to fail? What kind of twisted game was this guy continuing to play? Billy's anger was only tempered by his mother's pain. If she was to be believed, she'd already died, and this whole scene, her wracked in pain yet again, was for his benefit. It was like Billy didn't travel back in time, but more like time traveled to meet him, doubled him up. Made him and his mother have to endure a second painful demise. His emotions spinning out of control, he suddenly blurted out every single thing he thought he wanted his mother to hear. "I'm sorry Ma. So damned sorry. I ain't been the son you wanted…you deserved. I ain't been the man you thought I'd be. You was gone and I took to no good. Ain't no excuse why, ain't no reason. Just did. I did! Didn't even protect Josie none. I ain't the boy you thought I was." Billy broke down sobbing, as Catherine slowly put a hand to his head, smoothing out his hair. "Then I just did worse and worse. Just killed a man in Arizona. You believe that ma? Your own son is a killer. I ain't proud. I ain't happy. I ain't nuthin…" and then after a pause Billy could not stop himself from screaming at the top of his lungs, "I ain't nothing!!"

With her life force fading, Catherine was only able to drum her fingers gently on Billy's head. "But now I got me some good friends Ma. Teebsie, Rosie, and in some other life, or time…I don't even know, I got me a good woman named Maria. See I kind of turned it around, or I can. I'm not just what they say bout me Ma!"

As the sharp staccato of his mother's breathing increased, Billy knew it was time to say goodbye, "Ma, I love you. Came here to save you. Tried, but I just couldn't God damn do it!!" he screamed in frustration, "That book was sposed to get me here to help." Billy pounded the sides of the bed with his fists in anger and frustration.

"Book…yes…hhrrg….helps."

"How do you know about my book Ma? Who told you?"

"B….b…..bible." Catherine finally said as a trickle of blood ran down her cheek and pooled on her pillow. Then the enormity of it hit Billy. His mother knew nothing about his book. She knew nothing about Sergio Bachaca, she had been talking about the Bible the entire time. Billy had just laid bare his soul of all of his misdeeds, thinking his mother knew, only to find out that he'd simply burdened her even more.

Silently cursing himself, he saw Catherine's eyes flutter and knew this was it. She pushed her head closer to his to whisper her final words to the son she'd loved for 14 years, "father…." she gurgled.

"Antrim" said Billy.

Catherine barely shook her head, "no…f…hh..father"

"McCarty. Padraig….I know."

Catherine, knowing she was out of time, gulped in whatever air her lungs would allow and hissed, "no! fath…father….T…t…." and then the life left her body, finally going limp. Her glassy eyes stared at Billy, lifeless but beautiful and haunting at the same time. A final trickle of blood ran down and began to pool under her chin, finally relieved from the relentless pain. Billy waited in vain for whatever information his mother wanted him to have, but father T wasn't much to go on. Was she trying to tell him that father time comes for us all? That Billy shouldn't waste another day living a life that would not make his mother proud? There were an infinite number of questions, but the woman who held the answers was now gone, forever. Billy sniffled a bit, all of his real tears having already fallen. Not wanting for anyone else to see his mother like this, he searched around for clean bedclothes and a nightgown for her.

Taking time to carefully move his mother's body, he changed the sheets, and carefully dressed her frail, broken body in the nicest gown he could find. Propping her head up on two pillows, he never closed her eyes, hoping that she was still able to see some vestige of the boy that loved her so. As he was about to leave, he felt something amiss….as if he'd not completed his task. Taking a walk outside, he found a patch of wild penstemon and picked a handful. Back inside he wove the delicate purple flowers into a crown and placed it upon Catherine's head.

Satisfied that he'd done all he could, Billy simply stood there and stared for long minutes. She looked like an angel, waiting patiently for her ride to Heaven. He was unable to save his mother, but at least he was able to give her some dignity upon taking her leave from this world. Never wanting to forget this moment, or this scene, he started into her eyes, the woman that had given him life. Silently he vowed that he'd find a way to do better this time. To not die a broken, unhappy old man who sent his friends off, one by one, to be slaughtered, while he just watched. He didn't know how, but Billy was dead set on changing history, his…and the world's.

Realizing it was time to leave, he kissed his mother gently on the lips and slowly walked out of the door, fastening it behind him. Back inside, on those same lips was hidden a secret about Billy's father that she simply ran out of time to tell him. Somehow, even in death, those lips barely moved into a slight smile, knowing that somehow the boy would learn the truth. A last, single drop of blood escaped the dead woman's mouth and ran down onto her pillow, spoiling the perfect scene her son Billy the Kid had painstakingly created for her.

Catherine had done all she was able, to give Billy a map towards his destiny. Now it would be up to him to find out. As her soul lifted, freed from the prison that was her body, and began to rise toward the Heavens, she prayed that he would….sooner, rather than later. Had anyone been there to look closely, they would have noticed the tiniest tintype of a handsone, smiling young man tucked into the crown of penstemons, taken just days ago in Lincoln, NM.

44.

"Maybe in the outhouse? I'm sure he's got plenty of experience in there." joked Martin in response to Trisha's question about where the books might be. Remembering his own experience in the privy out back of the old store, he didn't relish the thought of peeking in there to find out. In any event, the first order of business was to find Kevin's keys, and both Martin and Trisha were scouring the 2nd floor of the courthouse in that effort.

"So he drives out of town, never makes Capitan, turns around and comes back here? Then he just goes to sleep on this old cot? I mean, there's not too many places those keys could be," reasoned Martin, "I know this is going to sound stupid, but did he ever check to see if he left them in the car?" Trisha's head poked around the corner, having been searching the old armory room in the back of the building.

"I don't know. I guess so?" she said more as a question than an answer, "Hey Martin, what was it like up here? Last week? On that day?" As quiet and peaceful as the place seemed currently, it was difficult for Martin to imagine the horror of it all.

He started tentatively, "It wasn't great. That's for sure. Bachaca was over there, near the judges desk," he said with a point of his finger, "and Farber's about here, where I am. We moved as fast as we could but I had Billy to take care of, he was in real danger of bleeding out, and Steve's head was laid open right down to his skull. We must have been some motley looking crew."

Trisha slipped onto one of the benches in the main courtroom, "Why do you think Farber didn't just shoot you all?" Martin looked up at the ceiling as if he'd never even considered the question, "You know, I don't know. He liked seeing people suffer, I remember that. Maybe killing us would be too quick and easy? Maybe he could have got one or two of us, but if we rushed him, someone was going to get their hands on him. I don't know, maybe he's like some superhero villain, that he's got to have some good rival in the world in order to balance himself out?"

Trisha contemplated Martin's answer, then asked, "So….to be clear, *you're* the superhero in this theory?" Her eyes danced and her smile lit up the room as Martin laughed, the butt of the joke he helped set up.

"Yea, that's about it. Let me just find a phone booth to slip into so I can change into my costume." They both laughed at the vision of Martin slipping into anything made of lyrca spandex. "Well, I don't think those keys are up here. We can check the first floor again if you like? I don't know. In the state Kevin was in, he could have left them anywhere and not even know it.

"This has been a hell of a day Martin, don't you think?" Trisha asked as she walked off towards the back stairwell, "You show up, Bachaca, the thing with Kevin. It's too much for just one day. How many more of these can I take?

"As many as it takes, Trisha, but there will be an end to it. I guarantee it."

They both trudged down the stairs, walking mostly in circles, covering ground they'd already seen. No magic books and no car keys were evident. Martin was struck by a question, "Trisha, can I get 'thru' to Rosita through you? Does anything that I say to you make it through to her?" Trisha walked towards the front desk where she'd spent hours during the past summer punching tickets. She was merely trying to buy time, as she didn't know the answer to the question. "I'm not sure Martin. It's not like she's talking in my ear or anything." Martin frowned sadly, his slim hope of sending Rosita a message all but extinguished. "But in some way, I feel like she knows I'm here, you know? Like on some level she can feel this experience, or this vibration, I don't know. I have the distinct feeling that Rosita feels like I do. Like some piece of her is misplaced. My guess is that she'd like that piece back. I would too, I guess. If I could explain it better, I would."

"Ok, I'm sorry. Forget it. I didn't….well, just forget it," replied Martin, "It's getting late. We should find those keys and head back to the house."

"What about the books? We need to find those too." protested Trisha.

Martin glanced at the young woman, before staring down the vacant main street, "Do you think he was really telling the truth Trisha? You think he actually wrote them? I kind of think he was just trying to save his own skin, give us some BS story about some hidden books so we'd keep him around. Or at least, wouldn't do him any harm. Something about the way he said it just seemed contrived. Phony."

"So he sends us on some unsolvable wild goose chase? We spend eternity here picking over every single inch of this place, never to find it, but always with a sliver of hope that we might?"

"Yea, something like that." answered Martin carefully.

"Somebody who would do that Martin, that's not a madman. That's not a puppet master. That would be the Devil him fucking self. And this would be Hell. So no, I won't allow that possibility to enter my mind. If I do, Bachaca won't be the only insane resident of Lincoln. I'll be #2 on the list, right behind him." Martin nodded, not wanting to push the conversation farther in any direction.

"Lemme just check inside the car again. I'll bet he panicked and dropped them under the seat or something." Martin said, walking towards Kevin's car. Sliding inside, he adjusted the seat backwards so he could even move his legs, given that he was a good 5-6 inches taller than Kevin. "How does somebody sit this close to the steering wheel!" Martin exclaimed. Trisha peeked in through the passenger side window, clearly amused at Martin's wrestling match with the tiny seat. "C'mon Martin! Show that seat who's boss!" she laughed. Wanting to roll the window, Martin reached for the switch and was instead met with a beep of the car's horn. Trisha smirked but Martin quickly looked over and f0und that Kevin's keys had fallen into the little well just behind the power window buttons. He'd pressed the 'lock' button inadvertently.

"Here they are," he announced as if they were a prize on some low budget game show. Trisha pointed at the door lock, urging Martin to allow her to get in. With the passenger door unlocked Trisha slid into the car next to Martin, and for good measure, adjusted her seat back all the way too. As she released the handle between her legs, she was met by a quick and sharp pain, "Ow!" she cried out, pulling her hand quickly away to judge the damage, "Dangit! Just a paper cut though." Curious, Martin slowly reached under her seat and pulled out a bound set of pages, with the simple title "The Martin Teebs Chronicles" on an otherwise unadorned cover.

45.

Billy rode for the best part of 3 days, intent on reaching Lincoln and settling the score with Bachaca. The sting of having to watch his mother die again fresh in his mind, he vowed to pay back the author in spades for every ounce of pain he had caused. There was no way Billy could accept that Bachaca's directive was for anything other than to cause pain. Billy could take it, but Catherine should never have been pulled into the situation again. A hundred scenarios of causing Bachaca the same kind of pain, or worse, floated through the Kid's mind.

Of course, that was the rub. Billy had just promised Catherine he was going to do better. He swore to himself he was going to remake his entire life, leaving every trace of being an outlaw behind. How could he have become so completely opposed from desire to rational thought? The decision tormented him every step of the way back from Silver City. As he ran every scenario through his head, he settled on the fact that he'd know, in the moment, what the right thing to do was. He vowed that whatever it turned out to be, he'd do it (or not do it), accept the outcome, and move on with his life. Entering town from the west, he rode carefully past The House and was just clear of the Wortley when he heard his name being yelled, "*Billito*!" Rosita yelled out happily, waving her hands at him from the portal, "Where have you been?" Billy pressed his eyes closed for second, knowing this was a conversation he was not prepared to have at that moment, but the happiness and hope in his friend's eyes compelled him to stop.

"Hey Rosie," he said, sliding from the saddle, "everything ok?"

"*Si, si Billito*," she announced with a smile, "but I was worried when I can't see you. Where have you been?"

Where have I been, thought Billy to himself? How could he even describe to Rosita the hope he held out to save his mother, coupled with the absolute devastation he felt when it could not happen? The clouds in his eyes caught Rosita's attention, "What is this *Chivato*? You are sad. What happens when you are away?" Unable to control his emotions, noiseless tears began to well up in Billy's suddenly red rimmed eyes. Each one slid off his cheeks and hit heavily on the dirt of Lincoln's only street. Rosita had not meant to cause any distress, and didn't even know what'd she'd said that struck such a nerve. She tenderly reached out a hand to brush some of Billy's tears away, "I am sorry for this. I did not mean to cause you to be sad. Let us not talk about this now, *si?*" For Billy however, he couldn't let it go. He had something to tell Rosita and if he didn't do it now, he was afraid that he might never.

"Rosie, listen," he said as he wiped his eyes clear, "bout this book and all. Can't happen no more, ok? I'm sorry but I can't do it no more." Rosita was confused. She hadn't mentioned Billy's book, Martin, time travel, or anything else. Just what had he been doing while he'd been gone?

"Is ok *Billito*, this we can discuss at anot...."

"No Rosie!" Billy said urgently, "Can't do it now or never. You start messing with things, wind up in places you ain't sposed to be, and you cause people to deal with pain they already dealt with!"

Rosita recoiled a bit, as if having been bitten, "But no, I'm not asking...."

Billy continued, as if he didn't hear Rosita speak, "All sounds like a good idea at first. Think you'll save someone. Think you'll find a way to make it better this time. You ain't saved anyone, and you sure as hell ain't saved yourself! You just got a front seat to watch em die and didn't do a damn thing about it! We been playing with something that shoulda been left alone Rosie! I can't do it no more. I love you like a sister, but I ain't gonna do it no more!"

And with that Billy descended into sobs, the final vision of his mother carefully tucked behind his own mind. Rosita, completely unaware of what had just happened, cradled the boy in her arms, feeling the desperate sadness in his movements. "Is ok then. Ok? Is ok. No more of the book and the time," she whispered into his year, "I won't speak of it again *Billito*. I'm sorry for your pain." Rosita stood there, one of the territory's most feared gunmen wailing in her arms, wondering if her chance to ever again reach Martin had just evaporated right in front of her eyes?

46.

"What does it say?" Trisha asked urgently, reaching for the manuscript, "Are we getting out of here?" Martin looked blankly at her, allowing the young woman to pull the pages from his hands.

"He's messing with us. This isn't the real book, it's just a warning shot." Martin replied.

"What do you mean?" Trisha asked, furiously rifling through the pages, which all seemed to be blank until she reached the last one, "What the hell is this?" The final page held forth on just a few scattered paragraphs, clearly chosen by Bachaca for effect:

Have you doubted me after all I've shown I'm capable of? You found this book, full of hope, optimism, and excitement, thinking it would be your salvation, and indeed, you might just discover that it is. My plan, children, was to make sure that should I suffer some untimely end, that you all learn the lessons that I've laid out for you. I couldn't simply leave it chance.

When I started this game, it was to settle a personal score, which has yet to see fruition, although I don't doubt it will. As I continued, I simply realized that I like playing God. I'm good at it. What I see for you, is better than the vision you see for yourself. I'm not your enemy, and I hope someday you'll realize that. It takes quite a bit of muster to change the course of one person's life, much less the multitudes that have been wrapped in this tragic opera. Still, I must see it through until the end.

No, this is not the book I spoke of. Did you think it was? Really? Under a car seat. Alas, I have done much better than that. This is only to allow you the prescience to understand that I'm still in charge, no matter where and when I am. Those books I spoke of are out there, even now. You would be wise to bet your life on that fact. You might be inches away from them and not even know, or, you could be a lifetime from discovering their secret embrace?

As for the children, Kevin and Trisha, I expect they will gain release from this setting once you, Martin, have tended to unfinished business elsewhere. As such, their salvation lies in your hands, and not mine. As far as how you get out of here to do that? Well, I'm certain something will come up to allow that shortly. As for me, I'm alive (or perhaps dead) on some other plane of existence, and shall watch your struggles fondly from afar, for the destination, in the end, shall be worth every bit of pain endured to reach it.

I've written myself only this one bonus life. Should you hear again of my demise, believe it, and know I'm gone. When I am, those stories shall direct your life in my stead. Or, they won't. I've spent a good part of my life on this project but even to me, some of the details are fuzzy. Perhaps one of you will be able to clear them up.

I certainly hope so.

Yours,
Sergio Bachaca

"So he's just a madman, and now he's probably dead," said Trisha, her hopes of seeing her family becoming more fleeting, "What the hell was Kevin thinking!?"

"He said I'm probably getting out of here? Some unfinished business? I don't know what that is, but whatever it is, I'll do it Trisha. Ok? Just help me figure out what to do?" Her hopes dashed, Trisha couldn't even bring herself to care about the book or its author any further.

"C'mon Martin, let's go back to the house please." Martin cranked the small engine, waiting for it to roar to life. "I wonder what Rosita would think of driving in a car with her man?" Trisha mused, "Maybe you could take her to a drive in huh? Maybe to Inspiration Point?" Martin was struck by the old pop culture reference, laughing quietly, "Inspiration Point? How the hell does someone your age ever hear about that?" he asked.

"My father loved 70s TV. I'm sure I picked it up there," Trisha said as Martin slipped the car into gear, "Hey, let's go watch the submarine races, ok Martin?" Trisha broke down laughing at the reference and Martin gave her a wry, amused look in return.

"You're in rare form. What's up?" he asked. Trisha didn't know why, but she felt slightly giddy. Maybe it was the release of expectation of finding Bachaca's book? Maybe it was her losing her sanity after a day in Lincoln that seemed to last a month. Whatever it was, she was done being serious for the time being. She reached her hands across the tiny console and put them into Martin's lap, "Well, maybe you in a minute Martin," a devilish smile crossing her face.

"Wait! What are you doing? Trisha!" protested Martin, but it was too late. The car inched its way down the street as she tore at his zipper, freeing him from the last protection he had against cheating on Rosita. Was it even cheating? This was Rosita, at least in some twisted way. This must be ok with her, being as she and Trisha were partly the same. It was far too late to change course now, as he grew in her soft hands. She quickly hopped up to reposition herself so she could kneel on the passenger seat, pushing her head across towards Martin's lap. His breath fired in short, rapid bursts as he leaned back in the seat, waiting for the relief of contact. Just as it was about to happen he heard a blood curdling scream;

"Martin!!!"

47.

Billy marched down the street, leaving his mare in Rosita's care for the time being. His sadness of the previous few minutes giving way to the anger that had burned at him for most of his trip back from Silver City. He worthlessly checked his Colt to make sure it was loaded, just as he'd done fifty times over the past 3 days. Reaching the Tunstall store, his boot heavily landed on the wooden planks of the portal, reaching a crescendo when he arrived in the doorway.

"Where is he!" Billy demanded of Sam Corbett, the store's shopkeeper. Corbett seemed surprised and in the moment it took him to not answer Billy's question, the young man stormed past the edge of the counter, turning right into Tunstall's private quarters. As he flung the door open, he was surprised to see John Tunstall, Charlie Bowdre, and Doc Scurlock enjoying an afternoon cup of tea. They sat on stools in a circle, chatting like perfect gentlemen, and were surprised by Billy's sudden intrusion.

"Hey, Billy, you're back." announced Doc calmly. Charlie's feet tickled a section of floorboards that had been cut away, leaving a rectangle shaped opening down to the dirt crawlspace underneath.

"He in there?" Billy demanded, pointing towards the darkness. Charlie placed his teacup down and rose. "Oh, uh no. We got em locked up back in the store room. C'mon, I'll show ya." Tunstall looked curiously at the young man he'd heard so much about, raising his cup and saying simply, "William." Charlie led Billy and Doc across the front of the store and into the storeroom on the west edge of the building. Grabbing the handle, Charlie pushed the door open, saying with a laugh, "We couldn't fit him under the floor. We tried. Too many tortillas and frijoles I guess." Billy silently nodded a thank you to Charlie, letting him know he'd take it from here. Doc gave one last questioning look towards the man, and then winked at Billy on his way out. With the door closed, Billy faced off against the man who'd occupied his every waking thought for the past 3 days.

"Well, based upon your current demeanor, I'm guessing things didn't go as you expected, now did they Billy?"

"What's your game?" Billy asked in a low and serious voice, "You knew I wasn't gonna be able to save my Ma. You sent me there to watch it all over again. You made her go through it all over again!"

"No Billy, I did not. I merely offered the power of suggestion. It was you who decided to go, I certainly did not make you." Engraged, Billy drew his Colt and cocked it, holding it just inches from Bachaca's head.

"You sayin this is my fault!?"

Calmly, Bachaca replied, "I'm saying it was your choice." Billy's trembling hand held the gun directly at the author's forehead, playing on what to do next.

"Well William? It appears that you hold all the cards. What do you plan to do with them?" Bachaca asked, without an ounce of fear betrayed in his voice.

"I'm gonna make you squirm, make you feel pain, make you afraid, just like my Ma felt."

Bachaca caught Billy's eyes, a look of compassion spreading across his face as he spoke, "No you won't Billy. My story is already written. What happens here changes nothing." Bachaca paused, waiting for a response that did not come. "You see, you're under the mistaken impression that I've done this to you, for you, whatever. I have not. My writings are only suggestions, like I gave you a week ago. Whether to follow them or not is always a matter of free will. I have no special powers or abilities. I've done my share of bad things in life, just as you have, but I'll leave those sins here when it's my time to move on." Billy's glaring eyes never wavered from Bachaca's. "I offered an alternate course to your life. To Martin's, to, well….everyone. If you want to be 'Billy the Kid' then so be it. If you don't, it's on you to change. I control nothing, you control everything."

"You wrote that shit book. That one that started everything." Billy said accusingly.

"And you read it Billy. What did you do with the knowledge you gained?" The truth of Bachaca's words hit Billy hard, and it was a truth from which he could not escape.

"Time travel can't change the past. That's a misnomer. It can only allow you to go back far enough to try to change the future, if you dare. This was never about Martin, or Rosita, or Farber. They were just spectators, caught up in the whirlwind, don't you see that? This has always been about you. The legend, and the man behind it." Billy looked straight through the man, seeing a black maw of nothingness behind his words. "Your mother wanted something better for you Billy. You lived a life that she'd never, ever want to know about. And you seemed to find any person, place, or thing to blame it on. But deep down, deep down Billy, you knew you were cut out for something different, didn't you? You felt it all along that you weren't living the life that you were destined for. You wanted a chance to make it right. John Tunstall didn't give you that, *I* gave you that chance!" Bachaca said, practically roaring now. Billy trembled badly keeping the gun trained on the man's head. Bachaca dramatically stood up, knocking his stool over, hands tied behind his back.

"You got the chance that everyone wants, and no one gets! You got a do over Billy Bonney!" he thundered, "You can piss it away like every other chance you've been given, or you can finally wake the fuck up!" Bachaca screamed loud enough that people outside were stopping to see what the commotion was about. Bachaca angrily kicked the stool across the room, it tumbling and clattering into Billy's boots.

"There! You want a reason to kill me, go ahead! Go back to whoever the fuck you were before I took pity on you!" Billy was shaking badly as he gritted his teeth. "Or you can cut this fucking rope off and say THANK YOU, and then get the fuck OUT OF MY LIFE FOREVE…."

The smooth action of the Colt flung the shell forward, straight as an arrow, making a tiny entrance wound in Bachaca's forehead, and then a millisecond later, creating a crater in the back of his head that spewed more brains that Billy gave the author credit for. The final, stunned look painted on his face, his body crashed backwards into the front corner of the building, disappearing to somewhere unknown, just before it hit the ground.

48.

"Look out!!" Trisha screamed, as Kevin's car careened towards the front west corner of the Tunstall store. What had a second ago been a fun, sexy escapade was now headed for a smashing conclusion as the car rocketed toward the portal. Martin, deep in the throes of lust for what Trisha was about to do, took his eye off the road and put his foot on the gas at precisely the wrong time. Just before the moment of impact, they were both stunned to see Sergio Bachaca come flying backwards, from the corner of the building, his brains dripping out of a massive hole in the back of his head. As the car sickeningly crunched to a halt in a shower of broken glass, only Trisha's agonized scream and the substantial thump of Bachaca's body hitting the floor were heard above the din.

49.

There was an insistent hissing from the front of the vehicle, coupled with clouds of steam, and maybe even smoke. Chunks of century old adobe blocks crumbled down on the hood and the corner post from the portal balanced precariously against the fender. A sinister muffled buzzing in Martin's ears told him he was alive, but he was barely able to make anything out around him in the mangled front seat. As his vision began to normalize his eyes were drawn down to his crotch, seeing himself fully exposed, but the promised deed incomplete. Before he could even do anything to cover up, words rang out from the seat next to him.

"What in the hell are you doing tossing around your junk Martin? At a time like this?" asked Steve in a gravelly voice as he was just coming out of his own shock, "Damn yankees got ways of doing things I won't never understand. Tuck it in and zip it up son, cause I ain't interested."

Martin dumbly looked around the smashed cab of the truck. Just a second ago, or was it a day, he and Steve had been talking about getting into Trisha Davis's house to get that last copy of Lincoln County Days out of the Feds line of fire. Having no idea what happened, Martin only remembered that Steve had veered wildly towards the corner of the Tunstall store, taking out the portal and destroying a small part of the building. When the airbags deployed, there was but a millisecond to see what was happening before both of their worlds went black. Martin was unsure about how long he was out, but it felt like a substantial amount of time. Checking his watch however, he could see it was no more than a minute. Two minutes tops. As people began to arrive on scene, someone wrenched open Martin's door, carefully guiding him out of the truck in the event it went up in flames. As he stood there, wobbly, cuts to his head and hands, he felt something was terribly amiss, like a heavy weight had been chained to his legs and was trying to drag him away. Seconds later, tiny slivers of memories of Trisha Davis arrived, he explained them away since he and Steve were headed to her house. The same could be said for Kevin Barrow, and even Billy, who obviously had a deep connection to Martin and Lincoln. Those memories popped and fizzed in the back of Martin's psyche, much like he'd experienced after 'The Dream' during his week in Lincoln. Distraught, Martin said quietly enough so he couldn't be heard, "I'm not doing this again."

The one face that subliminally blinked time and again, flashing like an annoying neon sign, was the author Sergio Bachaca. Why in the hell would Martin be dreaming about him, and why wouldn't that memory simply fade away like the others quickly had?

"You alright Martin?" Steve asked as he slowly limped around the side of the truck, "Sorry about that. Damn. Didn't you see the Barrow kid there? He was walking right there?" Steve pointed insistently towards the vacant lot next to the store, "Just caught my eye at the last second and I guess I lost focus. We need to find him before someone else does."

Kevin Barrow? Here in Lincoln? Martin hadn't seen a thing in the seconds before they crashed and only now stood there silently, taking in the scene, knowing something was drastically wrong. The more the moments ticked by, the less clear his memories became. With a few braces of clean mountain air, they were all but gone. Martin shook his head one final time and realized that, whatever it was, he must have imagined the entire thing.

50.

The crash had not been as bad as Trisha had feared, being that Martin had been driving relatively slowly. Still, Kevin's car had lost the front bumper and headlight in the affair. At the final moment before impact, she dived down onto the seat, and when she lifted her head up, Martin Teebs was gone. Unable to process how things had changed so quickly, she glanced around the car, both inside and out, trying to piece together what was happening.

For Trisha, it felt like moving in slow motion, the realization that she was again completely alone. The thickness of the air was much like she'd experienced after the shooting at the pageant, and like that night, here she was once again in a town with no people. So heavy were her eyelids that she was tempted to lie down on the portal and sleep, but night was rapidly approaching and she didn't feel safe. As she walked around the front of the car to see if Martin had somehow been ejected, she gasped when she saw the rotund body of Sergio Bachaca, a ghoulish mass of blood and brains in a puddle behind his head. She had distinct memories of grilling the man about Rosita during his talk at Old Lincoln Days just last week. Further, he had held court at the brewery that same evening, when Martin and that big cowboy Steve had gotten into it over something. Did Kevin do this? They'd all seen the man disappear after going through the house's plate glass window, but Kevin was still there in the house. Had been there the entire time? It looked to Trisha as if someone had blown the man's brains out of the back of his head. Even in his fit of rage, she couldn't imagine Kevin doing this? Was it Martin? In the margins of her fuzzy memory, she could see herself, smiling, about to please Martin as he drove slowly along the main road. In that last moment before they crashed, Trisha remembered just seeing Bachaca's body there, tossed at them as if from some other dimension. Questions multiplied but answers evaded here.

 Long past being able to do anything to save the dead man, she simply walked to the east toward her house. This day had seemed a month long, and all she wanted to do was lie in bed until such time as this nightmare might be over. She grimly hiked to the house, walked inside, and checked on Kevin, who was fast asleep in a guest room. Trisha had just enough energy to jot down a note before sleep claimed her.

Kev,

Found your keys. We had a little accident, sorry. Not too bad but your car is at the Tunstall store. That guy Bachaca is there too, dead. Somebody shot him. Was it you? I have no idea what happened to Martin, but I hope wherever he is, he's getting help. We didn't kill Bachaca (I don't think). I'm going to bed. Please don't wake me until this nightmare is over. I just can't anymore. Take whatever you need from the house. Nite.

Trisha

Leaving the note along with his keys, Trisha padded slowly into her bedroom, stripped off her clothes, and fell heavily into bed. The next time she woke, she hoped, would be the day she could leave Lincoln forever and go back to her family and life in LA.

The next morning Kevin rose, immediately seeing the note. Having slept for almost 14 hours did almost nothing, such was the tiredness in his body. He peeked in on Trisha, still sleeping deeply, before walking out of the house. He ventured up the road until he saw the front end of his car pushed up against the corner of the Tunstall store. Walking around the front end, he saw the bloated body of Bachaca, in even worse condition than Trisha had seen it the night before. Too tired to question or care, he slipped into the driver's seat, fired the engine and backed onto the road. Putting the transmission in Drive, he headed west out of Lincoln, bound again for his apartment in Capitan in a 'damn the torpedoes' move that would either land him at his apartment, or stranded in the middle of nowhere, dying of thirst, hunger, and exposure…as if Kevin really cared about any of that anymore. This time though, he made it, only to find the small town similarly deserted as the one he had just escaped. Unable to form a coherent thought, he parked his car, walked upstairs to his tiny room, and collapsed onto the bed, hoping that tomorrow….or someday….might prove better than the day he just had.

Back in Lincoln, a large wake of vultures flew in, most likely from the Fort Sumner area. Finding the remains of the substantial author to their liking, they picked his bones clean, finally dragging what was left of his carcass away from the damaged Tunstall store, and to the Bonito, where it would run downstream and someday, wind up most probably in the Gulf of Mexico.

51.

No one wanted to ask Billy what had become of the author they'd bedn keeping an eye on. They'd heard shouting, and some stools crashing, and then it seemed to just be over. Billy came walking out of the storeroom, completely detached. No one, including the man they'd watched for days, was left behind. Billy stared at both Doc and Charlie, nodded his head slightly in appreciation, and trudged out into the evening air. Walking steadily to Rosita's house, he had but one message to deliver before he found a place to spend the night. Even as his boots hit her steps, she heard him and quickly opened the door, trying to usher him inside.

"No Rosie. Can't," he said simply with a slight shake of his head, "just came to tell you it was over."

Rosita looked concerned, "What is over *Chivato*?"

"All of it," he said, holding up the worn copy of Bachaca's book, "The guy who wrote this…thing. He's dead. I just killed him. Don't think this will do nobody no good anymore."

Rosita was stunned, shaking. Trying not to betray her feelings, she simply nodded. Her chance to ever see Martin again was now surely gone. "Thank you for the news." she said simply and closed the door. Billy sadly stepped down to the street and walked slowly into the encroaching night.

"I tried Ma," he said into the darkness, "Tried to change things. Tried to change me. Guess when it comes down to it, your boy turned out to be nothing but a killer." Billy walked on, understanding that the Lincoln County War was coming, and he'd take part in it, just as the history books said he would. Everything would be the same. He'd be dead by the age of 21, the ventricles of his heart shredded by a bullet from Pat Garrett. He'd watch all of his friends die one more time, and he do nothing to change the outcome. He'd be buried on the desolate plains of eastern New Mexico, in an abandoned military cemetery, and his grave would be ignored for decades. When it finally wasn't, the world and countless history buffs would invent a life for him that reality could never live up to. He and his story become a legend, with the real life of Billy Bonney being subjugated to a mere footnote. No one would care about the truth, and the truth would fade away until it was as if the last wisp of smoke simply blew off into the sky. This is the way things were. This is the way things had to be. History demanded it.

As the night swept him in, Billy Bonney walked into a future that he could not escape. History expected it of him, and he belonged, almost like no other, to the history he helped create, and could no longer escape from.

52.

Martin and Steve walked slowly to the east edge of town. The wrecker that had been dispatched to get Steve's truck would be another 30 minutes, and that was their only ride back to Capitan.

"Well, there's the house up ahead. You sure you still want to do this Martin? I mean you go 10-62 and you might just spend a night in the clink."

Martin just glared at Steve as they approached the house. As they made their way up the walk, Steve stopped short, "Son of a bitch. Looks like somebody beat you to it." Indeed, the giant plate glass window at the front of the house had been shattered and the filmy drapes billowed in the breeze.

"You've gotta be kidding me?" Martin exclaimed, shaking his head. Having had enough broken glass, broken memories, and confusion for one day, he simply turned around and walked away. If the feds came for him, so be it, he'd deal with it then. Shuffling up the road he didn't even look back to mutter in his wake, "C'mon, I need a beer, and then I'm going home."

A knowing smile swept across Steve's face, "I knew I liked you for some reason Martin, and it sure ain't for you fiddling with yourself back in my truck either."

Martin kept walking, his shoulders slumped. Steve stopped when he reached the road and looked back at the house one more time. He contemplated telling Martin something, but decided against it. The guy had a long day and probably couldn't process it anyway. As Steve hustled to catch up with his buddy, he smiled, knowing that all of the shattered window glass was outside of the house. He knew, instantly, that no one had broken into the Davis girl's house. Whoever broke the window wasn't trying to break in, they were desperately trying to break out. Steve shuddered with a sudden chill of that meant, and put it out of his mind.

53.

4 Months Later

"Hi, Lil, I'm home!" announced Martin, as he entered the Teebs household. Smiling, Lilly came from the kitchen, having been working on dinner for the past thirty minutes. She noticed Martin held a grocery bag.

"What did you get, big boy?" she asked, peeking inside the rim of the bag.

Martin seemed almost embarrassed to answer. "Umm, chocolate fudge ripple ice cream?" he said, more as a question than an answer. "It was two-for-one at Shoopman's."

Lilly tilted her head to the side and frowned a little at Martin's dietary choice but said simply, "Okay, but go easy on these. I want you around for a *long* time, Martin Teebs!" She grabbed the bag and headed back to the kitchen, saying on her way out, "Dinner in fifteen minutes. I'm making your favorite: pot roast."

Martin smiled and danced upstairs to get changed, thrilled at the feast he was about to enjoy. Stripping off his pants, he grabbed his wallet, keys, and phone and tossed them on top of his dresser. As he opened a drawer to find a pair of shorts, his phone buzzed with a text message, most likely from Colin, his friend at work. He and Martin were planning a big bash to watch the NFL draft on the coming weekend, and Colin had volunteered to run to the grocery store after work to pick up some snacks. He was probably going to present Martin with the queso versus salsa question.

Tapping the appropriate icon, Martin's heart stopped, literally for a few moments, as he read the message from the contact in his phone labeled "T" for Trisha.

"*Martin*, I am with child. I need you, *mi amor,* please, I beg of you, come to me. I have waited. Come to me."

Epilogue

With winter quickly approaching, all sorts of creatures, both fur and fowl, made final plans to eat as much as they were able before the lean times that would sweep through the high mountain valley.

On this chilly morning, a juvenile coyote warily picked his way around Lincoln looking for scraps of anything to eat. A young prairie dog poked its head up from a place it should never have been, arousing the hunting instincts of the coyote. The coyote gave chase down the road, through a front yard, across the sidewalk and finally up a small hill. Seeing the prairie dog shaking in the tall dead grass, the young coyote stalked it menacingly. At the final moment, the prairie dog dived down next to a rock outcropping and slid down a shaft between the rocks and the dirt piled inside of them. Try is it might, the hungry coyote could not dig far or fast enough to reach its prey. As it dug, his paw hit and scratched a simple silver box that had been buried there, somewhere in the confines of what use to be a structure, maybe a house, many years ago. In the box were two manuscripts, wrapped in thick plastic and hidden years before, titled 'The Martin Teebs Chronicles' and 'The Curious Life & Times of Carl Farber'. The manuscripts have never been seen other than by their author, now long since dead. Whatever is contained in them remains a mystery.

Should they ever be found, one can only wonder what they might say about Martin Teebs, and Carl Farber. Perhaps the lucky reader might glean some information about the lives of these two forgotten men, and what they had to do, if anything, with the history of old town of Lincoln, New Mexico.

The End.

ABOUT THE AUTHOR

Michael Anthony Giudicissi is an author, screenwriter, and speaker from Albuquerque, NM. Michael hosts the internationally popular YouTube channel, "All Things Billy the Kid". In addition to the Back to Billy series, Michael has written a number of other books focused on personal growth, business, and sales.

Disclaimer: Due to the shifting nature of fiction versus reality, we're unsure exactly who is currently writing these books. Clearly a fictional character named Martin Teebs is not writing them, but who is Martin Teebs, really? Recent reports point to the fact that a Martin Teebs might just exist after all. We're not clear on whether Michael Anthony Giudicissi is a real person, or perhaps Michael Roberts might be the driving force behind the manuscript. It's possible, as disagreeable as it may seem, that even Carl Farber could be at the helm of current and future Back to Billy stories. Anyone with any information on this vexing puzzle is encouraged to contact the "author" at the links below.

To Contact the Author: billythekidridesagain@gmail.com

Books in the "Back to Billy" saga:
Back to Billy – 2nd Edition (Mankind Media, 2023)
1877 (Mankind Media 2021)
Sunset in Sumner (Mankind Media 2021)
Bonney and Teebs (Mankind Media 2021)
One Week in Lincoln (Mankind Media 2021)
4 Empty Graves (Mankind Media 2022)
Pieces of Us (Mankind Media 2023)

COMING SOON:
1950, Book 8 in the Back to Billy Saga (Mankind Media 2023)